A Dir

Whit looked at his watch. "Hit the pavement and talk to anyone you can find who knew her. The closer the better. I'll send Mark to the briefing, or would you rather have him with you?"

I winced discreetly.

"What's your problem with Mark?"

I made an attempt to be diplomatic. "There's a rapport you establish in an interview. Having someone else there blows it."

My editor rubbed his nose with the back of his thumb. "I covered one or two murders for the *Globe*. It's dirty business. Do you think you're up to it?"

This sounded like a reprimand. "I have the contacts," I said indignantly. "This is my beat."

"Mark's a big athletic guy. This may have been a sex crime. I have to be concerned for your safety.

I paused revealing a sliver of self-doubt. Whit's eyebrow went up. He was a master at reading inadvertent facial expressions.

"I can do it," I said tightly. "I want to."

Praise for *Exiles on Main Street*

"A debut of great promise and verve, with an unforgettable heroine to carry its provocative story. . . . A mystery for anyone who has ever tried to juggle family and career—and who hasn't?"

—Laura Lippman,
Edgar award–winning author of *In Big Trouble*

Exiles on Main Street

LISA KLEINHOLZ

HarperPaperbacks
A Division of HarperCollins*Publishers*

HarperPaperbacks
A Division of HarperCollins*Publishers*
10 East 53rd Street, New York, NY 10022-5299

ISBN 0-06-101411-7

First printing: September 1999

Printed in the United States of America

Visit HarperPaperbacks on the World Wide Web at
http: / / www.harpercollins.com

❖ 10 9 8 7 6 5 4 3 2 1

For Brittany, Siena, and Paul

Acknowledgments

For their generous help with research and fact-checking, I want to thank Long Bou-Chhung, Chethaketo P. Tan, and Lynne Weintraub. For invaluable feedback and support, I am indebted to my wonderful agents, Anna Cottle and Mary Alice Kier; my editors, Carolyn Marino and Robin Stamm; and my writing pals, Jeannine Atkins, Bruce Carson, Dina Friedman, and Judy Nikolai. For lighting candles in the darkest hours, I thank my good friends, David Ross and Aimée Dicker Ross. Finally, for providing fellowships for two interludes of blissful exile, I am most grateful to the Virginia Center for the Creative Arts, where much of the manuscript was written.

Plov veach kom boh bong
Plov naa trong kom duer hoang

The twisted path won't take you off course
The straight path may lead into the jaws of a tiger

—Cambodian proverb

Exiles on Main Street

1

Some blame the devil, some blame fate. I blame it all on rock 'n' roll. Because if it hadn't been for the music, chances are I would have lost the scoop—a matter of importance to me as a reporter for the local daily. I wouldn't have spotted the couple, or followed them along the crooked path into that murky territory on the edge of town, where souls are bartered, deals go down, and death awaits like a tiger on the hunt.

I had chosen the oldies station because I expected to hear something safe. Not this song. No, it was better to leave those old emotions buried. I didn't want to remember, but now that the music had begun, I was spellbound.

Delivered in a saucy, tough-girl taunt, the words hit me with two hundred joules of juice. So innocuous on the surface, they evoked so much.

"I'm riding in your car
You turn on the radio—"

Streaks of rose stained the frosted sky as the wounded sun sank behind the distant Berkshires. I pulled my ancient Civic—Honda's early boxy model, not the restyled sports-car wannabe—into a parking spot and gazed over the sprawl of one of the bleakest malls in Western Massachusetts.

I shut off the engine and sat listening in spite of the ache that had settled somewhere in the vicinity of my heart. That seductively straight yet sinister rhythm set by the bass and guitar, the relentless chink a-chink a-chink, sizzled with heat.

"You're pulling me close—"

In the dying light the vast lot merged with the surrounding farmlands, snow-blanketed and shimmering, and the present was momentarily extinguished by the past.

"I say I don't love you
But, you know, I'm a liar—"

Springsteen's "Fire," sung by the Pointer Sisters with a sultry innocence that harkened back to Ronnie Spector, was about sex, pure and simple. But lurking beneath the surface, a subtext spoke about a great deal more: about a young girl's ambivalence, about growing up, about fear, about resistance, about finally succumbing to the inevitable and letting go. Something I hadn't been able to do for a very long time.

What made the words endure was the ambiguity that all great rock lyrics shared. They provided latitude, space a listener could fill with her own private angst. As a teenager the love you reject, the love to which you are secretly and irrevocably drawn, is very often not romantic, but parental. That was the way it had been for me. "Fire" had hit the top of the charts when I was seventeen, the year my mother fell ill. More than fourteen years ago, yet the pain was as sharp as if it had been yesterday afternoon.

I'd been a runaway. Before I left, and even after I was lured back by the entreaties of my desperate father, I'd told her countless times that I hated her, but I was a liar. At the final moment, the last time I saw her, wasted and white, I had not been able to reach inside and find the generosity of heart to forgive her, to say, "I love you."

These were heavy feelings to be roused in this early twilight in my new hometown. As the final chords of the song faded away, I switched off the radio and gazed over the blur of cars in the packed lot on this last Tuesday before Christmas. I sat for a few moments, attempting to regain my balance, letting the present slough off the ghostly mantle of my past.

I had my own children now. I'd planned to spend a few moments doing last-minute shopping for their gifts before covering the Hallelujah Sing at the tacky central court of the mall. Such were the assignments I'd been getting as a rookie reporter on the small-town newspaper I'd been writing for since the spring, when Billy and I made a fast break from the fast lane and escaped to Greymont. It was a far cry from my glory days as a rock writer and Billy's as a musician, but that was what had attracted us to this sleepy college town.

We were refugees from rock and roll, and on most days the rewards outweighed the sense of loss. Sweet evenings with the fire crackling. Quiet. No more parrying with post-adolescent rude boys with guitars while I attempted to glean something that could be used in the reviews and short features I wrote for the rock press. No more lonely weeks with Billy out on tour and me in LA holed up with an infant, a two-year-old, a telephone, and a laptop. No more emergency calls from far-flung hotels and hospitals. No more glitter. No more frenzied search for the fountain of youth. No more all-night parties. No more bad contracts. No more last-minute tour cancellations due to sluggish ticket sales. No more lavish spending on borrowed time. No more creditors. No more lawyers. No more drugs. Yes, we had plenty to run from.

The mountains had melted into a washed-out smudge illuminated by one solo wisp of gold on the pale horizon. Most of the cars were driving with headlights on. The street lamps glowed like a string of pink jewels marking the highway that led toward Greymont's historic-landmark center. Last night's heavy snow covered the roadsides, and the plows and sand trucks were still out in full force. Snow was predicted again for tonight. It was time to let go of the past, to open the door to the frigid air of the future.

I had just turned my focus back to the task at hand, checking to make sure I had wallet, pens, reporter's pad, when I spotted the couple. An odd pairing, I thought, noting that they seemed middle-aged, the man dark-skinned, the woman white. But gesture, not skin color, was what sharpened the edge of my curiosity. The man paced hurriedly ahead, and the woman, in a frumpy green coat and blond fake-fur hat, slapped her hand to her mouth, shaking her head furiously. Neither noticed me as they beat a path in front of my Civic, where I was still seated.

When they reached the end of the row, the woman pointed to a big boat of a car, heavily laden with last night's snow, parked all the way at the outer perimeter of the lot. That was interesting, I thought. The automobile was the only one with such a heavy cover; clearly it had been there overnight during the storm. Something inside the car made the man spring back when he stepped up to the front window, dusted it off a bit, and peered inside. The woman, who hung far behind, put her gloved hands over her mouth.

They weren't too far away, but dusk veiled my presence as I watched from the Civic. The man drew a walkie-talkie from his pocket and spoke into it. The woman collapsed in sobs and shrieks. The man turned, glancing in my direction, but not seeing me, then took the woman by the arm.

Slowly they walked back toward the mall. As they passed under a light, I recognized the man as Dennison Brown, the security guard I'd used as a source on a car-theft story over the summer. I didn't know the woman. When they were only a few feet from my car, she grabbed Brown's arm and shouted something I couldn't quite make out.

"Get a hold on yourself, ma'am," I overheard Brown say.

When they were well down the row, I exited my car and locked it. Instinct told me not to be too conspicuous, so I slunk between two facing lines of autos as I made my way toward the snow-covered behemoth the security guard had inspected. When the two of them disappeared into the mall entrance, I made a beeline to the window on the driver's side and pressed my face to the glass.

A woman stared out at me through the frost. A trickle of blood had frozen at the corner of her mouth. I gaped, transfixed, into her blank eyes, and then realized with a start that she was dead.

2

Nothing in my past had prepared me for this. Once, on an interview for *Rolling Stone*, I'd opened the wrong door and found not one body, but two. However, they'd been quite lively, though somewhat muddled at the intrusion. This body, on the contrary, was decidedly dead, not something I'd ever expected to encounter in the relatively tame world of small-town journalism. As I stared at the corpse, my surroundings took on the surreal aura of cinema, removed from the normal by a membrane of disbelief. I watched myself in slow motion going through each take, perfectly calm, and marveled at how I managed to keep my head and maintain control. No panic. Not a trace. I suppose I was in semi-shock, but I didn't realize it at the time.

An unearthly heightening of the senses accompanied this altered state. Colors vibrated. Lights pierced the dusk with supernatural brightness. Snowflakes glimmered like sequins. Sounds reverberated against a velvet silence. I studied the corpse as if it were molded out of plastic.

Her dark eyes, staring through me to a place beyond life itself, stirred an odd flicker of recognition. A Cambodian, I surmised, examining the shape of the eyes and the tawny color of the skin. Had I met her? I'd just finished writing a long series on the refugees settled here in Greymont, so it was possible, but I couldn't place her.

I fished out my tiny flashlight and aimed the beam on the dead woman's face. Her broad mouth arced in a grimace of terror. Her crooked teeth were edged with blood. I imagined her screaming for help, the cries going unheeded or unheard.

My light fell on her torso. Beneath the blue-gray coat with a ratty fur collar, her coral-trimmed blouse had been ripped from her shoulders. Blood had coagulated into a black, gooey cascade over her naked breasts and stomach, which had been repeatedly hacked. The urgency of her last moments was etched into the strained clutching of her frozen hand at the window pane, open just a crack, with the tips of two purple fingers poking through.

I wobbled in my high-heeled suede boots. My knees, bare to where my skimpy pink dress started at mid-thigh, felt like ice cubes. I pulled my light wool coat around me, wishing there were a button at the top of the shawl collar. For a few moments I thought I would vomit. My legs swayed. *Keep your head*, I commanded myself, drawing in an icy breath, making up my mind to be brave. I'd seen bad things, but nothing like this.

A siren keened faintly in the distance. Knowing the police would seal the place off as soon as they arrived, I took out my pad and started to write. I wiped some snow off the fender, revealing a dark metallic green with patches of caked rust. I found the insignia at the back. The car was at least ten years old, a Chrysler New Yorker. Part of the trim had disintegrated. The door on the passenger side was beige. The front right fender had been mended with a thick swatch of Bondo. The kind of person who would buy a car like this—a luxury junker—had to be poor but with aspirations of grandeur.

I shone my light on the face again. She looked too old to be a student, but could have been anywhere from twenty-five to about thirty-five. My beam filtered dimly through the beaded ice on the window to the strikingly tidy back seat. The pale beige terrycloth covers and carpeted floor were spotless. Not a scrap of paper, not a leaf marred the neat appearance, in sharp contrast to the disgusting mess in front.

I squinted again at the corpse. She had typical Cambodian hair—black, coarse, and thick. Some loose locks had caught in the sticky mass of wounds across her stomach and breasts, and thick strands partly concealed the left side of her face. I examined her features, trying to conjure up an image of what she might have looked like minus the gore. Her cheekbones were prominent, eyes almost Tartar. Her nose was thick and flat against her pushed-in face. Her lips were generous, her crooked teeth small and square—like baby teeth. Yes, she was undoubtedly Cambodian.

I circled around the Chrysler and checked underneath for clues, until I could no longer ignore the wailing sirens and flashing blue lights as the police approached. I was taking one last glimpse inside the car when a large hand pressed my shoulder.

I turned to find myself face to face with Dennison Brown. The security guard was a portly African American in his mid-thirties, who'd helped a lot when I was working on the car theft articles.

"If it ain't Ms. Zoë Szabo, star reporter," he murmured with mock irony. "What are you doing snooping around without my permission?"

"Right now, trying to keep from keeling over."

"You seem to be holding up fine." He shone his light through the Chrysler window and shook his head. "Going to be a real carnival here tonight. You're dressed for it," he added, catching a glimpse of my pink silk. "Where'd you dig up that rag?" He liked to kid me about my Hollywood togs.

"Oh, back of the closet."

"I'll bet. Way back."

I smiled grimly, tying the sash of my coat in a double knot; it had no buttons. I wished now that I hadn't vogued up for the Sing, but there were so few dressy occasions in Greymont I hadn't been able to resist.

"Seen her before?" I asked, trying to slip it in casually.

"Nope. How about you?"

I shook my head. "I don't think so."

We had moved behind the parked cars away from the Chrysler. A spotlight invaded the darkness, flooding the area with a synthetic glow. Two police cars screeched to within a few feet of where Brown and I were standing. Several cops emerged from the vehicles.

"Will you give me a statement for the paper?" I asked.

"Later," Brown said, his tone growing more formal. "I've got to go talk to these gentlemen."

I took the cue, hanging back while he led the police officers to the Chrysler and showed them the window where they took a few moments to ogle the corpse. One swore softly. Radio static crackled in the air.

Some time later, accompanied by screaming sirens and flashing lights, several more police cars and an unmarked car drew up. A gangling white-haired man in street clothes, who I recognized as Bob Sodermeier, the Greymont police chief, jumped out of one of the cars. He jogged over to the Chrysler and shouted orders to the uniformed men. Moments later barricades were being erected around the automobile, which was now bathed in spotlights from several angles. Yellow crime scene tape went up along the rows of parked cars. Onlookers, drawn by the sirens and lights, had begun to gather at the barriers.

The woman in the fake-fur hat who'd pointed out the abandoned Chrysler to Brown was being questioned by a young officer. I watched as a couple of cars passed through the barricade at the outer edge of the lot and drove up. Two men emerged. Behind them another car door opened and a plump woman with a large black bag got out. The three conferred for a moment and then walked toward the Chrysler.

In the meantime, the policeman who'd been speaking with the fur-hatted woman had left her side. I seized the moment and stepped over to her.

"They tell me you found the body," I began.

Her mouth twisted, the only spot of color in her face. "It was awful."

"Can you describe how you noticed her?"

"I went to unlock my car. My packages must have bumped the window. I saw her out of the corner of my eye. At first I thought she was asleep, and then I saw the blood. I ran to get help. There was nobody at the information desk. This place is so badly run. Finally, the girl at the doughnut shop took me to the security phone. You know, they didn't believe me? They treated me as if I was crazy."

She brushed away her dark hair, which contrasted oddly with the fur hat. "The security guard finally showed up. I brought him straight to the car."

"What's your name?"

"May Stevenson." Her eyes drew together with suspicion as she noticed how I was dressed. "Are you with the police?"

"No, I'm Zoë Szabo from the *Greymont Evening Eagle.*"

Her forehead furrowed. "The newspaper?"

"Yes. Do you live in town?"

She nodded uncertainly. "This is the last time I ever shop here."

"It must have been upsetting."

"There's no security whatsoever. I mean, what is he doing? He should have been checking. It's an outrage!"

"Do you know who she was?" I asked.

"The dead one?" She pressed her lips together, shaking her head. "Do you?"

"No."

"She looked like one of those Cambodians to me."

Just then I caught sight of Dennison Brown. I took her number and excused myself.

"Do you have time for a few questions?" I asked, catching up with him.

"A minute. The woman you were talking to reported the body at five-ten. I walked out here with her, inspected the car, and called the police. That's Detective Brannigan over there next to Chief Sodermeier."

"Yeah." I scribbled the name down on my pad.

"He's head of the Western District, State Police. This is his jurisdiction."

"Has there been a murder at the mall before?"

"You kidding?"

"Any robberies, break-ins . . ."

He shook his head. "Well, the auto thefts. You know about that."

"People are saying security is lax."

Brown's eyes narrowed defensively. "I can't be everywhere. The stores have their own people for shoplifters, but other than that I'm responsible for the entire place. Fights, crazies, you name it."

"So you're saying nobody watches the lot?"

Brown shrugged placidly. "If a problem is reported, I check it out and call the police."

"They don't patrol?"

"No."

"Even with all these car thefts?"

"Talk to the manager. She'll want to put in her two cents, I'm sure." He nodded curtly and was gone.

A police photographer set up lights and began to take pictures. Forensic people hovered around the Chrysler. Near the edge of activity was Brannigan. Even before Brown had pointed him out, I'd recognized him from the press conference I'd attended when his appointment was announced over the summer. In his early thirties, he was young for the job—a short guy, flinty and close-mouthed. He covered the three counties that made up the Heritage Valley and oversaw homicides in all but the largest city, Springfield, far to the south.

Although it wasn't going to be easy to get his attention, I had to try. Now that the police were here, broadcasting on their radios, reporters would be all over the place soon. A murder might even draw television stations in Springfield and Hartford.

Uniformed men lined up, spread at arm's length, and began a meticulous search of the entire parking area. Walking twenty abreast, they combed the ground with their flashlights for clues, creating an eerie scene as flurries of snow drifted softly down from the murky heavens.

Brannigan headed away from me, his step brisk,

his head butted down like a billy goat. Even in the snow he wore no hat, and bristles of his short hair glistened in the lights.

"Detective," I shouted, jogging toward him.

He wheeled around and glared.

"What?"

"I'm Zoë Szabo, *Greymont Evening Eagle*. Could you confirm a few facts?"

"There'll be a statement at nine in the morning. My office." He spun around on his heels.

"Is this officially a murder investigation?" I asked, running to stay by his side.

"Looks that way."

"Who was the victim?"

"Don't know yet."

"A Cambodian? Town resident?"

He stopped short, faced me again, and looked me up and down with unconcealed distaste. His eyes lingered on my fashionable but impractical suede boots with their "What's-Love-Got-To-Do-With-It?" heels. After that he took a long look at my knees. I admit my skirt was a bit short for a thirty-one-year-old mother of two. But what probably threw him was my hair. Here in Greymont that seems to be the shocker. As a little girl I had dirty-blond waves almost as long as Rapunzel's. When I ran away from home at seventeen, I got fed up with the tangles and chopped it short. I go for the punk-glam look, though I've toned it down since we moved. When Billy and I met, I had a buzz cut à la Annie Lennox, and it was a lovely shade of baby blue. Now I settle for a close-cropped 'do bleached platinum, with a touch of color; this month it was a streak of pink. In California and New York, nobody ever gave me a second look, but here in Greymont, honest to goodness, people would drop their jaws and gawk. I'm an exotic in this neck of the woods; even though part of me wants to fit in, a deeper core can't bear to give up the style it's taken me so long to cultivate. I pulled my coat more tightly over my dress.

"You guys are supposed to be back behind the tape. How'd you get in here?"

I pretended not to hear his objection. "Can you estimate the time of death?"

His scowl grew darker. "No."

"The weapon?"

"I'm asking you nicely, Miss, uh—" He took in my outfit again, paused once more at my hair. I could read his thoughts, trying to figure out what planet I'd been hatched on.

"Szabo." I flashed him a quick smile. "The car's been here since yesterday. Has she been dead that long?"

The billy-goat head jutted forward. "What makes you think that?"

"I looked under the car. No ice or snow. It had to be parked before the storm."

"You print that, you'll tip off the murderer."

I softened my tone. "I don't want to screw up your investigation. Couldn't you give me a couple of facts I can use?"

He scrutinized me dubiously, then pointed to the

woman with the black bag, who was approaching the Chrysler. "The medical examiner will take a quick look here and do a more thorough job down at the morgue. It could take a day or more to pinpoint time of death. Off the record, please don't speculate about the weapon. Obviously, you've been poking around."

"Just one more question."

"Make it fast."

"Where do you start looking for clues?"

This was one he didn't mind answering; in fact, he relished the moment. "You comb through every flake of snow," he began with a grim look of importance. "You go through every used piece of tissue, every fast-food container and pizza crust in every garbage can for two square miles or more. You go through every mall shop and get the name of every person who's made a traceable purchase in the last twenty-four to forty-eight hours. You talk to every employee. You look at every scrap, every cigarette butt. You go down to the river and drag it for weapons. Because that way, just maybe, you get from zero to square one." He stopped and took a heavy breath.

"Now, I'm going to introduce you to my assistant. You tell him exactly what you saw, every move you made, since you've been here."

By the time they finally let me go, the ME had finished examining the body and was conferring heatedly with Brannigan, Sodermeier and a third man. As a cop escorted me to the barricades, the ambulance attendants approached the circle of police officers that surrounded the Chrysler. The parking lot was humming with activity as more onlookers crowded around the area cordoned off with tape and wooden barriers. Somewhere at the periphery cameras flashed. Behind that, a television news truck was parked, its generator humming. I walked toward it to assess the competition.

As I approached I caught sight of Mark Polanski, a Nikon hanging from his neck, waving a press card. Of all the reporters on the *Eagle* staff, Mark was my least favorite and, with a shiny late-model Miata sporting a police-band scanner, the most likely to show up. A former baseball jock at the State University, he'd been hired to cover sports, but lately had been maneuvering his way onto my beat, which was local politics and the arts. At twenty-six, he was five years my junior and never let me forget it.

"Hey, Szabo!" Mark called to me, accenting the final syllable. *"Qué pasó?"* For some reason he found my Hungarian surname funny. The forced rhyme, pronounced in a fake Mexican accent, had become his familiar greeting during the eight months I'd been on the paper.

"No game tonight?" I asked, ducking under the police line and nodding to the officer who'd escorted me.

"How did you get through?"

"Mole on the force," I stage-whispered.

He guffawed dismissively. "Right."

Mark was a big, athletic guy and despite his annoying personality, I found his physical presence comforting. I'd been more shaken than I realized.

"Get any photos?" I asked.

"Sure—of police cars. They won't let us close. How did you get in there?"

"Not even her?" I asked with a nod toward Carolee Clark. We print people considered her to be a prima donna because she anchored the evening news on TV and rarely wrote her own stuff. When she ventured out of the studio, she expected to be treated like royalty.

"Nope." He dropped his voice lower. "Man, was she pissed."

"I got the whole story," I crowed, unable to resist bragging.

"No kidding?"

"Yeah. Complete with quotes from the detective and the woman who found the body." The blood began to pump as I reflected over the fact that no other press had managed to interview even a minor spokesperson. I had a fantastic head start.

"I wish we could get some pictures." I scouted around to see if I could find any way to frame a decent shot. "Have you questioned anyone in the crowd?"

"A few. They're saying there was a shooting."

My pulse ratcheted up a few beats per second. No one even knew that it was a stabbing. The word *scoop* chimed in my ears like a tiny cymbal.

"Take a picture." I poked Mark, indicating the ambulance, awash in lights from the press and police. As the attendants lifted the corpse out of the Chrysler, Mark slapped on a long lens and shot. After what seemed like forever, the ambulance finally drove off. Watching it turn onto the highway toward Sheffington, I remembered the woman, her wide mouth arcing in a silent scream. I ached to know who she was, why she had died. I don't believe in ghosts, but something out of the ordinary had touched me. I had caught fire.

"Guess that's it for the Sing," Mark said.

His words sent me plummeting back to earth with a thud. I'd been scheduled to interview the Sing's organizer at five-thirty. I'd also promised Billy, who had a gig, that I'd be home by seven to watch the kids. I gazed up at the pitch-black sky. It grew dark very early here in New England in winter.

"What time is it, Mark?"

"Eight-oh-five."

I swore under my breath.

Mark smirked ungenerously. "Supposed to be somewhere, Szabo?"

3

Inside the Heritage Mall everyone seemed oblivious to the drama going on outside. In contrast to the dull concrete exterior, the interior was kitsched up to resemble a quaint New England town. The stores and food stalls had false fronts simulating old-fashioned shops, and the central food court was arranged around a "bandstand" of molded white vinyl. Matching planters with plastic tulips were dispersed strategically among the tables anchored to the green outdoor carpeting.

Town shopkeepers waged a constant PR war against the artificiality of the mall, but it was a losing battle. Greymont's retail space melted into restaurants, and the shops closed. I liked the authentic charm of the town center with its Colonial and Victorian buildings, its nineteenth-century brick town hall and storefronts, but I was also a sucker for all things glittery and fake. It was a continual source of conflict with Billy, who, now that he was a reformed sinner, had adopted the pure, organic way of life. He scoured labels for chemical ingredients and went out of his way to buy local produce. I was more laid back about what I ingested. And I missed the guile and superficiality, the synthetic glamour of California. I also pined for the light, the scent of the sea, and the beach.

I pushed through the hordes of shoppers to the bandstand, where I discovered to my relief that the Sing had been postponed to accommodate the police. Then, concerned about the fate of Billy's gig and my kids, I hurried down the dimly lit corridor toward the phones.

My stomach turned over slightly when I heard the telltale sound of a child breathing, then my three-year-old daughter's faint, high-pitched, "Hello?"

"Smokie?" I said. "It's Mom. Can you get Daddy?"

"Hello?" Smokie repeated.

"Can you get Daddy on the phone, honey?"

More breathing.

"Smokie?"

"Daddy's not here."

My stomach twinged. "Can you get Keith?"

"Mommy?"

"Yes, hon."

"Mom? Keith won't let me play with his Legos."

"Is somebody there with you?"

The phone seemed to go dead. My stomach began doing cartwheels.

"Hello?" It was Morgan Swan, our next-door neighbor.

"Morgan! I'm so glad to hear your voice. I got tied up with an emergency. It's a breaking news story."

"Zoë?" A semi-retired physics professor, Morgan was partly deaf. I suffered a pang of guilt, the kind only a mother feels when other people are caring for her children.

"Yes."

"Billy had to get to a *gig*." Morgan leaned on the last word. He was totally enamored of my ex-rock star husband, and he got a kick out of using the lingo. He played a fairly decent blues harp and was always after Billy to "jam."

"I'll be home in fifteen minutes," I shouted. "I'm sorry to have troubled you."

"Oh, no trouble at all."

I got off the phone as fast as I could and looked around. Mark had vanished. Digging into my wallet, I extracted another quarter and called my editor, Whit Smythe, at home. As we spoke I tried to imagine the lonely workaholic, wedded only to his job, in the grandiose Georgian manor, with formal gardens and carefully-tended fields in the south end of town, which had been passed down from his ancestor and namesake who'd founded the paper.

"There's been a murder at the Heritage Mall," I told him. I gave him a brief rundown and described the victim. "The police haven't released an ID."

Whit was quiet. "A Cambodian?"

"Yes."

"How do you know?"

"I saw her."

"They let you that close?"

"Not exactly, I—"

"Never mind. Look like anyone you've met?"

I hesitated. "I don't know. Maybe."

"Forget the police. Go to the community. Get interviews."

"Brannigan's having a press conference in the morning."

"That's too late. As soon as they release the name we'll know about it over the wires, and so will every other reporter in the state. The police know who she is right now. How many Cambodians are there in the county? Hundred, hundred-fifty?"

"Something like that."

"Go knocking on doors. Take Mark. I don't want you working alone."

"Now?"

"Yes. We'll hold the front page till the last minute. Dig up as much as you can tonight. We'll update the story just before press time tomorrow."

"Okay," I agreed, trying not to betray my panic. I had no idea how I was going to find someone to watch the kids while I chased the story tonight. Whit, who was single, didn't have children and had no idea what was involved. I'd once tried to plead off an assignment because both kids had chicken pox and Billy had a gig. "Get a baby-sitter," had been Whit's response. That was my third week on the job, and the story had been the high school graduation, not a murder. Daily journalism, I'd learned in an instant, was like the theater. No matter what, the show must go on.

"Too bad you didn't recognize her," Whit added. "You could go straight to the family now."

"I can check with the monk. He might know something."

Whit grunted approvingly. "Good idea. Call me anytime."

When he hung up, I called home again. Morgan put on five-year-old Keith, who promised to cooperate—not his strong suit—and go to bed. I told him I'd kiss him goodnight when I got home later. Once he heard about the murder, Morgan assured me he could hold down the fort.

By the time I was finished, Mark had materialized.

"Hey, Szabo, I found two Cambodian kids coming out of the movies." He flipped through his notebook. "They don't want anything to do with the police. I had to promise not to use their names."

I shook my head. That was the wall I kept running up against with the refugee series. Nobody wanted to be quoted.

"What did they say?"

"They didn't see anything today. *Yesterday* they witnessed an argument."

Yesterday, I thought. The killing could have happened then. The car had been there overnight, even Brannigan conceded that.

"Yeah?"

"Between a Cambodian woman, mid-to-late twenties, and a skinny guy they called 'Loony Toons.' Also Cambodian. Very thin, late teens or early twenties."

"Here?"

"Outside the arcade."

"When?"

"They weren't sure. Later, they said, the guy was causing a commotion in the arcade. Playing *Mortal Kombat,* or one of those killer games. They didn't see what happened because other kids complained and someone went for the security guard. They didn't want to get mixed up in it, so they split."

"Sounds like they speak pretty good English."

"One has a bit of an accent, but, yeah, they're fluent."

"How old?"

"Fourteen, fifteen."

I nodded. The kids were all fluent in English, while their parents barely spoke a word. The older generation was caught in a time warp, blocking out anything that happened after the Cambodian holocaust, unable to adapt to a new culture, unwilling to emerge from the past, while the kids couldn't put the past behind them quickly enough. They wanted desperately to be American, postmodern, cool.

"What are their names? I'd love to get a better description of the couple who were arguing."

Mark balked. "Uh, well . . ." he stammered.

"You have the names, don't you?"

He smirked condescendingly, feigning sheepishness, the ex-jock pose, at which he excelled. There wasn't an ounce of humility in that large, muscular frame. I let out an exasperated sigh.

"Unless someone else corroborates, this is useless."

"Why?"

"Because anybody can make up anything. They've got to be willing to stand by what they say," I added, "or we have to have independent confirmation, preferably both." *It's Journalism 101, Mark*, I thought.

"Why don't we let Whit decide," he countered slyly.

"Okay." I wondered if he actually had the names and didn't want to tell me. He was sneaky like that. He'd stolen stories from me before.

"You going home?"

"No. I talked to Whit. He wants us to cover this together, if you're willing."

"Whatever you say."

"I have to ask security a couple more questions. You want to find more witnesses? Maybe somebody else saw the fight."

"I'll look for those kids. See if they'll cough up their names."

I acknowledged this concession with a reluctant grin, which Mark breezily returned. We agreed to meet in ten minutes, and I went off to find Dennison Brown.

Nine-thirty seemed a bit late to go calling on a Buddhist monk, but the venerable Bou Vuthy was such a logical starting point that I put aside my sense of propriety and took the chance he'd be willing to receive us.

Mark followed me in his shiny red Miata after I managed to get the Civic started. The temperature had dropped about fifteen degrees in the last few hours, and the Civic, having lived most of its thirteen years in California, was allergic to New England winters.

The familiar chords of the Beatles' *White Album*, which I automatically slipped into my cassette deck whenever I was troubled, soothed my spirit. Growing up, I listened to the Beatles the way most kids clung to blankies and stuffed animals. The advantage was that I never had to give up my childhood security item. The Beatles have managed to endure and listening to them has never lost its appeal. George Harrison's guitar gently wept—with help from Clapton—as I cut onto back roads that wound past farms and into the more rural sections skirting Greymont's center. With only a few sprinklings of stars peeking from behind the clouds, the night was dark. Electric candles burned in windows. An occasional house sported colored lights. Trees decked with strings of Christmas bulbs marked the trail to my destination, the Normandy apartment complex, where a unit had been rented by a group of Cambodians to house a makeshift temple.

On the way I mulled over what Dennison Brown had told me. He didn't remember an argument between the crazy teenager and a young woman. But he had been summoned to the arcade by the manager and found the boy talking to himself. He'd intended to call the police, but an older woman, white, lean but vigorous, gray-haired, hawk-nosed, had appeared. The boy seemed to calm down instantly when she spoke to him in his own language. It was this last bit of information, that she spoke Khmer, which told me without a doubt that the woman was my friend Cletha Fair.

Cletha and I went way back. She was actually the reason Billy and I had moved to Greymont. A Quaker activist, a long-term resident of the town, she had been a friend of my parents. My father, a Broadway song-and-dance man, had done many benefits she'd organized. Having escaped from Hungary in '56, he was an unabashed supporter of human rights. She'd started calling him in the late sixties to perform at anti-war events in various cities, and they'd stuck together through subsequent campaigns over Nicaragua, Somalia, and South Africa.

When my dad was sick, Billy had filled in at one of Cletha's rallies here in Greymont, and he'd fallen in love with the town. Not too far from Boston, where he'd grown up in a large Irish family, it seemed to embody everything that America at its best was supposed to be: small-town, human-scaled, picturesque, and at the same time worldly, with its college population and culture. That was why we'd decided to settle here after the crisis. And I guess this is as good a time as any to talk about that.

The "crisis" is my shorthand for a series of events that almost led to the end of our marriage. For Billy it was a near-death experience, and for me it was the demise of whatever youthful illusions remained after eight years of writing on the rock circuit. It involved a combination of Billy's touring, debt escalating like inflation in prewar Germany, and heavy doses of cocaine and pills, which landed Billy in one hospital after another for about a year.

We had met at the tail end of Billy's run with success. He'd been the bass player for a band called Alamo, which had a couple of hits through the late seventies before falling out of fashion in the early eighties. They'd been trying to make a comeback when I was assigned to do a story on them for *Rolling Stone*. I'd been a cocky and irreverent twenty-three, twelve years younger than Billy. I was already a regular LA correspondent, after serving a stint as a staff writer in New York, thanks to family connections and a healthy dose of chutzpah.

Billy and I had some kind of music going even at that first meeting. Rock 'n' roll guys would often come on to me as part of their macho act, and the guys in Alamo employed the standard innuendo-drenched repartee that I'd grown to expect whenever I did interviews. I'd become adept at deflecting the comments. To my slight disappointment, Billy Harp, the sexy bass player with the bedroom eyes, didn't come on at all, although the corner of his mouth creased appreciatively when I got in a good zinger in response to one of the none-too-subtle comments of his mates. That egged me on, and I elicited some deliciously sophomoric quotes from the guys that I used to great effect when I wrote the piece. It was an acidly tongue-in-cheek treatment, lumping Alamo together with a couple of other bands I considered over-the-hill. I was into punk and new wave, and they were like

Eagles wannabes. My editor thought it was funny and put it on the cover, along with a picture of the band.

A few days after the story appeared, I got a call from Billy. Wanted to take me for a latté to discuss a few "quibbles." I suggested he write a letter to the editor. He upped the offer to dinner. I told him I was on a diet. He said he knew a great place for salad. I said, "I don't date guys I write about." He said, "How about guys you trash?" I hung up. He called back. The fourth or fifth time, I agreed to have tea. It turned out to be a pretty long cup of tea.

We'd fallen in love and made the terrible mistake of getting married almost immediately. Although pregnant with Keith, I wrote more and more. But even as my name started to get known, I was growing dissatisfied, feeling like I was no more than a cog in the music industry PR machine. Around the time when Smokie was born I went through one of those "What am I doing and why?" moments. My heart went out of rock writing. Of course, maybe this was my response to having two little kids and a husband who was constantly on tour, racking up debt at a fearsome rate, and becoming increasingly distant even when he was home.

The crisis came—after several warning tremors during the previous two years—late one night about six months after Smokie was born. I got a call from Japan that Billy had OD'd after a concert outside of Kyoto. They didn't know if he was going to make it. Ever try to get last-minute reservations to fly halfway around the world with a three-year-old and an infant? Well, I loaded up the last credit card to the limit and made the trip. Billy survived.

Once he was out of danger, I told him I'd had enough. The sweet dreams were all played out. I went home to my dad in New York and tried to sort out my life. Billy went into rehab. A few months later, he followed me to my dad's, clean, wanting to get back together, swearing he was quitting the band, drugs, touring, and the LA rock 'n' roll rat race. It took over a year to deal with the debt, sell off everything, get out of the bad contracts he'd signed over the years. I'd been offered another staff job at the *Rolling Stone* New York office. But Billy wanted to move to the country. I weighed the choices and, succumbing to his charm and the fact that I'd never completely fallen out of love even though I should have a million times over, I threw my lot in with Billy again.

Somewhere along the way my dad died, a grand old man of the Broadway musical. Those two years were such a nightmare that I block them out as much as I can. I miss LA and the wild life, but I don't miss the loneliness and the tears. Some nights when the kids are asleep and the house is quiet, I blink like a reverse-image Dorothy after the tornado. We're not in Oz anymore. How did we manage to survive, and is the storm really over?

Billy spends his time playing bass with local groups, just for fun, writing songs with the hopes of coming up with another hit, and watching the kids. I've taken up journalism with the closet intention of eventually writing something serious, some kind of investigative news thing. When I was a kid, one of my heroes was Lois Lane. I'm probably the only person in the world who bought the Superman comics just because of the reporter. I thought she was much braver than Superman; he had special powers and an impenetrable skin, whereas all she had was her wits. She'd go to the ends of the earth to track down a story, to nail a great scoop, no matter what obstacles stood in the way. She cared about people, about conquering evil. That's what intrigued me about news: It had an effect on the world, it wasn't just some glossy fantasy created to sell a product. Your words had meaning, they weren't just glitter and lies. Of course, I'm torn. The glitter is so beguiling, so pretty, a drug in itself, and the truth can be so plain, so deflating, so harsh. I guess that's part of growing up, learning to wean yourself from illusion without losing hope, which is what I've been trying to do for the last year and a half.

When I was undecided about getting back together with Billy, I'd confided in Cletha. She'd come down on a weekend when my father was very ill, and one night I just spilled it all out in a torrent. She urged me to reconsider the divorce I was planning, to take the kids out of the city to someplace like Greymont with good schools and fresh air.

Cletha was the only person in town who knew the whole dirty story about the crisis, and for that reason, even though I'd known her most of my life, there was a whisper of tension between us. My fault entirely; she'd seen us at our worst, and I was ashamed. Not that she would ever talk about it. If you could trust anyone to keep a secret, it was Cletha.

A feisty widow in her mid-sixties, she was the most persistent and principled person I'd ever met. She had led the drive to settle the Cambodian refugees in Greymont. She'd hounded—gently, of course—my editor, Whit, to do the series on the Cambodians and planted the idea in his mind that I'd be the perfect person, as the daughter of a refugee, to write it. But after I'd started probing into the terrible problems in the community—unemployment, spousal abuse, drinking, post-traumatic stress—she'd bombarded me with objections to the tack I was taking. The whole thing had been problematic. I wanted to do right by Cletha, who'd gone out on a limb to provide me with something meaty to write about and who'd helped Billy and me settle here, but I also wanted to do a professional job. And that meant telling both sides of the story.

This fall she adopted a foster son, Prith. After several years of struggle she'd brought him over from a Thai refugee camp as an unaccompanied minor. With a tremor, I wondered if he was the boy involved in the fight. I hadn't seen much of him, but I suspected he was troubled.

Knowing that she'd been at the mall last night worried me. As I approached the Normandy apartments, I tried to convince myself, hoping against hope, that Cletha must have taken Prith away before the murder occurred.

4

The door creaked open and the scent of incense wafted into the cold night air. I put my hands together in a *sompeah* and did my best to pronounce the greeting Cletha had taught me when I'd started my refugee research. *"Jum reap sua, Loak Sang."* Roughly translated, this meant "Greetings to you, venerable monk."

Bou Vuthy, a wrinkled, bald-headed man in long saffron monk's robes, bowed gravely. Wizened with age and sorrow, he stood only an inch or two above my own five-foot-four, but his presence filled any room he entered. He was a formidable character who had traveled widely and defended his people courageously.

"You are taking lessons in Khmer, Miss Szabo?" he asked, after I introduced Mark.

"Did I get it right?"

"Quite good," he said, closing the door.

Mark and I slid off our shoes, placing them with a row of other footwear beside the door, and followed the monk into a small room bare of furniture but covered with beautiful fabrics of many different colors and weaves, complementing heavy drapes over the windows. A poster of the Buddha was centered on the broadest wall. Nearby on a low table were an assortment of silver bowls containing betel chew, fruits, rice, and flowers, surrounded by dozens of candles of all shapes and sizes.

The flames danced in front of the mirror over the low table. I could see our reflections in the glass: me in my glitter makeup and short platinum hair with the streak of cerise; Mark in his down vest and khakis; the old monk with his thin brown arms and orange-yellow robes. I held my impractical teal coat tight so it wouldn't fall open to reveal my skimpy dress.

Bou Vuthy sat on the floor. Mark and I followed suit.

"There's been a death. A Cambodian woman," I explained. When he didn't reply, I added, "The police think it's a murder."

"You come to tell me this," Bou Vuthy asked after a long time, "or to gather information for your newspaper?"

There was no reproach in his tone, but the words stung. He'd been a frequent, though reticent, source as I'd worked on the series, and I'd learned to read his oblique manner.

"To gather information. Mark and I are on assignment. We want to find out who she was." I guessed at her age, described her face, her clothes.

The silence was suffocating. It echoed through the

room that served as a temple for the hundred and fifty lost souls who had found themselves on these shores after wandering the hell of Khmer Rouge Kampuchea and the purgatory of the refugee camps of Thailand.

The monk's face betrayed nothing.

"What kind of car?" he asked at last.

"A green Chrysler. Very old. Very big."

Though his face was impassive, his shoulders tightened ever so slightly. I watched him carefully as I continued. "One door was tan. The left rear fender was patched, but not painted."

The room grew colder. The candles seemed to sputter as if the spirit in the room that kept them dancing had faltered.

"Do you know the car?" I asked.

The old man's brown lips barely parted. "Yes."

"Whose is it?"

The impassive expression spread over his entire body.

"*Loak Sang*, the police will not be happy that I've told you this much."

"Many in Greymont would like us to go away," he said. "They make speeches and write angry letters to your newspaper."

"I know," I said, remembering some of the anti-immigrant rantings the series had provoked. It would be worse now, with the murder.

His eyes wrinkled at the corners. "Words have power. Please use them carefully. People can be hurt."

I wondered if this was a veiled warning, or if it was just a cryptic extension of the ongoing argument I'd been having with Cletha over my coverage of the refugees. As a reporter I had to present a balanced view. She wanted all the sordid things either ignored or softened with layers of sugar.

"We report the facts," Mark interjected. *Please shut up*, I prayed silently, but Mark blundered on. "News isn't censored here in the United States."

I was dumbfounded at the utter rudeness of his remark.

Bou Vuthy exhibited dignified surprise. "Of course not."

An aura of opposition crept into the air and mingled with the smoky incense. The monk spoke again. "Let me not waste your time. I can tell you nothing."

"If you know this woman," I pressed, "if she or other Cambodians were threatened, it might be important."

He slowly lifted his hands, his delicate fingers curled gracefully. "We must think first of her family." He stood up, signaling that the audience was over. Mark and I scrambled to our feet. After I'd zipped up my boots in the narrow vestibule, I couldn't resist one final attempt.

"Without mentioning any names, could you at least indicate whether this is a woman I might have met, or interviewed?"

His left eye seemed to twitch inadvertently. He shook his head no. Yet the face of the corpse swam back vividly. I *knew* I'd seen her. I just knew it.

* * *

It was after eleven when I parked in the tiny garage next to the rundown Cape Billy and I had barely found a way to afford when we'd sought safe harbor in Greymont. Clouds drifted across the soft circle of the rising moon, casting a sheen on the snow-crested roofs. I trudged up the unshoveled path to the house. On the other side of the yard, Morgan Swan's walks and driveway were neatly cleared. His three-story Victorian resembled a Christmas card with its delicate gingerbread, generous porches, the great wreath on the door, and the electric candles glowing at every window.

The sixty-eight-year-old professor was snoring lightly, seated in our big old recliner, a thick text open in his lap. On the floor lay his trusty PowerBook. He was a dyed-in-the-wool Mac man, a physics professor, amateur philosopher, and musicologist. He'd surprised me already when he'd recognized some veiled allusions of mine to little-known seventies punk bands (I used to hang out at CBGB's as a teen, which was one of the things my artist mother, a devotee of classical music, and I disagreed about). He had a vintage vinyl collection that made me drool.

A widower who'd lost a child many years earlier, Morgan enthusiastically agreed with me that Keith was a budding genius and had embarked on the project of teaching him to parrot the periodic table of the elements. I said to Morgan early on, "Why on earth does he need to know the valences of titanium when he's rockin' on guitar like his namesake?" Billy had told Morgan we'd named our son after Keith Richards, whom he'd met briefly when recording a demo in Canada.

"Zoë," Morgan responded, "rocket scientist isn't a bad day job." Which, of course, I had to concede.

Tonight, though, the professor was all tuckered out. Asleep in the recliner, he wore baggy tweed slacks and a nubby cardigan with leather patches on the elbows. With his thinning gray hair, droopy eyes, and sagging cheeks, he reminded me of the anthropomorphic creatures in the Mercer Mayer stories Smokie (as in Smokey Robinson of Motown fame) insisted on reading over and over again.

"Morgan," I whispered, touching his arm gently.

His eyes opened after a moment, but it took a few seconds for him to get his bearings. "Oh, Zoë."

"How were the kids?"

"Fine, fine. They tried a bit of mischief, but I kept them in hand. Tell me about your adventure."

I gave him a capsule summary as I helped him collect his things: the text, notes, and PowerBook, which he was rarely without.

"It was pretty gory. Whoever killed her must have been out of control."

"Sad business."

"Yes." I helped him on with his heavy overcoat. "Thank you for pitching in at the last minute."

"My pleasure, dear. You must start those children on instruments. Early music training increases intelligence. There are new studies."

"You might have mentioned that," I teased. He

pushed the music lesson theory every time we spoke, and I humored him. But I had no intention of following through, remembering the tortured piano practices during my own childhood with my exacting mother, for whom nothing less than perfect had been acceptable. She'd given up on me by the time I turned ten.

"Smokie's already picking out tunes," he responded, catching my tone. "Seriously, think about it."

"I will. Oh, I've got something for you."

"Really?" He was so pleased. Poor man was lonely. His only relative, a niece, lived in the Midwest somewhere. I ran to the kitchen and brought him a little basket of Christmas cookies I'd made over the weekend with the kids.

"Thanks again," I said.

He gave my shoulder an awkward squeeze. "Anytime."

"They can be loud."

"Enjoy the noise, dear. Be grateful."

After donning a muffler and mittens as slowly as a little kid, he departed through the mudroom. I watched to make sure he didn't slip on the way across our yard to his house. The light went on in his hall, and the porch went dark.

I was standing by the kitchen table. The dinner dishes with the remains of lasagna, Billy's specialty, were still out. I took them to the sink to soak. Then I distractedly thumbed through the mail, which lay out on the counter. Mostly bills, a couple of Christmas cards. One unopened letter was hand-addressed to Billy, postmark California. There was no return address. I lifted it to the light. Inside there seemed to be a handwritten note. Perhaps another Christmas card. I put it with Billy's mail and made a mental note to ask about it later.

I was eager to go through my files, but first I checked on the kids. Smokie had tossed off all her blankets and clutched a stuffed rabbit against her chest. I covered her, smoothed her hair, and kissed her, enjoying the sweetness of her soft three-year-old skin. *Such a cuddly little one*, I thought, melting slightly. She frowned in her sleep, shrugging me off. In Keith's room, I had to navigate a fleet of pirate ships and dinosaurs to reach his bedside. Unlike Smokie, he slept peacefully, his expression calm and angelic. I kissed his cheek and his eyes fluttered open. He reached his arms out and embraced me with a sensitivity that made up for his little sister's abruptness.

"Night, Mama," he whispered.

"Good night, darling boy," I echoed back, wiping the pale sweaty hair from his forehead.

He smiled dreamily, then drifted back to sleep.

You name kids, I thought wistfully, *imagine all kinds of things about them when they're born, and then they set about growing up and proving you wrong.* Keith was an introverted kid, a dreamer, a thinker, nothing like his namesake at all. I should have been thankful, but I felt a twinge of disappointment that he wasn't more of a boy's boy. If anyone was going to end up a rocker, it was Smokie. She was energetic, joyful, full of jokes and cheer. It was she who kept getting to Billy's bass, who picked out melodies on the MIDI keyboard. Still, Keith was the one who brought out the nurturer in me. I kissed him again before tiptoeing out of the room.

Downstairs, finding I was too late to catch the news on TV, I turned on the best local radio station to see what they had on the murder. In one corner of the living room stood a stack of file crates where I stored my clips and old notes. Keeping an ear tuned, I dropped to my knees and found the crate devoted to the Cambodian series. According to the radio, very little had been released so far. No victim ID, no time of death, no clues.

Knowing I still had more information than anyone else gave me a second wind. The feat was to publish it before they could beat me to it. With competition from big regional dailies and radio and TV, this feeling was all the more exhilarating. It wasn't as great as the first time I saw my byline in *Rolling Stone*; after that I'd walked on air for a week. But when I'd been on staff, I'd been one of the peons, not one of the VIPs. If I could score a bona fide scoop on the worst murder that had ever occurred in town, I could end up as one of the local stars.

Might as well start at the beginning, I thought, digging out the story on the lavish Cambodian wedding that had kicked off the series. Most of the refugees living in the area had attended, so it was a logical place to start.

I found four notebooks on the wedding, a tape with

some of the ceremony, and a few short interviews. The article itself, in the October 15 issue, had gotten a small lead on the bottom of the front page, linked to a big spread inside with lots of pictures taken by Kate Braithwaite, the *Eagle*'s staff photographer.

In a large center photo the bride and groom smiled radiantly from under a huge fringed pastel parasol. The bride was definitely not the victim. She was prettier, thinner, younger.

There were shots of her father, a muscular man named Rok Boeng, marked by a deep scar on his cheek; her mother, Saw Boeng, a wiry woman with one arm missing; her aunt Ly Touch, Saw's sister; along with assorted other relatives. All the women in the pictures were younger, older, thinner, or fatter than the victim I'd seen tonight. They wore Cambodian-style sarongs, tight blouses, and fancy coiffures. Everyone was smiling.

The only ones I remembered were Ly Touch and her daughter Song, who was a junior in high school. At the wedding, Song had offered to translate for me. I was charmed by her openness and intelligence, and later in the fall I'd done a mother-daughter profile.

As I browsed through the photos, I found one of the whole wedding party gathered around the bridal couple, who were seated before the monk, Bou Vuthy. The faces were too small to make out much detail. But as I perused them, something began to nag at me. Finally, I found a magnifying glass and went over the photo again face by face. After a few minutes I put down the glass with a sigh. The picture was too fuzzy.

Frustrated, I began to pace the room, picking my way through the clutter. Against the wall were two Fender basses, one in a case, the other on a stand, a Peavey amp, and a Stratocaster guitar. On the floor near Smokie's high chair snuggled a family of stuffed rabbits and a little calico house. By the door sat a pile of newspapers ready to be set out for recycling on Wednesday, next to a paper bag full of empty soda cans and seltzer bottles. Not without reason did Billy call this the hard-hat zone. I began to reorganize the scattered magazines and toys, thinking that cleaning up might help me sort the faces in my mind. As an accompaniment, I put on the Beatles' *White Album* again. That always boosted the brain cells.

Logic told me that the victim had probably been at the wedding. But two months was a long time in a reporter's life. I'd talked to dozens of Cambodians since then, met scores more, not to mention all the other stories I'd researched and written. Daily news was more demanding than anything I'd ever done. You hammered out story after story, day after day. In rock writing, you schmoozed a whole lot more, took time massaging your phrases, and drew better pay.

I washed the dishes I'd collected in the sink, letting my mind rest. I put down the last dish, wiped my hands, and went back to the old paper to reread the piece.

The wedding had been a three-day affair with lots of colorful pageantry and sumptuous costumes. I'd attended the biggest ceremony and stayed most of the day, watching the bride and groom appear in different changes of costume and undergo several separate rituals: one with candles; one with dancing, songs, and ritual haircutting; one with the monk; one with the *ajah*, or master of ceremony, lecturing the couple on how to have a happy marriage.

While the bride and groom went to change, I'd interviewed guests, listened to the live music played on native Khmer instruments and sampled the all-day outdoor feast. Food was barbecued over open pits. Dishes were washed by the tubful with hoses. Things looked much the way a festivity of this type would in Cambodia, except that the backdrop was a New England autumn with flame-colored maples instead of the rice fields, palms, and tamarind trees of the Southeast Asian tropics.

The article itself said little about the participants. It named the bride and groom, their parents, gave a brief description of their exodus from Cambodia, and spent several inches describing the pageantry and symbolism.

I flipped through my notes and found a wealth of material that never made it into the final story. My eyes fell on a description of fabrics.

Bmaids lace bls, tight bodice, puffy slves—dk blu pttrned silk "pantaloons" (name?). Bride headdress—big. Not move. Groom gold cape, green silk pants, tunic. Musicns JWlkr Red. Singing coupl story angels, rich mn's marrge, haircut. Symbol?—ask.

I closed my eyes and saw the shabby living room of the townhouse where the bride's family lived. It was empty of furniture, except for a few mats on the floor and a low table laden with fruits and ceremonial objects. I was watching *pithi kat soh*, the haircutting ceremony. A couple performed an elaborate dance, singing a story. They concluded by clipping the hair of the bride and groom and mixing the bits in a bowl. I'd later found out that this symbolized cutting and throwing out impurities, not blending souls as I'd first imagined.

Gradually, a face seemed to emerge from the mist. She was a bit older than the other bridesmaids. She wore a white lace blouse, blue silk pantaloons which puffed out at the hips and stopped around the knees, and high-heeled shoes dyed to match the pants. Unlike the others, she wasn't smiling. Her mouth was open in a grimace. Her small square teeth were crooked. Her black eyes seemed wary.

The face hardened in my mind. I saw a trickle of brown blood at the corner of the mouth. The black eyes stared blankly through the frosted window of the battered old Chrysler. My stomach knotted with a jolt.

I glanced down at the newspaper photo, going over the blurred faces again with the magnifying glass until I stopped at one of the bridesmaids. There she was. Short, somewhat stocky, a pushed-in face with exaggerated Khmer features, very wide cheeks, tiny crooked teeth.

I read the caption, my eyes gliding over the list of difficult foreign names. Chram. Yes, that was her name. Chram Touch. *Touch?* I thought. *Like Song and Ly.*

I closed my eyes, trying to focus my memory

through the fog. I thought of Song's bright face when I'd interviewed her. Then, my memory pricked, I recalled first meeting Song at the wedding. She was standing beside Bou Vuthy, interpreting the monk's words. Peter Albright, chair of the Asian studies department at the university and a good friend of Cletha's, was introducing me to Song's mother, Ly. I tried to put the face of Chram from the photograph together with this slender recollection. I remembered the warmth of the Indian-summer day, the sun on my shoulders as I spoke with Song, Ly, and Peter, the scent of barbecuing meat and curry, the sound of gongs and Cambodian music. A brief flash of the flat profile. The wary eyes.

But the flash faded and a seemingly unconnected moment floated to the surface. I was outside, sampling lemon-grass beef and hot curry with coconut sauce, chatting with Cletha Fair and Peter Albright. I'd nicknamed them the "defenders" because they double-teamed me, always trying to put the best face on anything I might end up writing. Peter and Cletha had traveled many times to Thailand to help relatives of Greymont's Cambodian families obtain the necessary papers to immigrate to America.

I shook my head, trying to rid myself of thoughts of Cletha and Peter, wanting to focus on the Cambodian faces. But the memory of our conversation persisted, and with it the other glimpse I'd had of Chram.

"Zoë," Cletha had been saying, trying to avoid a question I'd asked her about drinking among the musicians. "I saw you talking to Ly Touch. That's a sad story with a happy ending."

Throughout my research for the series, Cletha and Peter had plied me with "happy endings" and "success stories." They didn't want one negative drop of ink on the refugees, and shamelessly lobbied for a very upbeat group of articles that would generate support for more assistance.

"Yes," Peter agreed. He was a big, blustery man in his late fifties with a square red face, a thatch of white hair, and a hearty laugh.

"She and her husband lost four children under the Khmer Rouge. It was a miracle they got out alive with Chram and Song."

"Right," Peter concurred gravely, a hint of sadness showing in his eyes as it always did when the subject of the Khmer Rouge came up. He'd told me about colleagues in Phnom Penh, where he'd worked during the war, who'd perished in the Khmer Rouge camps. "Chram was the eldest child, Song the youngest. They were the only two to survive. Song is smart as a whip and made all-state running track."

Cletha added, "And Chram is engaged to one of Peter's students, Stephen Giles. A lovely young man, very promising."

Peter beamed, and Cletha flashed her big horsey teeth at him.

"There they are over there," she added, pointing out the bridesmaid, who had changed into a bright orange skirt and gold lace blouse. She stood a few yards away, just beyond earshot, beside a tall blond man who wore a loose white jacket and slacks and a

Cambodian shirt. His hair was long and very golden. He was lean and elegant. Early thirties, I guessed.

"Stephen's the pretty one of that couple," Cletha remarked dryly.

"Chram is a bit masculine, isn't she?" Peter said, echoing my own impression as I studied the woman's fierce expression. The couple were engaged in heated whispered conversation.

The three of us watched as Chram and Stephen moved away down the grassy slope toward a smoky barbecue pit where three Cambodian dowagers roasted chicken wings and lemon-grass beef on bamboo skewers.

They walked slowly and didn't touch.

Once she wobbled on her heel, which stuck in the soft earth, and he ever-so-slightly supported her elbow with the tips of his fingers. Even though the touch was small, it seemed tremendously sensual. She turned her face toward him. Her eyes, even from a distance, flashed. He bent over and whispered in her ear. She seemed to melt. The intensity between them had struck me, and the moment stood out sharply in my mind.

5

I must have dozed off, because as soon as I curled up on the sofa for just a minute before typing the article, Billy was shaking me. His mass of dark hair gave off the pungent scent of stale smoke from the bar gig he'd played that night. I opened my eyes. "Hi, honey," I murmured. "What time is it?"

"Around three. What happened tonight?" His lips tensed peevishly, accentuating smile lines that had deepened as he'd grown older. At forty-three, he wasn't quite as handsome as he'd been when we'd met eight years ago, but the rock-star appeal shone through the careworn features.

"What's wrong?" I asked.

"Babe," he said, an edge in his usually soothing voice. "Where the hell did you disappear? Luckily, Morgan was home. As it was I missed the sound check."

"Billy, you'll never guess what happened." I sat up. "I found a body."

"A *what?*"

"There was a murder. A Cambodian woman."

I blurted the whole chain of events: hearing the song on the radio, spotting the security guard, inspecting the car, discovering the corpse.

"Why didn't you call?"

"I did."

"When?"

"Around eight. If I'd left sooner, the police never would have let me back in."

His chiseled lips registered doubt, and his eyes creased. "Well, you could have broken away before eight. You were supposed to be here by seven." He drew the words out, as if trying to be reasonable. "I was waiting. So, when did you get home?"

"Around midnight."

"Jesus, Zoë—"

"Whit begged me to stick with the story. Morgan was delighted to help with the kids."

"So what does this mean?"

"What do you mean, 'what does this mean?' "

"You're telling me when you get a hot story, I can't— no, *we*, the kids and me, we can't count on you."

"That's not what I'm saying."

"What if there'd been a baby-sitter waiting, and you didn't get home till midnight?"

"I called as soon as I could."

"Babe, I had a gig."

"So did I."

We glared at each other for a moment. Annoyance pulsated in his dark brown eyes.

"Where are you going?" I asked.

"Get something to eat. You hungry?"

I followed him into the kitchen. None too daintily, he cut a piece of leftover lasagna and tossed it into the microwave.

"Billy, this is the biggest thing I've ever stumbled on."

He nodded in a manner I found patronizing.

"I couldn't let it slip through my fingers."

"Okay," he muttered. "Let's let it go."

One of our porous silences ensued.

The microwave buzzed, and Billy took out his meal. "Sure you don't want some?"

I tried not to show my distaste. "No, thanks."

He sat at the counter and opened an old copy of *Rolling Stone*. I suffered a pang of envy. The guy who'd written the cover piece had been a lowly researcher the year I'd met Billy and my career got put on pause. I tolerated a few more moments of benign neglect, then went to the table and sifted through my notes. The mail, which I'd left next to my papers, had been moved. I looked up at Billy, wondering about that California letter, but decided to wait until he was in a more hospitable mood. With a sigh I switched on my Compaq portable and started drafting my piece.

Billy glanced up, then went back to the magazine. He removed his white silk vest, draped it on the back of his chair, and rolled up the sleeves of his dark blue shirt. A careful eater, he wiped his mouth, then turned a page of the magazine with his long, thin fingers.

I finished the draft quickly, surprised at how easily it had come together. There were only a few outright guesses, which I could check in the morning. I wondered briefly if Mark had gone home after Bou Vuthy's, or if he'd tried to gather more news. Then I glanced at Billy, and our eyes meshed.

Taking him in, I was struck by the change time had wrought. Our romance had begun at a point in his career when he was fairly well-known and complacent about it, despite the fact that album sales had been slipping. He'd been a great-looking guy with fine-hewn Irish features loaded with wry charm, and seemingly not a care in the world. His magnetism had nearly engulfed me, and I had to fight to keep from being swallowed whole into his force field.

That he had been so much older gave me a bit of an edge, because I realized (more than he did) that his group had had its day, although this didn't stop me from being flattered by his attentiveness. I'd enjoyed the fact that he'd kept calling, and I liked the way he looked me over when we finally met for that "cup of tea." Over lemonades—not tea, as it turned out—we continued the verbal sparring we'd begun over the phone. Of course, he did bring up the article, putting forth a theory that perhaps Alamo wasn't the has-been group I'd made it out to be, asking whose stuff I did like, and then making snide remarks about the acts I mentioned. We finally found common ground when he quoted a Smokey Robinson lyric. I loved the old Motown stuff and so did he. We kept talking until I realized I had to get to an interview, and he offered to drive. The whole way there and back, we chatted about Chuck Berry, Marvin Gaye, the Supremes. When we finally reached the lot where my car was parked, he made the pass that I'd been half-expecting and suggested we continue the conversation at his place.

"Maybe some other time," I answered.

"Why not now? Life is short."

"Not that short. I'm no groupie."

He laughed.

"You seem surprised," I said.

"I didn't think I was treating you like that."

"Listen," I said, "in this town people will walk all over you if you give them half a chance. I don't intend to become a major thoroughfare."

He laughed again. "How about dinner? I know a nice place by the beach. Far from the beaten path."

We negotiated. Finally, I agreed, on the condition that after dinner I would go home alone. We had a nice lazy meal at a cheap seafood place on the beach, enjoying a gorgeous salty sunset, and then we took a long walk as a lavender dusk melted into an inky star-strewn night.

Our conversation switched from music to our backgrounds. He told me about his big Irish family, his father who worked for the Boston transit system as a conductor on the T, his brothers and sisters, the difficulty they all had with his success and his own nagging guilt about leaving them behind. I told him about my dad, his stints in the *Fantasticks* and in summer theater on Cape Cod when he wasn't in some

Broadway production. He told me about his reading—he dabbled in poetry and philosophy, stuff I had never touched. By the end of the evening, I was in love. Not infatuated, not beguiled by the poise, the attitude, the grace, but really in love for the first time in my life.

It was two in the morning when we parted, and he was at my door, knocking, at dawn, saying he couldn't sleep. It was the only really magical time I'd ever had with a guy because I'd always picked such losers before: bad boys with rotten attitudes, guys who wore macho threads and felt compelled to prove their masculinity by treating chicks like dirt. Billy wasn't like that. Maybe it was because he was older, or more successful, but he didn't seem to need to prove anything. He was tired, he said, of tarty types who wanted to make it just to say they'd done it with you or worse because they thought you could help further their career, which, of course, you couldn't.

We went back to the beach and walked, watching the sun rise over the city and admiring the pewter sea in the vanishing half-light.

No matter how bad things have gotten since, the colors of that night and morning have never faded from my memory. It's like a film, the way I see it. As the credits roll, a sexy, synthy tune loaded with sensual overtones and a bitter, dazzled drum, beats on relentlessly. Echoey sopranos sigh while a wanton diva croons a sultry lyric. Annie Lennox, maybe, singing "Sweet Dreams."

Through all the tears, all the anger, that sweet

dream remains, like a scrim fluttering unseen in a darkened theater.

His late snack done, Billy brooded, still slightly testy, though I could tell his mood had begun to mellow. His soulful eyes were rimmed with red from too many hours in a smoky bar with poor ventilation.

"This is an incredible scoop," I told him.

"Looks that way." His tone was unconvinced.

"This may not be a big paper, Billy. The woman who died, her family, this little community of refugees—they may not be movers and shakers, but they've been through a hell of a lot. My leads are golden. I can bring something to this story no one else can."

When he didn't object, I pushed on. "But it will involve long hours. There will be times when I won't be able to get to a phone. Somebody else at the paper could cover this murder. Mark would just die to be in my shoes. But that means I lose a chance that will probably never come again."

"So," he finally asked, "what are your leads?"

I told him about Chram and her family. "I want to talk to them first thing in the morning. They know me. And then there's Cletha. Her foster son, Prith, has been behaving strangely. She picked him up after a fight at the mall the other night, close to the time of the murder, I think. It's not confirmed."

That hooked him. Billy thought the world of Cletha. He nodded. "She's good people."

"She might be in pretty deep. I hope not, but, well, she was there and so was Prith."

"You don't think she did it?"

"Of course not! Cletha wouldn't hurt a fly."

We both fell silent, thinking the same thing but not saying it.

"I was going to call her tonight," I added after a moment. "But I want to have more facts before I do."

"You sure you want to work on this, Zoë?" Billy asked quietly.

"Yes."

"Even if—"

"Cletha's not involved in any way. It just can't be."

"Well, don't worry about me and the kids," he relented. "We'll manage."

The softness in his voice touched me. "Sorry about tonight."

He went to the fridge. "Hey, I've done worse to you. Sure you don't want some of this lasagna, it's really good."

"No. I don't think I can sleep. I'm so psyched."

"Here, this will help." He poured a glass of California semillon and handed it to me. Took a beer for himself. Billy never was much of a drinker, but being Irish, he likes his microbrew. Now he is careful, even with beer and wine. We both watched as he poured today's quota, from a tiny brewery in Maine, into a glass.

I took a sip of wine and my solar plexis unclenched. I hadn't realized how much I wanted his support. It would be difficult enough to juggle my job, child care, and the holidays. Being Jewish on my father's side, I'm pretty ambivalent about Christmas. My first inclination is to ignore it. My father always made sure there was Hanukkah gelt and that the Menorah candles were lit; my mother, a lapsed Catholic, gave a gift or two at Christmas, though we never had a tree, which she considered wasteful. But this year Billy and I had agreed to do it up right for the kids and to put the past behind us.

"I have a couple of gigs," Billy volunteered, checking his calendar. We'd moved to the living room and were nestled together on the sofa.

"Maybe Morgan can help."

"Yeah. And, remember, we promised to go to my folks right after Christmas."

I nodded. "It'll work out." I silently determined that it would.

He draped an arm round my shoulder and touched his forehead to mine. We shared a kiss. Just a teaser.

"Oh, by the way, honey," I whispered. "What was that letter about?"

"Hmm?"

"The one from California. It was on the table. Did you open it?"

"Yeah. Oh, it was nothing."

"No, who was it from? I'm curious."

"Just, you know . . . fan mail. Where were we?" The old charm surfaced momentarily in his grin, and the synthy beat picked up.

"Your folks."

"Uh-uh."

"Christmas?"

"Here, let me refresh your memory."

His breath was like a dusting of frost on my lips. I

slipped closer. The rest . . . I promised to keep off the record.

I let my hand dangle down till it touched the phone, and to quell the persistent ringing I grasped the receiver in my fingers and brought it to my ear. The voice was Whit's.

"Mark just called from the police station. They've notified the next of kin. They're not giving us the name yet, but they should soon."

"Chram Touch," I muttered groggily, making myself sit up. It was dark outside the bedroom window. Beside me, Billy, who slept in the buff, rolled over and groaned, pulling the down quilt up to his naked shoulder and the pillow over his head.

On the phone, Whit hesitated. "You're sure?"

I grinned to myself. He was impressed. Whit was one of those close-to-the-chest New Englanders, whose praise consisted of small visual signs and slight pauses. "It's an educated guess."

Billy groaned again, tossed back and forth on our four-poster bed. I took the hint, carrying the cordless phone into the bathroom, grabbing my fleece robe on the way.

"I met her briefly," I added to Whit, after seating myself somewhat uncomfortably on the rim of the old-fashioned tub. It was a big bathroom which we shared with the kids, this being a prewar house built before America fell in love with multiple toilets as status symbols. Instead there were two medicine cabinets, a large linen closet, and a huge sink with brass hardware. I'd stripped off the yellow fish wallpaper that the previous owners had put up, painted the walls white, and decorated with bright cornflower blue rugs, hampers, towels, and shower curtain. And I think it was my favorite room in the house. A large window across from the tub looked out over the backyard into the huge old maple and across at a neighbor's swing set. Now most of the branches were shrouded by darkness, although a bright moon lit some of the snow-laden limbs.

"Have you talked to her family?" Whit was asking.

"No. What time is it?"

"Four-fifty."

"No wonder I'm having trouble keeping my eyes open."

"They'll release the name too late to run in the morning papers," Whit exclaimed. He sounded positively ecstatic. The *Eagle* was one of the last afternoon dailies in the country. "I need your copy as soon as possible. Then I want you at the Touches'."

"How about the press conference?"

"They've pushed it back to ten. At the Hotel Carnarvon."

"I want to go."

"We'll talk about it when you get here."

If I was going to a press conference at the district attorney's headquarters at the hotel, I figured I'd better dress respectably. Generally, I go for slinky dresses and Matterhorn heels. Today, I toned down my look to retro-fifties coed, picking out a soft blue angora sweater and gray skirt with matching suede pumps. I checked out my hair, with its streak of cerise. After doing my makeup, I grabbed the scissors I used to cut the kids' hair and snipped out the brightest spots of pink. *There*, I thought, I looked a little less alien. Of course, short of a total makeover I was bound to stand out; however, today's ensemble had a nice hint of *noir*, which seemed appropriate for investigating a murder. In the kitchen I grabbed my computer disk, left a note for the kids and Billy, downed some vile coffee reheated in the microwave, and ran out the door.

It was nearly five-thirty when I arrived at the *Eagle*'s office on Main Street. The double entry of the old Victorian opened into a large hall where the receptionist's desk stood. It was empty at this hour. A set of pocket doors off the hall led to the main area, composed of three large rooms that had originally been a parlor, a living room, and a dining room. Here the reporters had desks with computer terminals and phones. To the rear was a kitchen leading onto a huge back porch, glass-enclosed in winter and screened in summer, where we sometimes ate lunch and where the smokers on staff retreated for their breaks.

I hung my coat on the rack near the doors and climbed the massive oak staircase. Whit's office was neatly kept, with a large bay window overlooking the Commons. His desk was angled so he could get light from the windows without having glare on his monitor. The room was lined with books, antique prints, and old front pages from important moments in the paper's past.

Everything about Whittimore Covington Smythe III was tasteful, tidy, and quiet, including the way he dressed, usually in an Oxford shirt, V-neck sweater, and tie. His furniture was old family stuff that looked lived-in but good. Whit had inherited the paper from his father and grandfather. He'd grown up in this town, moved away after college, dabbled in poetry, found a job working on a paper in upstate New York, then moved to the *Globe* for a couple of years. When his father died, he'd tried to sell the paper. My suspicion was that he'd set an inflated price because he subconsciously couldn't bear to let the paper out of family control. Then he hired an editor to run it, attempting to stay in the background. When the paper began to go under, he came back to town to try to revive the tired old rag.

And he succeeded, although things were touch-and-go at slow times of the year. He shifted the emphasis from small-town gossip to hard-hitting regional stories with lots of local sports. He hired eager young writers and gave us a lot of free rein. Instead of the traditional editorial page with wire copy from national syndicated columnists, he went for the heavies on the local political scene and urged them to write punchy opinion pieces. His editorials were the clincher. He tackled local, national, and international issues of the day with wicked, incisive language that made people boiling mad, but kept everyone coming back for more. It was a great local paper, and I was proud to be on staff.

Whit sat at his desk, studying the computer

screen. As usual for this hour, he was doing a last-minute edit on items that had come in at deadline last night. These would be transferred to the compositor by modem, and the paper would be made up within the next hour or so, with space reserved for a late-breaking story on page one. By ten all the changes would be made, and the paper would be printed and ready for distribution by noon.

He tapped the keys, his brown hair cut close, his face narrow, patrician, pale. Although only a year older than Billy, he was light-years apart in style. Billy was the counterculture; Whit old-fashioned Ivy League. Billy was a natural flirt; Whit, a bachelor, prim and reserved.

Without looking up, he said, "What took you so long?"

I knew Whit well enough to know he was too impatient to listen to an explanation. So I just started reading.

"Chram Touch—pronounced 'TOO-it'—who survived Cambodia's brutal killing fields and the slow death of a refugee camp on the Thai border—thought she'd finally found safe harbor when she arrived on the shores of the New World two years ago.

"Late yesterday afternoon that safety was shattered when Touch's body was found slumped over the front seat of her 1979 Chrysler New Yorker. The car, according to police estimates, had been parked at the Heritage Mall for nearly twenty-four hours before the body was discovered by May Stevenson, fifty-six, of Greymont.

"Death came after a struggle, according to Chief

Detective Kevin Brannigan of the Western District State Police. Touch, who was twenty-eight years old—I have to check this—had recently become engaged to Stephen Giles, a graduate student in Asian History at the State University at Greymont. She apparently died from multiple stab wounds to the chest and lower abdomen. . . ."

Whit listened while I spoke, folding his hands together as if praying. His elbows rested squarely on the mahogany desk that had been in his family for six generations. He studied his fingers. When I broke off, he looked up.

"How much can we print?"

"I have to verify my facts with the state police. Everything on Stevenson and Brown I can use, and the quote from Brannigan. I might run into trouble on time and cause of death."

Whit picked up the phone and dialed. He identified himself and asked for Brannigan's office.

"We're about to go to press," he said. "We need an official response to a few facts." After a moment's wait, he read the pertinent sentences over the phone, scribbled some notes, and then hung up.

"Okay. We can go with most of it. Of course, they're mad as hell that we came up with the name. They say Touch was thirty. We can confirm that with the family. They say they won't have cause of death until the preliminary autopsy report becomes available tomorrow at the earliest. But they corroborate the stab wounds, and"—his mouth twitched in a partial smile—"though they're not certain, it looks like she died sixteen to twenty hours before the body was found. Could even have been twenty-four. Seems the cold makes it hard to set time exactly. They're still working on it."

"That means she was dead by midnight on Monday."

Whit nodded.

"Leave your disk. I'll get it into the computer. We'll hold page one till eleven. Go to the Touches' and get me a quick profile of Chram, maybe a photo if they have one. Reporters are going to be crawling all over the place within a very short time, so you have to work fast. How well do you know the family?"

I handed him the clip on Song and Ly.

"We can take this escape story and recycle it. Can you get me some new facts?"

I nodded. "I was hoping to go to the press conference."

He looked at his watch. "No time. Go to the Touches', then hit the pavement and talk to anyone you can find who knew her. The closer the better. I'll send Mark to the briefing, or would you rather have him with you?"

I winced discreetly.

"What's your problem with Mark?"

I made an attempt to be diplomatic. "There's a rapport you establish in an interview. Having someone else there blows it."

Whit rubbed his nose with the back of his thumb. "I covered one or two murders for the *Globe*. It's a dirty business. Do you think you're up to it?"

This sounded like a reprimand. "I have the contacts," I said indignantly. "This is my beat."

"Mark's a big athletic guy. This may have been a sex crime. I have to be concerned for your safety."

I paused, revealing a sliver of self-doubt. Whit's eyebrow went up. He was a master at reading inadvertent facial expressions.

"I can do it," I said tightly. "I want to."

"Why?"

"Why?" My mind raced, as I realized this was my cue to pitch. Whit never gave you more than one shot. "Because this woman had just begun to put her life together. She was in college. You know how hard it is for a Cambodian immigrant to do that? She was a teenager at the time of the Khmer Rouge takeover. Under their rule there was no education. Instead they had brainwashing. They murdered every teacher, every knowledgeable person. Bou Vuthy, the monk here—I think I can get him to talk, by the way—he's one of the few who eluded their grasp. Think of it. Cinderella of the killing fields, engaged to this handsome grad student. And Stephen Giles is a knockout. Let me tell you, he fits the part of Prince Charming.

"Then, Monday night, days before Christmas, the season of peace, love, and redemption, someone sticks a knife into her. I saw the body. She must have been stabbed twenty or thirty times. I can't get the blood out of my mind. Whit, I have to find out why she was murdered."

He weighed what I'd said.

The wind picked up in the trees. The snow shaken

from the branches was tossed by a gust against the office windows. The frozen flakes at the glass sounded like fingernails scratching, as if there were a ghost out there, pleading for sanctuary from the cold and pitiless dawn.

6

I walked through the old center of Greymont to my Honda, which was parked in the lot next to the Commons, across from the landmark town hall with its slate roof and clock tower. Nearby stood the sprawling, eighteenth-century Lord William Inn and the stone Congregational church. Two blocks to the south rose the Ivy League spires of Greymont College. To the north on the same block as the *Eagle* office stretched a row of shops and bookstores. To the east an old-fashioned bank faced a large modern one, where more small shops and restaurants ran the length of Stanhope Street. Though the names and types of stores were different, one hundred years ago the buildings had been nearly the same.

The Civic started without a hitch, and I drove around to Stanhope. When I passed Wingate's, the big stationery and news store on the corner, I reminded myself to stop in later to buy the stamp sets Keith wanted. There were only four shopping days till Christmas. Somehow, I had to finish purchasing and wrapping my gifts. Luckily, I'd bought Billy's already, and the kids were young enough to be satisfied with little things that could be picked up in town. I didn't relish a return to the mall.

The drive to the Touches' apartment, located in the same complex as Bou Vuthy's temple, was absolutely shimmering. I rarely found cause to be up at dawn and was smitten by the faint pinks and lavenders, the half-light reflected by the snowy fields, rooftops, and trees, as my Honda tooled along the well-cleared road through the south of town, past the old library and the colleges, toward conservation land and farms.

But as I turned along the curving road that led toward the Touches' building, my sense of calm evaporated and qualms began to nag me. The last time I'd interviewed them, it had been for an upbeat profile on Ly and her teenage daughter, Song, highlighting the girl's success in school and on the track team. Now I had to go back and probe their wounds. In rock journalism your subjects were eager to publicize upcoming ventures. They wanted to talk to you, although they didn't always like what you wrote. But in straight news, you had to interview people in their rawest moments. Suddenly the superficiality of celebrity journalism seemed almost laudable and hard news morally questionable. What drove my desire to ferret out and tell the truth? Was it a noble commitment to justice or merely ghoulish curiosity?

I shut off the ignition and watched the fiery tentacles of sunlight glint across the far mountains. Lois Lane, I reminded myself sternly, wouldn't have entertained doubts. She would have rushed in headlong, finding ways to pinpoint the villain, getting herself—of course—into an unimaginable mess, from which Superman would have to rescue her. But the culprit would be nabbed, the crime solved, the righteous risen victorious. Crime reporting wasn't for wimps, and part of the toughness required was the willingness to ignore the victims' feelings. I was not going to let my fear, sympathy, or any odd mixture of the two, get in the way.

As the door opened I immediately recognized Auntie Saw Boeng—not because of the coal eyes that lit the ravaged face, the sharp, angular frame, or the shiny black hair rolled into a taut bun, but because of the pinned-up sleeve that hid her amputated left arm.

I was about to explain who I was when I felt her one hand on mine. She clasped it with fierce energy.

"*An djunn jol,*" she began, a phrase I'd heard often in the past few months, meaning "Please enter." A string of Khmer syllables followed. "Come," she repeated.

After leaving my suede pumps in the hall, I entered a room that had not been as cleverly transformed from the drabness of poverty as Bou Vuthy's "temple" a few buildings away. When I'd been here to interview Song and her mother, the apartment had not seemed so threadbare. The stained mustard carpet was only partly hidden by Cambodian mats, and these were well worn. A television cart stood in the corner of the room, and the top of the TV served as an altar, with photos of dead family members, wilted flowers, and candles. The walls, badly in need of paint, were pasted with travel posters of Phnom Penh and water buffalo. Yellowed and curled at the edges, they looked as ancient as the tranquil scenes of prewar Cambodia they depicted.

Near the rear window in a white lacquer chair sat a thin old man in faded blue pajamas. His hair was gray and several teeth in his lower jaw were discolored. He gazed at me. No, he looked right through me. In one hand he held a glass filled with an amber-colored liquid that appeared to be whiskey.

I nodded and said, "Hello."

He scowled toward Saw, who let out a string of popping consonants and deep vowels that I recognized as Khmer.

He mumbled malevolently, then wobbled toward the stairs, which were partly visible through the archway, and shouted. The only word I could make out was "Song." Then he shuffled back.

Against the far wall was a bureau, its cream-colored paint chipped. The top was covered with an orange-and-gold silk runner, more photographs in cheap metal frames, mirrors, and bright gold-and-silver footed bowls filled with mangoes, tangerines, and lemons. In the center stood a photo of a child in formal Cambodian attire, a sarong of iridescent purple and a white lace blouse with puffy sleeves and a Chinese collar. She looked like a very young Chram

Touch, about four or five years old. Before the photo, a long thin candle burned.

Auntie Saw spoke again, this time to me, saying, "Sit. Sit." She indicated the vinyl sofa. One of the seams was ripped and there was a large, soiled spot on the center cushion. I sat down.

"Tea?" she asked. "Caffee?"

"Just a little."

"Caffee. No trouble."

She disappeared through the archway to the kitchen. I was alone in the room with the man.

"I'm Zoë Szabo," I spoke slowly. "With the *Eagle*, the newspaper."

He held his glass forward, eyeing me uncertainly. To my surprise, he spoke. "My name Phroeng Touch." His accent was so thick, I had to strain to understand.

"Are you Chram's father?"

At the mention of the name, a spasm shot through his face. In slow motion, his mouth widened. I thought he was about to laugh or scream. But no sound came out. After a pause, his mouth closed in a stiff grimace. He drank the rest of the amber liquid and gazed at the large photograph with the flame dancing before it. Then he turned toward me, glowering, the gray hair a soft halo about his deeply-etched face.

I shrank back against the sofa, enveloped by all the emotions I'd promised myself not to give into.

"I'm so sorry," I stammered, groping.

Still, I wanted to establish his identity, get a quote,

but I wasn't sure how much he knew, how well he understood English, or how drunk he was.

"Ay," he said finally. "My beautiful child. Number one." He held up one finger, smiling with his mouth, grieving with his eyes. "She live so much. Much terrible thing. You know?"

His English was almost unintelligible, but as I deciphered it, I nodded.

"Here. She die"—he raised his voice as if struggling to find the words—"safe."

He shook his head in disbelief and dropped his arm. It hung by his side lifelessly.

"You mean she died in safety?"

He grunted. "Safe here, right?"

"May I say that in the paper?" I asked, slipping out my pad.

"You say." A long pause and a bleary stare.

I wrote it down.

From the kitchen I heard Auntie Saw speaking. She came out followed by Song, who glanced at me with a flicker of recognition, then looked with concern toward her father. She spoke to him quickly in Khmer and he responded, sounding dismissive and very drunk.

"Hello," she said to me, her expression troubled. "You're from the paper."

"Yes." I mentioned the profile I'd done of her and Ly.

"I remember," she said. Her simple clothes were clean and freshly pressed, but threadbare. Her long black hair, falling to below her waist, had a slight wave and was held neatly in a barrette at the back of her head. Tall for a Cambodian, she had long limbs and a lithe, athletic body. Her smooth face conveyed a placid acceptance far beyond her seventeen years.

"My aunt thinks you are coming to express your sadness at what happened to my sister." Saw was standing to the side holding a tiny plastic cup. Another man entered the room, moving up behind Saw. I assumed he was her husband, Rok. Short, muscular, and menacing, he wore a well-cut gray suit, newer and more expensive than the clothes most refugees wore. A thick curl of hair hid one eyebrow. On the other side of his face a purple scar traveled down his left cheek like a tear track, beginning under his eye and stopping just below his protruding ear. His features were exaggeratedly Khmer, skin a dark tan, face and cheeks very wide, nose flat, lips full.

He nodded curtly and moved toward the bureau where the photo and bowl of fruit were placed. He selected a fresh candle, borrowed fire from one of the flames on the dresser top, and lit several candles in small glass cups. He chanted.

"Uncle Rok is praying for Chram's ghost," Song explained, "that she will go to a calm place. That she won't wander. Those who die violently can wander and become angry and cause trouble."

She stopped speaking and lowered her eyes. Her aunt offered me the cup of coffee. I thanked her and smiled, in an attempt to be polite.

"Do you mind if I take a few notes?" I asked. I wanted to make sure I had all the names right.

"You are here for a newspaper story," said Song.

"Yes." I asked her for everyone's age and the spelling of their names. Phroeng was forty-nine, she said. I couldn't believe it. He looked closer to seventy. Saw was forty-six. Rok was fifty.

Something heavy fell upstairs. I heard a cry.

"Excuse me. I need to help my mother."

Song disappeared behind the partition. I heard her footsteps on the stairs and, after a few moments, voices above.

In the meantime I took a sip of the coffee, which was undrinkable, and smiled at Saw, who watched as if trying to gauge exactly how many drops I'd consumed.

"When did you find out about Chram?" I asked.

Her face tightened. "Chram," she said loudly, her intense eyes zeroing in on me. "Dead."

The two men, Rok still praying at the makeshift altar, Phroeng in a stupor, turned and stared. I felt a deep discomfort.

Phroeng began to speak in Khmer. Rok interrupted sharply. I couldn't understand any of the words, but Rok sneered, uttering a tense, guttural, and apparently stinging phrase. Phroeng left off, his haggard mouth hanging open. His glazed eyes floated toward the photo of Chram as a child, and tears trickled down his cheeks. This seemed to anger Rok, who barked at him. Saw shouted something at the two of them. Then suddenly everyone was still, and I heard slow, faltering footsteps.

Song appeared on the stairs, holding the arm of

her mother, Ly, a large woman who moved very slowly. Clinging to the banister, Ly wore a pale sarong and loose cardigan sweater over a Chinese-style blouse. Her short hair was freshly combed. She moved quickly to me, her wide face a mask of disorientation.

"S-s-soë," she said in a hoarse voice. "You came!"

"I'm so sorry," I said.

She took my hand in both of hers beseechingly, then grabbed Song's hand and put it with mine, while Song cringed with embarrassment.

"Take care. Take care. This baby only one left. Only one." Ly pulled Song close, clutching the teenager's head against her bosom and patting her cheek. "Please," she said, her brown eyes meeting mine. "Don't let them kill her, too."

"Mother—"

"No. I no speak English good, but—you take. Take care her."

"I'm not in danger, Mother." Song calmly shook her head, smiling at me as if to beg indulgence for her hysterical mother. She took Ly's face in her hands and whispered quietly to her in Khmer.

Saw hovered beside them, speaking in a loud singsong that seemed to be an attempt at soothing persuasion. Phroeng shouted something, still sitting, staring at the empty whiskey glass. Rok studied me coldly.

I stepped back. The family was distraught. Song was the only one who spoke English well enough to give me any usable information. The father was certainly drunk. The mother I considered momentarily irrational, although she'd seemed very clear when she'd said, *Don't let them kill her, too*. But she had reacted to my presence as if I were a close friend, when I'd only spoken to her at length once before. Either she had a warped perception of my relationship to her family or she was so stricken by grief that all barriers were temporarily down. The journalist in me was whispering in my ear, telling me to find out who Ly meant by "them," whether she meant someone specific was after her children, someone here in Greymont, or whether this was just the agony of a mother losing her child to a violent death.

"Song," I murmured when the others all began talking at once, "is there a place we can speak in private?"

With a relieved expression, she nodded toward the front. I followed her into an L off the kitchen, furnished with a Formica table surrounded by metal chairs.

I noticed the flaking green paint, the tired linoleum flooring, and the prints of Buddha and a gold-domed pagoda on the walls.

Song stood by the window, the morning sun flooding the sad room with an incongruous cheer. We could hear the others arguing in the distance.

"You might think that I am cold and have no feelings," she said, her large black eyes scanning my face. "I have to be strong. I think this is the end for my family." She composed herself and continued. "I have to be strong. You see what they are like.

"I am afraid to call Cletha," she added. "Uncle Rok says he will kill her."

"Why?"

"He's angry. When we called last night, she had a problem and couldn't come, but he says she refused. Now, he blames her for everything. For meddling, for encouraging Chram to go to school and marry Stephen. He won't let me or my parents see her anymore."

A mild tremor passed through her body. But when I put my hand forward to comfort her, she jumped as if I had made a move to attack. She gazed at me, in shock.

"The police," I said quietly. "When were they here?"

Song eased herself into one of the chairs, the sun orange in the window, her face in the shadow. She let out a sigh.

"They came around midnight. Maybe a little later. My mother was in bed. At first she thought it was a terrible dream. That the policeman was a ghost. Not a real person, you know, and that the whole thing was revenge by some dead person. A wandering soul who had died violently."

"Then what happened?"

She looked confused.

"When the police came," I prompted, "what did they ask? What did you answer?"

"They called first. My father answered the phone. He didn't understand what they were saying, so I talked. A man asked if this is the residence of—" She mimicked the police officer's clumsy American pronunciation of her father's name, saying "Frank" rather than "P'rong" and "Touch," rhyming with "hutch," rather than "TOO-it."

"I said 'Yes.' He asked if this was the family of Chram Touch." She again mangled the name, American-style, enjoying it, almost laughing at how silly it sounded. The smile faded. "He said they were going to come to see us. I said, 'Now, tonight?' He said 'Yes.' I didn't understand. I wanted to know more. He asked if we would need a translator. I said I knew English. He asked my age and how I was related.

"As soon as I hung up, I called Cletha and told her the police were coming. She was very upset. She asked if we had seen her foster son Prith. I said no. I told her that Chram had not come home the night before, or even in the afternoon to take my mother to the doctor in her car. I had to leave school early yesterday to take my mother on the bus. Cletha always tells me that my parents are too dependent, that they shouldn't ask so much, but it's the way we are. The parent is the most important god for the parent gives the child life. You have to take care of your parent."

She looked at me as if I could help with this problem. I ignored the rush of sympathy and guilt, the urge to compare my own immaturity at her age, and pushed on.

"So, Chram was gone all day yesterday?"

"And the night before."

"Did they know she hadn't been home?"

"No. I lied for her."

"Did you try to find her?"

"I took my mother to the doctor. I helped make dinner. After we ate, I started to get worried, but she'd stayed away a few days before, and I had to study for a chemistry test. There was so much to do. I didn't think about Chram." She looked at me shamefaced.

"When exactly did you last see her?"

"On Monday. I was doing my homework right here at this table. My mother was cooking dinner. Chram got a phone call. She said she was going out. She told me not to wait, that she might take a long time. I asked was she going to see her boyfriend, Stephen. There had been some problems between them. She said, 'I'm going to visit an old friend.'"

"Did she say who?"

Song shook her head. I suspected she wasn't telling everything.

"That's all she said?"

Song nodded. "The police asked these things over and over. I had to translate for my mother, for my father. Then they asked me the same questions again. The whole thing is so crazy."

"What time Monday did she leave?"

Song shrugged. "I don't know. Maybe five o'clock."

I paused. "What kind of car did she have?"

"A big green American car. Rok bought it for her." Song smiled. "It has air-conditioning and buttons to push to make the windows go down. Chram said it made her feel like a rich American."

"Why couldn't Cletha come?"

"Last night? She needed to stay home for Prith to return or phone. She was beside herself. She told me to call Professor Albright. I woke him up, but he finally came just before we went to the morgue. He helped Rok calm down. It was very confusing. I didn't want to wake my mother, but the policeman said I had to. Two men came to the door. One showed a badge.

"Aunt Saw ran over from next door. She was crying because she said a ghost had woken her and she knew at once something bad had happened. And Uncle Rok was here saying awful things. But luckily the police didn't understand. It was so frightening . . . like in the camps with the soldiers. I still have memories from when I was small."

Her expression was imploring. A long, difficult moment passed. There were no tears, but as a precaution I found a tissue and handed it to her. She took it and twisted it between her fingers.

"I tried to hold my mother but she refused to be touched. The police said a woman had been found. They thought she was Chram. She had been killed."

Song gazed off at the distance. "You see, I knew this and I had to translate and tell my mother that her child was dead."

Her eyes met mine.

"My mother lost four children," said Song. "I am the last one left. We don't talk about my brother. He was the oldest. When I was born, he went to the hills. He became Khmer Rouge. My father says he's as good as dead.

"All the children who died, my father says, it was a payment for this one Khmer Rouge child."

And then she came back to full awareness of who I was. "No," she added rapidly, "don't tell that part."

"So your brother is still alive."

"He is dead for us," she said.

"Is he in the country—here, the United States?"

A panic crept into her. "Why did I talk to you? Are you going to print this in the newspaper?"

"Only what you agree is on the record," I assured her. "I won't put the things about your brother. Who knows about him? Cambodians in the community? Anyone else?"

Her eyes clouded with suspicion. "My father drinks. When he does, he says things other people shouldn't hear. We try to forget what happened back there. I was very young, but I remember living with the Khmer Rouge in the labor camp. And then in Thailand in the refugee camp. But the happy days before the war, I don't remember.

"My father and mother are different. They remember so much. They remember what they lost. For them, to come to America was a chance to give a life to their children. And now what happened there has followed us."

This was precisely the interpretation Hal Gaffney and his odious group of xenophobes, the Greymont First Coalition, would put on the murder. They'd been the ones who'd been making speeches at Town Meeting and bombarding the paper with anti-immigrant letters and op-ed pieces. Gaffney had a regular column, owing to Whit's determination to give everyone space to air their views. I'd been trying to counter them with my articles, but they'd taken my words, my facts, and twisted them to their own narrow purpose. And at this moment, like Song, I found myself partly in agreement with one of their most insidious arguments: that with the refugees had come trouble and danger.

My thoughts drifted to Cletha, who'd done so much to help the refugees. She seemed to be inextricably tangled up in this. Her name kept being mentioned, first at the mall, now here.

"Afterward," Song was saying, "They took us to see the body of my sister."

"Oh." Nausea hit me as the grotesque face of the corpse swam momentarily before my eyes.

"You think it's very terrible. But we are so used to seeing our loved ones dead."

"Who identified the body?"

"My mother. They won't give Chram back. They have to do some tests. And her spirit won't rest until she's cremated. We have to carry the ashes to the temple." She laughed wryly. "But that's all right, because there isn't any temple."

I thought of Bou Vuthy, and she must have read my mind because she pointed to the poster of the pagoda on the wall. "I mean, a real temple."

"Have your parents gotten any sleep?"

"Professor Albright brought some pills, but they refuse to take them. I am so worried, Zoë. I don't know what to do. I am so tired of this. I've carried on, and carried on. What should I do? What do you think I should do?"

The exhaustion of the long night seemed to hit her all at once. Perhaps it was the burden of the past seventeen years. How much she'd gone through. Her exhaustion pulled me in and twisted me the way her anxious fingers tugged and knotted the tissue in her hands.

"I wish it had been me," she said. "It would be so much easier to be dead."

We sat in silence. I could hear muted crooning through the wall.

"Song," I said. "Do I have your permission to use your name and write the things you've told me?"

"Don't tell about my brother." Her voice was a whisper.

"What about the rest?"

"Go ahead. Maybe it will help."

"Do you have any idea who could have done this thing?"

Her head snapped up. For a brief instant I thought she would offer a clue or suggest a name. But then a curtain seemed to pull shut. Her expression closed.

"No," she said. "How could I?"

"Was anybody angry at her?"

"Chram was very good. Very sweet. A good daughter. No one would have a reason to hurt her."

I sensed she was hiding something, but I decided not to push it.

"Were you with your mother when she identified the body?"

"Yes."

"What time did you get home?"

"Five o'clock."

"Have you slept?"

She shook her head. "When I try to sleep I feel that there is someone pressing down on me, trying to kill me, push the breath out of me. It's a common thing with us. A common kind of ghost that visits you. We call it *khmauch songkot.*"

"You need somebody here with you. I have to go back and file this story. Can I call someone?"

She shook her head, her face seeming so young, so fragile. "No, Zoë. Chram is dead. No one can help."

"Try to get some sleep," I said, reluctant to leave her unprotected. "And don't open that door for any reporters. They're going to be swarming all over this place in no time."

"Like you," she teased, her eyes lighting a bit.

"Yes," I admitted, "like me."

"You don't have to worry. I'm strong."

"I know," I said. Strong, I thought, but not street smart. As soon as I got back to the office I would call Cletha. She'd know someone who could come down here and help these people hold the other wolves at bay.

7

Outside, navigating the icy path, I was struck by how empty the walkways were. No reporters had appeared; however, neither had any friends. The Cambodian community was tight-knit and interrelated, yet only Aunt Saw and Uncle Rok had come to lend support.

As I unlocked the Civic and waited while it coughed to a start, I wondered why Chram's fiancé, Stephen Giles, wasn't there. On impulse, instead of driving out of the complex, I pulled into the lot in front of Bou Vuthy's "temple."

When he answered the door, the old monk bowed his shaven head, beckoning toward the temple room beyond the vestibule. I slipped off my pumps and followed him inside to the mats on the floor.

"The police have confirmed that Chram Touch was the victim."

He indicated with a slight motion of his eyelids that he was aware of this.

"I just spoke to her parents."

"You work hard. We talked late last night. Now, early in the morning you are here again, asking your questions."

I smiled, despite his wry tone. "Could you comment on the murder?"

He took a moment to gather his thoughts. "I feel sometimes an evil monster is intent upon devouring my people. Even a monk sometimes asks: How can this be?"

"What can the citizens of Greymont do to help the Touch family?"

"Pray for the peace of Chram's soul and for the one who has killed her. This person must be in terrible torment."

"Do you think a Cambodian might have murdered her?"

"That is a question for the police."

"Is there a place to send donations?"

He didn't seem to understand.

"Money," I explained.

"Ah. I will find out. Perhaps the Quaker Rescue people would know."

"The family seems very isolated. No one is there except Rok and Saw Boeng."

"I am on my way to visit. Others will come later."

"Will there be a funeral?"

"Yes." He stood up. "I will have someone call you after I talk to the family."

Cambodian monks, I'd learned in the past few months, followed strict rules. They lived by begging, and could eat only two meager meals a day. They couldn't touch women or even look them straight in the eye. They weren't allowed to drive cars or use a telephone, although some refugee communities relaxed the rules a little. Life in America was almost unmanageable without a car and a phone.

"I can't get over how alone the Touches seem," I said to him before leaving, aware that the question you ask after the interview appears to be over often receives the most revealing response. Although he'd weathered interrogation by pros like the Khmer Rouge, Thai border patrols, refugee camp guards, and U.S. Immigration, I figured there was a chance he might get sloppy against so minor an opponent as me. "Is it usual for people to stay away when a family experiences a tragedy like this?"

"After the camps, people tend to shrink from trouble."

"But even her fiancé isn't there."

He regarded me shrewdly, having caught onto my method.

"Did you know him well?" I asked off-handedly.

His smile was uncomprehending.

"You have nothing to say about Stephen Giles?"

"I have said enough for today." He bowed again, the skin on his neck wrinkling.

Reluctantly, I moved toward the door, where I turned and nearly caught his eye. "Why won't you talk about Stephen?"

"Because there is too much sadness in the world already. Your newspaper does much harm."

"My newspaper didn't kill Chram."

"You write a series on the Cambodian people, telling our secrets. Then a young woman is found dead. How do you know your words didn't set the deed in motion?"

His statement reverberated in my mind as I left, so much so that I didn't notice that I'd slapped the *White Album* tape into my car's cassette deck with the "Revolution Number 9" side on. My reveries were interrupted by John Lennon's maddeningly repetitive, "*Number nine, number nine, number nine.*" Whenever I considered retaping the album to leave out the few songs I didn't adore, I hesitated, considering it somehow sacrilegious to mess with the artistry of the whole. However, after a few more *number nines*, I made a concession to my nerves and reversed the tape. Paul was singing about being "Mother Nature's son." Then came John with "*Everybody's got something to hide*"—a suitable sentiment considering my upcoming interviews.

On my agenda after writing up the Touches' interview was calling Cletha Fair to find out how much she knew. The prospect worried me. I didn't look forward to confronting this old friend of my father's about what role her new foster son might have had in the murder. I also wanted to run into Wingate's for Keith's stamp set and something with a bunny motif for Smokie. "Wabbit" had been one of her first words, and she went wild over anything with long ears. But that had to wait until after deadline. Right now, the first order of business was to file my story. Once at my desk, I quickly typed my piece and updated the murder story.

Whit read over my shoulder, talking me through a fast edit, and then transmitted both pieces to the compositor, along with one by Mark on the press conference ("Mall Stabbing Stumps Cops") and a photo of Chram, cropped out of a group picture that staff photographer Kate Braithwaite had dug out of her files.

Afterward the four of us went into the back kitchen to plan our next move over sandwiches from the sub shop next door. Whit had been listening to the radio all morning, checking the wire services, and keeping an eye on the local TV stations. We'd scooped everyone with our interview of the family, but he wanted to keep the heat on because the killing had been mentioned by CNN, and he'd just gotten word that the wire services had picked it up for nationwide distribution. The anti-immigrant sentiment had reached a fever pitch this year, and politicians and radio talk-show hosts were calling for repeal of refugee assistance. Some Vietnamese fishermen's boats had been destroyed and fisherman had been beaten up in Biloxi, Mississippi, a couple of months earlier; and this murder was being played as another racist attack.

Mark, super-jock today in an old baseball shirt, faded jeans, and hightops, stopped chewing a huge Italian sub long enough to mention that all three local TV stations, including the farthest away, in

Hartford, had cameras at the press conference.

"Brannigan hates the press," he added, his mouth half full. "Called us vultures."

Kate Braithwaite, my closest pal at the paper, laughed. "If you think about it, the term is appropriate. We're all circling over a dead body."

The only other female under fifty at the paper, Kate had befriended me instantly the first week of my arrival the previous spring, giving me the low-down on all the staff members and warning me to watch out for Mark's tendency to encroach on other people's beats. He'd already wormed his way into a position as the paper's backup photographer.

Kate was a sporty brunette with a healthy complexion and long thick hair which she wore in a dangling braid down her back. She was one of the jeans-and-baggy-sweater set, but on her the look worked. A cross-country ski fanatic, she had hiked most of the Appalachian trail, and in her not-too-distant college days had set records on the equestrian team. Mark and she had a kind of mutual put-down thing going on, which I expected to grow into forthright flirtation, but so far it hadn't. She came from a local farm family and had an on-again-off-again romance with an old high school boyfriend. From the few details she'd told—just sailing into personal confidences as if I'd been an old college chum—it seemed she was trying to find a nice way to end the relationship.

Kate said she'd recognized a stringer from the *Globe* at the press conference, as well as a couple of magazine freelancers. "You know who else was there?" she added, daintily tearing off a piece of her bagel and cream cheese.

"Who?"

She named a well-known reporter for the *Times*. Nobody said it aloud, but their presence meant we were competing against some pretty heavy hitters, as Mark might put it.

Whit met my gaze. "How's the family holding up?"

"They're not."

"Can we get a picture?"

I winced openly, hoping to arouse some sensitivity in him. "I gave Song specific instructions not to let any reporters in. Bou Vuthy lectured me about the newspaper doing harm. He thinks one of my stories triggered the murder."

"Did it?"

"I don't see how. There has been almost no mention of Chram in the paper. Her picture appeared only once, in a large group photo of the wedding."

"You did the profile on Song and Ly."

"Right. But Chram wasn't in it. Okay, her name was mentioned."

Whit slipped something out of a manila folder in front of him. He hadn't touched his turkey sandwich, which Mark eyed hungrily. Kate, who was constantly on a diet, offered Mark half her bagel, which he swallowed in two bites, chasing it with root beer. He drained the can, then deftly crumpled it in his fist in one motion and tossed it with a hook shot into the wastebasket next to the soda machine.

"Here." Whit handed me a clipping after leveling

a fastidious glance in Mark's general direction. It was my interview of Song and Ly. Chram's name and age were printed, along with the fact that she'd worked in Peter Albright's office and was a student in the hotel and restaurant management school. Some of the details on the family's escape through the jungle into Thailand were described, along with their varied attempts to enter the USA. Also mentioned were the other siblings who had died. Of course, I knew now that one of them was most likely not dead. I wanted to check my old notes and see if there was any more on Chram. I vaguely remembered that her mother had named a number of Chram's jobs.

"Have you talked to Cletha?" Whit asked.

"Not yet."

"Call her today." His narrow face reddened slightly as it did when he felt pressured. "I want a piece on the support people around the Cambodians. Get statements from everyone who knew her from that angle."

"How about a 'man in the street'?" Mark broke in, not noticing Whit's flash of annoyance. Whit hated to be interrupted, although he did his fair share. "I can go back to the mall, interview shoppers, ask them if they're taking any precautions with a murderer loose."

Good, I thought, that would keep him out of my hair.

Whit pursed his lips. "Okay, Mark. Zoë, call the Touches. Tell them Kate's coming down to take their picture."

Realizing he wouldn't take no for an answer, I nodded reluctantly.

Whit stood up. "I'd like to see something on my desk by tonight. Mark?"

"No problemo." Mark was one of those guys who thought speaking in a phony accent added to his allure. He winked mischievously toward Kate, who appeared not to notice.

Whit turned to me. "Sure," I said, already thinking of who I could call. The difficulty was the season. A lot of people were out of town for the holidays and most of the University people were gone for intersession. Peter Albright was around. And there was another professor I'd used as a source, a Vietnamese woman named Cecily Chen.

"Cletha," he reminded me.

"Yes." A vague dread passed through me when I said it. The reason I hadn't called Cletha already was that I feared what she might say.

Mark set out for the mall. I called the Touches and got through to Song, who gave a trusting okay on the photo, which wrenched my heart. I picked up the phone, about to call Cletha, and suddenly lost my nerve. Instead I called Billy.

"Hey, babe. How's it going?" he asked cheerfully.

"Okay. I'm going to need the car, if that's all right with you. I may have to drive to some interviews. How are the kids?"

"They built a snow fort. We're having soup. I'm going to try to convince them to take a nap. Everything's copacetic."

"I don't know when I'll be home. Whit wants a new story by the time I leave. Depending on who I round up, it could be late."

"If you get a chance, we're low on milk."

"I'll pick some up."

"Good."

"Any interesting mail?"

"What do you mean?"

"I don't know. Did I win the Sweepstakes?"

He laughed. "Haven't checked, but I'll call you right back if you did."

I got off and quickly dialed Cletha before I had a chance to change my mind. The phone rang a long time. I was just about to hang up when I heard her cautious "Hello?"

"Cletha," I said with false heartiness. "This is Zoë."

Long pause. "How can I help you?"

"I assume you've heard about the murder—"

"Yes. Shocking," she murmured in a voice that seemed very weak for her. She was usually a powerhouse, despite her sixty-odd years.

"Whit wants a piece rounding up reactions from the refugee support community. I'd like to drop by and have a chat."

"I don't really see the point."

"You knew Chram quite well." I hated pushing her.

"Not really. Have you talked to Stephen?"

"No."

"Well, you should start with him, don't you think?"

"Not for a refugee supporters piece."

"Why not?"

"He was her fiancé, not a member of Quaker Rescue." I was thinking as we spoke how odd it was that she was resisting. Usually she did the opposite, tried to get the paper to cover one injustice after another. She was a publicity hound, not a retiring flower. When in doubt, I thought, try flattery. It's amazing how well it works, even with people you'd expect to be immune. "You're a leader in this community. People want to know your opinion."

Her breathing was heavy, as if she were attempting to hold back emotion. "Zoë," she said finally. "This is not a good time. I promise we'll talk, but give me a day or two. The news has hit me quite hard."

"All right," I answered, stymied by her directness. If someone is being evasive I can push through it, but honesty is hard to counter, especially in a friend. "Oh, there is one favor I wanted to ask."

"What?"

"The Touches are so vulnerable. Do you know anyone who could help them fend off the press?"

Normally, Cletha would have crisply asserted her own willingness to run down and stand guard. Now, after another pause, she breathed quietly into the phone. "You could try Eleanor Kerr. She might be a source for your story, too, come to think of it. And, of course, Peter."

After I hung up the phone, I stood thinking for a few moments. Cletha had never sounded so troubled in the entire time I'd known her, which dated back to when she and my parents were friends. She'd always been strong, vigorous, and outspoken. The problems that consumed her were world affairs—civil rights, unjust wars, the defense of the downtrodden. In my memory, she'd never displayed such low spirits. Of course, my memories were selective. I'd seen her when my parents hosted activist affairs or my father performed at her benefits. I knew little about her personal life. Her husband had been a doctor. He'd died a decade earlier, and I'd only met him once. She had no children and had been really excited about adopting Prith as a foster son this fall. But even that had seemed more an outgrowth of her activism than fulfillment of a personal need. Perhaps I'd misjudged her feelings.

Should I just drive out and see her? I wondered. Lois Lane would have. Without a statement from Cletha, I couldn't produce the story Whit wanted. I decided to finesse it by coming up with something else for tomorrow's paper. I promised myself I'd get to Cletha tomorrow. Being ruthless was not as easy as I'd envisioned.

As I was mulling over who to call next, I heard a commotion in the reception area in the hall. Someone with a strident voice was arguing heatedly with Whit. I heard my name mentioned and Whit's soft-spoken reply. I went to see who it was. By the time I reached the lobby, Whit had escaped up the stairs, and I found myself face to face with the town gadfly, leader of the Greymont First Coalition and all-round pest, Hal Gaffney.

No matter what the issue, Hal had an opinion, usually one I considered outrageous. You name it, he and the GFC opposed it: taxes, of course; school funding; ESL programs in the library; foreign languages; all immigration from "non-European" countries, which didn't share our "Western values"; vegetarians; anti-hunting sissies; gun control of any type; government in general and Town Meeting in particular, because it was a "breeding ground" for anti-American ideas like environmentalism and public services. In the interest of balance, Whit had invited him to do a weekly column, which Gaffney produced like clockwork, spewing hot air that was cheered by about a quarter of the people in town and made the rest cringe.

"Zoë! Just the person I wanted to see. Your boss said you weren't here."

The owner of one of the bars in town, he was a stereotypical Irishman: a drinker, formerly well-built but going to fat. He wore a well-cut overcoat, looking very much like the politician he aspired to be. He'd run twice for the state assembly and lost. The capillaries in his left cheek seemed to have burst and there were faint purple lines in a circle that resembled a slap mark. His eyebrows were thick, his hairline receding, and his nose seemed to grow more bulbous each passing week. I suspected he'd spent most of his adult life making up for the fact that he'd either been ignored or bullied as a kid.

"I was just on my way out."

"Zoë, sweetheart, you have to stop this habit of misquoting people. That story yesterday."

"I read that sentence to you twice, and you okayed it."

"Out of context as usual."

"Hal—"

"You made me sound like a jerk. You know what I'm talking about. And you got my age wrong. I'm forty-five, not forty-seven."

In a weak moment he'd mentioned his own nightmares, and I had quoted, thinking it would be nice to contrast post-traumatic stress among vets to that suffered by the refugees. He'd been a prisoner of war. He was haunted by memories of friends who'd died during the last month before they'd been released.

"I thought you sounded human for a change, Hal. Excuse me."

"What's this 'for a change'?"

"Hal, I'm on deadline, so—"

"Are you working on the murder?" His pale eyes glinted with curiosity.

"Yes."

"How's that going?"

"I've got about a thousand people to call."

"I hope the message won't be lost on your co-workers."

I gazed wistfully up the stairs wondering how Whit had managed to escape so quickly.

"This has mobilized us," he continued eagerly. "GFC is having a press conference tomorrow. And a rally."

"Drop a press release by the office."

"I'm faxing it this afternoon to every reporter

within two hundred miles. You should be happy I'm telling you first. Did you see the *Globe*? We're drawing national coverage. Citizens speak up against the foreign hordes."

I inhaled slowly and counted to three, a technique I'd learned when Keith was going through his "terrible twos." Gaffney had a point. Angry citizens protesting immigrants was what all these out-of-town reporters were looking for. "When's your press conference?"

"Two tomorrow. At the community center."

"I'll be there."

"You won't be disappointed."

"Wait a second, Hal."

"Yeah?"

"How about a statement on the murder?"

"You've got to be crazy. After that misquote?"

"Had you ever met Chram Touch?"

His eyes narrowed. "Sweetheart, I don't know where the hell you root up your information, but somebody's been feeding you some heavy swill."

He turned on his heels and swung abruptly out the door.

I shared a look with Sharon, the receptionist.

"What's eating him?" she asked.

"Oh, you know. The usual."

He'd neatly evaded the question about whether he'd known Chram, which I'd asked on a whim. They were such unlikely acquaintances, it was worth following up. Maybe Cletha or Cecily Chen would enlighten me. I dialed Chen's home and work numbers and got her answering machine in both places.

Then I called Peter Albright, with the same result. I left a message asking for an interview, adding that someone from Quaker Rescue might help the Touches fend off the out-of-town press corps. Cursing quietly to myself, I wondered how I was going to have a story for tomorrow's paper when none of my sources could be reached. Vaguely I wondered if I should drive out to Cletha's. No, I'd wait till tomorrow. I owed her that much. Figuring I had nothing to lose, I dialed Stephen Giles. As luck would have it, he answered the phone.

8

The rambling old Victorian on Waverly Street, just off Restaurant Row on Stanhope, occupied a small lot not far from the State University. A thin woman with dark hair pulled into a messy ponytail answered the door and let me in without bothering to inquire who I was. She held a large textbook and wore a pencil in her ear.

"He's in the kitchen," she said with a remarkable lack of interest when I asked for Stephen. She turned to go back through the pocket doors into a small parlor, dominated by an enormous metal desk with books and papers piled knee-deep around it.

Although the exterior of the house was unassuming, the inside was clean, unlike many student residences, and the furnishings, though Spartan, were tasteful. I was taken by the maple wainscoting, the beautiful grain protected by a satiny layer of well-polished varnish.

Along the staircase a row of coats and jackets dangled from brass hooks. I hung up my coat and kicked off my pumps, as requested by a prominently-placed photograph of shoes neatly grouped on a floor. Attached to the picture a handwritten note read: "Please do the same." Below I counted eight pairs of shoes and three pairs of boots. I matched up the sizes and decided there were four housemates, probably all grad students. The weather was good for boots, I thought, regarding the salt stains on the suede heels I'd been sliding around on all day. As soon as I had time, I decided ruefully, I was going to sit down with the L.L. Bean catalogue and pick out something waterproof. The years in California hadn't prepared me for ice, snow, and slush.

I found my way to the kitchen through the dining room on the other side of the stairs. On the mantle over the fireplace stood a number of handsome Asian artifacts: a stamped tin platter with a lotus design, two celadon vases, and a white teapot decorated with cranes. The display of antique weapons on the wall above aroused my curiosity: a bow carved in the shape of a dragon; five silver-tipped arrows; two ivory-hilted swords; and between them a knife about the size of a machete with a wide blade and a silver handle inlaid with ivory.

Stephen Giles wasn't in the kitchen itself, but in a sunny room behind it. He sat on a U-shaped window seat, legs tucked in a lotus position, staring out at the snow-covered roofs of downtown Greymont. The house was chilly, and he was dressed appropriately: heavy wool socks, gray sweat pants, a blue chamois shirt, and a gray and brown vest that looked hand-knit.

He continued to stare out the windows, breathing in a quiet but regular fashion that I remembered from my short-lived fascination with Buddhist meditation. I waited.

After a while, he turned toward me partway, unfolding one leg and wriggling his toes. Giles was built like a dancer, lean and muscular. His forehead, nose, and jaw were well-defined and strong. Abundant blond hair curled behind his ears, but was cut close in front. His cheeks were unshaven, the blond bristles revealing about two days' growth.

Not until he lifted his head did I notice his best feature. His eyes were a spectacular turquoise, translucent as two bright gems. Fixing them on me with a full dose of bad-boy charm, he reached over and shook my hand. "Hi. I read your pieces every day."

I covered my attraction with professional crispness. "Where would you like to do the interview?"

"Here's fine." He studied me with almost whimsical detachment, as if attempting to detect how I responded to his looks. This was something I had encountered in a few superstars I'd interviewed, but it surprised me in a grad student.

"Would a tape recorder bother you?" I'd already taken it out and switched it on. The micro-recorder was about the size of a cigarette pack.

His blue-green eyes flicked from my face to the tiny machine. "Yes, it would."

I switched the thing off and put it away. An interview is a subtle battle for control. You press a bit, kind of testing for where their hot buttons are. When they start pushing back, you yield, ask a few easy questions, and they wind up telling you stuff they wouldn't confide in their mother. Once interviewees have managed to get you to turn off the recorder, they seem to think what they say is private, but I'm fast enough with a pen to get what I need without the machine if I have to.

We began with background. He'd grown up in Ohio, traveled in India, trekked in Nepal, taught English in China. Four years ago he'd come to the State University, where he was a doctoral candidate in Southeast Asian history. His thesis adviser was Peter Albright. He was thirty years old.

"When did you meet Chram?" I asked once the preliminaries were over.

"Three years ago," he told me. "I'd just started working on my thesis. I wanted to learn Khmer and Vietnamese, so I volunteered as a tutor in the library program. Phroeng, her father, was my first student. Can't say I did a great job. His English is still halting."

He gazed out again at the snow-topped roofs.

"As a tutor you can get pretty involved. I must have driven six midnight trips to the airport to pick up extended family members. As a favor to Phroeng, I drove Ly and Chram to the airport to pick up Ly's sister and brother-in-law, Saw and Rok, when they came from Thailand. Want spellings?"

"No, I've got them."

"We had to go twice, because the first night they

missed the connection from New York. Chram sat up front with me so Rok, Ly, and Saw could talk. They'd been separated since the last days of the Khmer Rouge."

He pulled one knee to his chest, letting the other swing loosely off the window seat. "I was probably the first American her age she'd met who spoke Khmer, even as badly as I did. Her English was barely passing, but good enough so if we didn't want the elders in the back to understand, we could manage.

"Later, of course, after she started to work in Peter's office, we got to know each other better."

"What did she do for Peter?"

"Secretarial stuff. It was basically a make-work position. He wanted to help out the family. She'd been working for the University food service and a couple of lousy restaurant jobs. But after she enrolled in college, it was just too much. Peter came to the rescue. She quit this fall. Wanted to make it on her own. The girl had pride."

I studied him for a moment, trying to discern his emotions. He seemed pale, tired, somewhat dazed, but not grief-stricken. His leg jiggled nervously.

"What attracted you?"

"Well, the pride for one thing. And she had a great sense of the absurd. Maybe because of all she'd been through. She was a fighter. Plus, I knew a lot about her culture. That made her comfortable. She could talk about what had happened, and I was curious—you know about the Khmer Rouge and all the atrocities. I gave her space to vent."

"So you started dating?"

He grimaced. "Dating is unheard of. Usually the parents arrange a marriage."

"How did you get around that?"

"I went along with some of the traditions. Made myself useful. As time went on I spoke the language better. Phroeng liked me. You know he's a drunk? I sneaked him a bottle every so often—the expensive American stuff he likes. They gave Chram a hard time about going to school. Girls aren't usually educated in Cambodia. I talked them into letting her go for her high school equivalency, and then I helped her study."

He winked at me, a mischievous schoolboy who'd put one over on the old folks. Then he seemed to remember what had happened, and his face went white. His fingers trembled as he put them on his knee to stop its shaking.

"When did you become engaged?"

"It's a long story."

"I have time."

"Yeah, I'm sure you do." He laughed scornfully. "Bet you don't get a murder story every day."

His eyes met mine in a fixed stare. I waited noncommittally.

He composed himself and went on. "It had come to the point where Chram and I just couldn't keep sneaking off on the pretext of going to the library to study. The family caught on. First they hinted around to Chram, who ignored them. Chram has a rebellious streak that was really pronounced with certain family members, Saw in particular. And Saw is an interfering busybody. Very controlling. She rules Ly and henpecks Rok."

I didn't say anything, but I found it hard to believe anyone could henpeck Rok.

"Finally," he was saying, "the grand melodrama. Phroeng and Ly brought us to visit Auntie Saw. She was holed up in her bed, in a stuffy room with candles and incense all over the place—no electric light. Fancy tin bowls filled with all kinds of symbolic offerings. Rok was there, giving us the evil eye. She screams at the sight of us, but makes us come real close. She's sick, she says, her spirit has been invaded by ancestors. They're complaining of my behavior with Chram. If Chram and I don't stop, she'll get worse, might die. She and Rok accused us in a roundabout way of having sex."

He laughed. "No kidding. This really happened. I found it amusing, but Chram was furious. Saw practices a kind of Cambodian witchcraft. She knows all about herbs, and this tight little community treats her like a queen. Even Rok is afraid of her.

"Well. Chram wouldn't stand for it. She called Saw names. Rok threatened her with his fist, but Saw stopped him. She said Chram would be lost to the family. The ghosts would take over her body as well as Saw's. Saw made as if she was dying. Ly burst into tears. Phroeng took a swipe at Rok. Chram and I left in the middle of it, and Ly ran after us. She was so pitiful that Chram promised to apologize, which she did a few days later.

"It took a couple of months to sort this out. Saw

kept complaining about me to Ly and Phroeng. Doing some sort of magic, which I think was intended to ward me off. Tried to slip secret concoctions into Chram's food.

"Finally, I talked to Phroeng and asked if I could marry his daughter. We got formally engaged. Auntie Saw and Uncle Rok weren't happy, but the rest of the family was satisfied."

"Saw and Rok disapproved of the marriage?"

"That's what the police zeroed in on. They had me down at the station from four this morning till just before you called. I spent the whole night answering questions."

So that was why he hadn't been with the family this morning. I wondered if Saw or Rok spoke English well enough to communicate suspicion to the police. His lips curved in bitter amusement as he waited to see what I would say.

"What did you tell the police?"

"You going to print this?"

"Maybe."

"I have a hypothesis."

The silence grew heavy. Curious what his reaction might be, I asked, "Who killed her?"

He leveled the turquoise eyes on me. "Somebody who had a score to settle."

"Is that what you told the police?"

"Something like that. Yeah.

"What kind of a score?"

"An old one," he said in a dramatic stage whisper. He was leaning toward me, his pallor heightened by

He swallowed, met my gaze again, the brilliant eyes watery and dense. "We met at a coffee shop," he answered. "Took a walk, had an argument. She told me she didn't want to see me anymore. Didn't want to get married. Refused to discuss it. Wouldn't explain." His voice grew strained. "'Fine,' I told her. 'See you around.' I figured, let her cool off. I'd talk about it again in a couple of days." A muscle in his face intermittently tensed and relaxed. "I guess she was killed later. I waited nearly two days for her to give in and call me. . . . The whole time she was dead. I didn't even know until the police woke me up this morning."

"Who told you?"

"Detective Brannigan. They banged on the door around four this morning. 'You know Chram Touch?' Brannigan asks. I say, 'Yes. She's my fiancé.' I thought she'd gotten into some kind of trouble. 'When did you last hear from her?' 'Two days ago.' 'Haven't seen her since?' 'No. Has she disappeared?' 'Why do you ask, lover boy?' 'Lover boy? What's going on?' 'Mr. Giles, your fiancé was found dead. We'd like to ask you a few questions.'" He smiled sarcastically, emotion flushing out his former pallor. "That's how I found out."

In spite of my distrust, I was moved. "That's cruel," I said softly.

"Yeah."

His fingers went to his forehead again.

"Did anyone know you were having problems?"

"Auntie Saw. I wouldn't be surprised if she engineered the whole damn thing."

"The murder?"

"The break-up. She hated me."

"Why?"

"I'm not Cambodian. The ancestors weren't pleased. The reality of this hasn't quite sunk in," he added, bowing his head, blond hair glinting in the glare from the west-facing windows. It was after four, and the sun was low in the sky, the light gold. "There's a good chance I'll be arrested."

"What for?"

"The police think I killed her."

"Did you?"

His answer was swift, sarcastic. "Sure. That's why I'm here talking to you."

I stopped taking notes, feeling a chill.

"Tell me about Chram," I continued, breaking the gaze. "Her personality. Her history. Her hopes for the future."

He hesitated, seeming to frame his response. "She wanted to be a real American. She was ambitious. We both were. She had plans to open a restaurant, wanted to employ her family. She used to talk about it constantly, wanted to emulate the success of new Chinese immigrants. She'd worked in a couple of eating places—bars, sandwich shops, not Chinese. She latched onto the restaurant idea. Some of the owners struck her, you know, as not particularly smart. She figured if they could do it, why not her.

"That's why she was in school. She was sold on the American dream. She passed her GED and was about to get citizenship. All the papers were filed. We were just waiting for a final determination from the INS.

Regular white Americans look at someone like her and totally miss what's there. She seemed so shy, so quiet, but behind that veneer was a dynamo. She would have made it."

"When did you plan to marry?"

"We approached Bou Vuthy. He had to consult the heavens. Cambodians have their own system of constellations. They never do anything unless the stars are favorable."

"How long had you been engaged?"

"Fourteen months."

"In closing," I said, "would you like to comment on how you feel?"

He seemed about to answer the question, but then said, curtly, "No."

"Can you think of friends of Chram I should talk to?"

He mentioned Cecily Chen. "She runs a support group for Asian women. Chram had some brutal experiences in Cambodia. Cecily helped her handle the memories. Eleanor Kerr was overseeing the citizenship application. Chram didn't make friends easily. I can't think of anybody her own age."

"No Cambodian woman she might have confided in?"

"Only Song."

"You've been very helpful," I said.

He led me to the door, through the dining room with its display of Asian weapons. On our way he commented on it. "The ceramic vases are museum reproductions, Sung dynasty. The platter is Burmese. An export piece. The bow and arrows are Japanese, eighteenth century, a gift from my father on passing my comprehensives. The swords are Thai, early twentieth century. The knife is Cambodian. About a hundred years old. Belonged to a minor prince."

"It's a nice collection."

"Thank you." His voice was tinged with irony. "The police thought so, too."

9

On my way back to the office, I took a half-hour break to do some last-minute shopping. I knew it was going to be a long evening at the paper, and I wanted to pick up gifts before the stores closed. My first stop was Toys for Tots, a kids' store owned by the mother of Keith's best friend in kindergarten.

Even though I'm too attached to sassy skirts and shock-effect lipstick to be in any position to object to fashion dolls, I had groaned inwardly when Grandma Harp informed us by phone a few weeks ago that she'd gotten another for Smokie this year. The one she'd bought last Christmas, though admittedly generous considering the fact that Billy and I were on the verge of divorce, had been a disaster.

A "collectible" doll on a stand with clothes that were glued on, it had been totally inappropriate for a toddler, no matter how precocious. Of course, Smokie wanted to play with it. I'd finally given in and let her hold the doll. Then, I'd gotten involved with some toy Keith was trying to assemble and the next thing I knew, the clothes had been ripped off and Smokie was scribbling all over the doll's face and neck with a ball-point pen. She threw a tantrum when I tried to rescue it from total destruction. This year, I'd bought an inexpensive baby doll for her to do with what she desired, so Grandma's "collectible" could be set on a high shelf without undue trauma. However, I wanted to get my little bundle of energy something more active. She wasn't the dolly type. She liked noisy, bashable, movable things.

Plenty of wonderful choices greeted my eyes, but the problem was I had to shop without plastic, and most of the meager balance in our checking account was earmarked for things like electricity, heating oil, and January's property tax. During the crisis, although Billy had avoided bankruptcy, his credit had been totally wiped out. Anything he earns from radio-play or covers of old tunes goes toward repaying a mountain of debt. My salary barely meets our basic expenses, and what my dad left bought us the house. So we're continually stretched. Billy, who grew up in a working-class family, knows how to do without, but I find it hard to live on a budget.

I spent a good deal of time playing with the Brio train set, but it was too pricey. So were the huge stuffed rabbit family, which Smokie would have adored, the smooth wooden blocks, and the Playmobil pirate ship that Keith had begged for the last time we'd been here. Instead, I bought Smokie a colorful doctor kit and a cute bunny puppet with a pink nose and sad eyes. For Keith, I found a swashbuckling pirate puzzle and a Play-Doh ice-cream sundae set with an extruder.

It was late afternoon when I left the shop, and white lights twinkled in the bare branches of the crab apple trees. I loved the decorations, but still I felt lukewarm about Christmas. My ambivalence came partly from being brought up half-Jewish and partly from the way my show-business Dad and artist Mom used the holidays as an excuse for a round of parties and performances that largely left me out. I'd be stuck in a bedroom on a bed piled high with fur coats, in front of a TV set watching movies while the grown-ups had fun. Or else, I'd be left at home with a matronly baby-sitter. For an only child in the New York theater set, the holidays can be quite lonely.

There were some good moments. We always went downtown to Rockefeller Center to see the tree, and my mother would make an exception to her agnosticism and take me into the mysterious St. Patrick's Cathedral across the street, with the candles, the incense, the stained glass windows, and the statues of saints. These were probably the best memories I had of my mother. She'd been forty when I was born, and although she'd wanted a child, she didn't know what to do with me once I'd arrived. She worked desperately hard at her art in a studio downtown. She and my father loved each other with a romantic intensity that most marriages lose after the honeymoon. Sometimes I envied my friends with divorced parents because they seemed to get the attention I craved.

Adding to my negative feelings was the fact that my mother had died on the twenty-sixth of December. When the days grew short, I began the dreadful countdown to the anniversary of her passing. When I had my own kids I'd expected the pain to diminish, but it increased. I'd developed the nervous habit of comparing my nurturing skills to my mother's. Would I pull away, as she had? Here I was, I thought, pursuing a murder story on the very week when I should be home baking cookies. Billy and I hadn't even bought a tree, I suddenly remembered. In California, I'd put up a little tinsel one. Things were so hectic with Billy's touring and drug problems that I'd felt heroic just getting them fed every day.

This year was supposed to be different. Billy and I had planned an old-fashioned holiday. He was very earnest about it and, even though I'd never experienced one, I'd wholeheartedly embraced the idea.

Looking back, I realize what a tall order this was: giving my family a warm, magical, New England Christmas, while continuing to pursue this murder investigation with the dedication of Lois Lane, who was single and had a super-powered friend. I began to panic a bit, thinking that I had only four days. I told myself sternly, *Just do it*.

Women's magazines labeled this compulsion the Supermom syndrome. These were the same magazines with headlines screaming that you could lose ten pounds in two weeks, cook nutritious meals in ten minutes (that even picky eaters will love!), make your own dried-flower wreaths, and supervise your kid's schooling, while accessorizing your wardrobe, lobbying your boss for a promotion, and making sure your husband wasn't cheating. At least when I wrote for *Rolling Stone*, I was pushing albums, not expectations so overblown that they could lead only to the nuthouse or Prozac. Sex, drugs, and rock 'n' roll suddenly seemed much healthier than the lifestyle promoted as the ideal for today's working mothers.

At Wingate's I bought the stamp set for Keith, a colorful bouncing ball for Smokie, and a music notebook for Billy. I knew he wanted the new B.B. King album and went to the music store for it, tossing in a pack of the thirty-minute cassette tapes he used for songwriting and demos. I'd already bought him the big gift, a yummy sweater from the upscale men's shop in Sheffington, which I'd found on sale at half price during the summer and which I'd kept hidden in the back of my file drawer at work for the past four months.

By now it was completely dark, and the Christmas lights, strung on the trees lining the sidewalks and on several of the large maples in the Commons, blinked cheerily. Nightly for one month a year this little town full of activists, vegetarians, and scholars was clothed in the gossamer garb of fairy tale, and I was transported back to LA and glamour.

My last errand was to the convenience store next to the sub shop. I picked up milk, glanced at the headline on the fresh copies of the *Eagle*, and noted with pleasure that it was in 36-point type and under it was my byline.

* * *

Instead of the quiet I'd expected, I pushed open the door of the newspaper office to find the joint jumping. Phones rang. Computer terminals flickered. The only staff member preparing to leave was Sharon, the receptionist. Everyone else was camped in for the night. I wondered, what with all the resolutions I'd made about Christmas and sitting down quietly tonight to plan with Billy, whether I would get home any time soon.

"Here," said Sharon, handing me pink message slips. "Hal Gaffney says it's urgent." She laughed when I wrinkled my nose. "And Cecily Chen called about an hour ago."

"Great, I want to talk to her."

"Detective Brannigan's office called, too. I switched them through to Whit. Mark wants to talk to you. And Whit says to give him a buzz as soon as you've got a story logged in. Let me warn you, he has no sense of humor tonight."

"Thanks. I better go to work."

"Don't mention it. I'm going to make my escape while I can."

I went to my desk, turned on my computer, and began making phone calls. I tried Billy first. The line was busy, so I checked the notes from my interview with Song, circling some facts about Chram that hadn't made the paper. Together with the information from Stephen Giles, I had a good start on a profile. Despite what Cletha had said this morning on the phone, she knew the Touch family well. She and Peter Albright had brought them here from the refugee camp in Thailand. With regret I realized that I needed both of them for the Chram profile as well as the refugee support article. I dialed Peter. Again the answering machine. I considered phoning Cletha, but decided against it. I'd stop in on her tomorrow on my way to the office. If I caught her in the right mood, I could add to the story before drop-deadline.

I called Cecily Chen. She had helped me with the refugee series this fall. From an upper-class ethnic Chinese family, she'd been raised in South Vietnam, educated in France, and emigrated when the Americans had evacuated Saigon.

"Professor Chen," I began. She was not an informal sort of woman, despite her petite stature. "I suppose you can guess why I called."

"Yes. Truly horrible, this murder."

"How well did you know Chram? I'm doing a profile for tomorrow's paper."

The silence on the other end dampened my spirits.

"Could this wait until tomorrow? I'm late for a dinner engagement."

"Oh, please answer a quick question or two. I'm on deadline." I'm not above begging. Although this technique isn't taught at Columbia Journalism School, without it much of the news would not get written.

"All right, one question."

"Can you tell me about her involvement with your support group for Asian women?"

A moment of dead quiet. "I'm sorry, Zoë. The support group has to be a safe place for women to bring their most painful secrets. I have to be careful not to break confidences. I'd be happy to give you a full interview tomorrow. We're planning an Asian Women's Night Walk on Friday or Saturday. We'd appreciate publicity."

Ah, the old quid pro quo. "Okay. How about one o'clock?"

"Could I get back to you?"

"It would be easier if we could arrange something now. I might be out most of the day."

"Then let's say one at my office."

"Good. See you then."

I shuddered slightly when I hung up. Unlike Cletha and Peter, Professor Chen, though reticent, was willing to be critical, so it was worth jumping through a few hoops to talk to her.

As a last resort, I called a couple other people at the University, finally reaching Chram's restaurant management professor. He effusively praised her business and math sense, and gave me the name of one of her classmates, who echoed the professor's sentiments, giving me the angle I wanted for my profile. The portrait of Chram was acquiring color. She was no longer just a helpless exotic, but a human being with ambitions and unexpected talent. Things were beginning to cook.

I called Albright again, and this time he answered. I was overjoyed. The story was too complex, he said, to do a rushed interview over the phone. We arranged to meet in his office tomorrow at four.

Suddenly, I had a full day ahead of me: I'd get this

profile logged tonight, dig up a few extra facts from Cletha tomorrow morning, if she let me in the door. Then I'd talk to Chen, do the press conference, interview Peter. Tomorrow night I'd write the refugee support story and maybe a follow-up, depending on what emerged.

Before starting to hammer out my story, I dialed home.

"How's the fort?" I asked Billy.

"I, uh, think the injuns are winnin'," he goofed in his best John Wayne imitation.

In the background I heard Keith and Smokie hollering. I experienced a weird sense of relief that it was Billy, not me, who had to try to tame them. "They sound hungry."

His voice echoed away from the phone. "Who wants pizza?"

In unison, they stopped fighting long enough to shout, "We do! Yeah!" at the top of their lungs.

"Can you pick one up on your way home?"

I paused, afraid to tell him how long it would be before I could leave.

"You've had the car all day," he added, taking my silence for disapproval. "I couldn't get out to shop."

"How about lasagna?"

"We finished it last night. Remember?"

"Okay, but it's going to be at least an hour. Maybe two. I did get milk, by the way. And enough presents to keep them happy on Christmas morning."

His voice softened. "That's sweet of you. I've got a few surprises myself."

"Nothing expensive, I hope."

"Well—a surprise. Let's just leave it at that."

"Billy? You up to some kind of mischief?"

"So, what's for dinner, Mom?"

"Neat change of subject. Isn't there some packaged macaroni and cheese—Annie's Organic or something?"

"Oh, yeah. There it is. How long you going to be?"

I looked at the clock. It was after seven. "Don't expect me before nine or nine-thirty. Why don't I pick up a pizza for the two of us, you give the kids the macaroni now?"

"Deal. Zoë?"

"Yeah?"

"Go get 'em," he whispered close to the mouthpiece.

Out of the corner of my eye, I saw Whit approaching. "I'll do my best," I said softly.

As I hung up, Whit said, "How's the support piece coming?"

"It's turned into a profile of Chram," I said, trying to sound upbeat. His lips flattened with annoyance.

"Whit," I added, "just listen to tomorrow's schedule. In depth interviews with"—I bit my lip, hoping it wasn't a lie—"Cletha Fair, Cecily Chen, and Peter Albright. Today, I've got one of her professors, a classmate, and her fiancé all talking about Chram's ambitions, talents, and what she did on the afternoon before the murder. I'll also write up the Giles interview as a separate piece. Heart-to-heart with the distraught fiancé type thing."

Somewhat placated, Whit growled, "When am I going to see copy?"

"One hour. At the outside. Promise."

He pointed to the clock, noting the time, and without another word stormed off to chew out Mark.

I have one surefire technique for writing on deadline. It's called a Walkman. I put on the earphones, tune into a top-forty station, and crank it up loud. For the next forty-five minutes or so, I tapped at the keyboard to the heavy beat of tunes familiar to fourteen-year-olds nationwide. Once I get all my facts, I'm a fast writer, especially when I'm listening to music. Virtually none of my sources had been contacted by other reporters. That sense of being on top, added to the prospect of tomorrow's interviews, gave me a rush of energy. The words, facts, and quotes fell into place automatically.

When I was done, I rang up Song to see if the funeral had been set. Saturday or Sunday, she told me, complaining that her building was under siege by reporters.

"Have it on Sunday," I advised. "It's Christmas. Most papers will be short-staffed."

"I'll tell Bou Vuthy. He's making the arrangements."

"Did anyone come from Quaker Rescue?"

"Cecily Chen came for a while. Eleanor Kerr is here now. She brought us Kentucky Fried Chicken."

My anxiety level must have declined because all of a sudden I was starving. Even greasy KFC sounded good. "If you remember anything about Chram to fill out a profile—come to think of it, what do you know about her restaurant plans?"

"Oh, Chram," Song laughed. "She had all kinds of ideas. She wanted to be a rich American with fur coats and jewelry. She was after me to learn to cook, not just Cambodian but Thai and Vietnamese. I said, I'm going to college. I want to be a teacher, not a cook. She even asked people to lend her money to get started. She went to the bank to find out how much she would need."

"When did she do that?"

"Not too long ago. The last few weeks."

"Did she succeed in borrowing money?"

"No. The bank said come back when you graduate and show us your business plan. She started writing one that night."

"Did she ever mention Prith?"

"Cletha's foster son?"

"Yes."

"I don't think so."

"Had you met Prith before coming to the US?"

"You mean in the Thai camp?"

"Yeah."

"No."

"Chram didn't say she recognized him?"

"I don't think she said anything about him."

"Did anyone in town recognize him from Site II or the Khmer Rouge camps?"

"Do you want me to ask?"

"If you can do it unobtrusively. Oh, my line's lighting up. I'll talk to you tomorrow."

It was Whit.

"I just logged in two pieces."

"Good. Come on up."

I wanted to call Song back. I'd forgotten to ask if she'd noticed anything weird about Prith at the wedding. I vaguely remembered him, and I'd thought he seemed a bit aimless, but my mind had been on so many other things. However, there was no putting off Whit. I ran upstairs.

"Find out anything new?" he asked without looking up. He had my profile of Chram on screen.

"Aside from what you'll read in the story, a couple of things. The police had the boyfriend down at the station for over six hours this morning, and he thinks he's a suspect."

He squinted at me. "Prince Charming?"

"Today's Prince Charming is tomorrow's Bluebeard. Happens all the time."

His mouth twitched slightly, which was as close to a smile as he ever came. "What's your angle on Chram?"

"Not-so-local girl makes good." I told him about the restaurant, and he turned back to the monitor and scanned the story, nodding in a manner precariously close to approval. He fixed that by catching a grammatical error and moving a paragraph near the end up to the top after the lead.

"Okay," he said, pulling up the story on Stephen, which he read with a frown. "Needs balance."

"I'm talking to Peter Albright tomorrow. He's Stephen's adviser."

Whit gave a dissatisfied nod. "Check with Brannigan and make sure this guy isn't about to be booked. We don't want to look stupid."

"Did Mark come up with anything?"

He called Mark's piece onto the screen and I read over his shoulder. The murder weapon hadn't been found and the police wouldn't speculate on it. The time of death had been fixed. There had been a receipt in Chram's pocket. Monday, December 19, at 6:17 P.M. She'd died sometime between then and midnight. The body hadn't been found until Tuesday evening. Nearly twenty-three hours after the killing. A cold trail. There was no mention of the kids Mark had interviewed in the video arcade.

"Mark's downstairs," said Whit. "Why don't you two stop in before you leave."

I agreed and went back to my desk, where I called the Touches again. Song didn't remember anything about Prith at the wedding.

"While I'm thinking of it, did Chram ever have anything to do with Hal Gaffney?"

"Oh, the man who writes the angry things in the paper?"

"That's the one."

"He owns a bar. She worked there once. A long time ago."

"Do you remember why she left?"

"No. My mother might. Or Uncle Rok. I think maybe Rok made her quit. That was when she went to work for Professor Albright."

"Oh. Where'd she go after she left working for Peter?"

"The Lord William Inn. She planned to quit that, too."

"What was she going to do instead?"

"Open her restaurant. She'd just found a space."

"Even without money? Where?"

"There was an empty spot on Stanhope near the pizza place, where the Sandwich Shoppe used to be."

I hadn't realized that she was so far ahead in her plans. Odd, I thought, that Stephen hadn't mentioned it.

Song gave me the name of one more college friend of Chram's. I called the young woman, who was quite talkative. She told me an anecdote about Chram taking a swimming class the previous year. Chram had wanted to learn to swim, but her parents forbade her because bathing suits were indecent. Instead of outright defiance, Chram took the class wearing long johns to avoid exposing her shoulders and legs. In my conversation with the woman, I sensed she was holding something back. I didn't pursue it, figuring I'd make an appointment to see her when things got slower. There were just so many leads you could follow. Thinking about it later, though, I found it funny that Chram would bow to her parents' wishes about bathing suits, while sneaking around behind their backs with Stephen.

I logged in the story, tagging it as having been changed so Whit would be sure to reread it, then shut down the computer and found Mark in the kitchen heating up a hot dog in the microwave. It was eight-thirty. With luck I'd be home when I'd promised.

"*Qué pasó*, Szabo?"

I poured a cup of coffee.

"Want a bagel?" He nodded toward a white bakery bag on the table.

I took one and sat down. "Thanks."

He opened his arms. "Hey! We're partners, right?"

I half-expected him to give me a sporty pat on the back, but just in time the microwave chirped. Mark withdrew the hot dog and pushed it between two halves of an onion bagel. After slathering it with ketchup and mustard, he brought it to the table and edged his oversized frame into the metal chair.

I sipped the stale coffee.

"Whit wants to talk to us before we leave."

"We need to split up the territory," Mark explained when he'd consumed half his sandwich.

"Whatever happened to those kids you found at the mall?"

He shook his head, chewing and swallowing before he spoke. "Couldn't find them. I've been there three times today. Whit won't use the statement without their identity, and no one else saw the loony guy until later."

"Have the police mentioned the loony?"

"Nah. I asked Brannigan point blank. He told me to stuff it."

The conference in Whit's office lasted all of three minutes. I asked about the cause of death. He told me the autopsy was being performed today or tomorrow. Results from some tests might take as long as six weeks.

"Anything else?" Whit asked.

Mark shook his head. "They say they're following a number of leads, but I think they've got *nada*."

I told them about the emerging plans for a funeral.

Whit consulted his calendar, a large black leather book that always lay open on his desk. "The University press office called, working late just like us. They're planning a memorial for Friday at noon. They're hoping for lots of coverage and a big turnout. Zoë, pin down the time of the funeral and take Kate with you to cover it. Mark, talk to the University PR people."

"We ought to clarify," Mark began, pushing up the sleeves of his baseball shirt, "like, who's covering what. We should carve up the territory so we don't retrace each other's tracks."

Whit frowned. "Zoë's working the personal side. We'll keep you on the police angle. How are you getting on with Brannigan?"

"Super."

Whit suppressed a smile. Brannigan didn't suffer fools gladly, let alone a sports reporter investigating a murder.

"It's a wrap," Whit concluded. "Go home. Get some sleep."

Later, as I put on my coat, Mark sidled up to me.

"Where you off to?"

"Home."

"I'll buy you a beer."

"You've got to be kidding."

"I've got some angles I'd like to bounce off you."

"I have to go home and give my kids some attention."

That didn't faze him. "How about I swing by later?"

I didn't have the energy to object. Besides, I wanted to know what he was up to. All his concern about splitting up the territory made me suspicious.

While waiting for the pizza, I wandered down the street to the empty Sandwich Shoppe. I cupped my hands and peered inside. This was the spot Song said Chram had rented—or had she just hoped to rent it? Illuminated by a faint fluorescent bulb in back, the moderately sized space appeared to be pretty grubby, the paint chipped, the linoleum scuffed and torn, but Stanhope was a prime location. Around the corner was a fancy Chinese restaurant that always had lines on the weekend, across the street a new brew pub, next door a moderately priced but comfortable American-style place. There were two Indian restaurants in town, another Chinese, a burrito place, a Texas grill, a couple of Italian restaurants, and a vegetarian cafe. A Cambodian-Thai place would fit in well. Chram's idea might have worked, if she'd been able to secure the necessary capital. That was the key question. How was a Cambodian immigrant whose parents were on refugee assistance going to come up with the tens of thousands of dollars necessary to open a restaurant?

10

The first sight that met my eyes when I finally kicked shut the door to the mudroom and entered the kitchen was the colored paper all over the floor. A pair of scissors and a box of markers lay in the middle of the room. The TV was on with the sound off, and the thudding of a muted electric bass could be heard. Giggles and the gush of running water emanated from the bathroom.

I turned the oven to two hundred degrees, popped in the pizza, hung up my coat, and traded my heels for cozy wool slippers. Around the corner I spied two faces poking through the doorway.

"Mommy! Mommy!"

Keith and Smokie were upon me with shrieks, climbing, pulling me, until I knelt down to their level. With a green line down her tiny nose and red zig-zags on her round cheeks, three-year-old Smokie was made up like a 1950s Hollywood Indian. She threw her soft arms around my neck and pulled my face close. Keith, older at five, shyer, hung back, tugging at my arm.

"Can we paint your face?" Keith asked.

"Yeah!" shouted Smokie. "Let's paint her face!"

They ran to the bathroom.

"Turn off the water!" I called after them.

The bass still thumped away in the living room. I opened the refrigerator and found makings for a salad. I had just finished mixing the dressing when I felt two warm hands on my shoulders. Billy put his arms around me, and I leaned into his heat.

"I'm going to do it!" shouted Smokie.

"No! I am!" insisted Keith.

The two munchkins scrambled into the kitchen.

Billy bent down to kiss me, pulling my hips close to his. "Mmm," I murmured.

"We've got an audience," Billy whispered.

"Yay!" shouted Smokie. "Family hug!"

She and Keith jumped up on us. Billy and I lifted them in our arms and we all hugged and kissed.

"Ready for dinner?" I murmured softly, smiling at Billy through the blur of our children's heads.

He grinned sleepily. "Nice to see you, stranger."

"She's not a stranger," Keith corrected him. "She's Mommy."

I got the kids to calm down by allowing them to paint my face. While they did, Billy poured me a glass of California Zinfandel. Afterward we took the kids upstairs, read them stories, and put them to bed.

I lay for a few minutes with Keith while he told me in his tentative, hesitating manner about a secret snow house he'd made for the squirrels that afternoon.

"The problem is, Mom, that the foxes want to know where the squirrels are hiding. So they could catch them. That's why I had to keep the trail secret. So they won't know where the squirrels are going."

"Oh. That's pretty clever."

"Think there are any wolves out there, Mom?"

"No. There aren't any wolves in Massachusetts."

"There was a bear in the middle of town. You wrote a story about it. Do bears eat squirrels?"

"That's a good question. I'm not sure. They like berries, honey, and fish."

We were quiet for a while.

"Mom?"

"Yes, sweetie."

"Maybe you should buy a gun."

"Why?"

"I heard you talking with Dad. You're writing about someone who got killed."

"Honey, I'm perfectly safe. I just talk to people on the phone and take notes."

"Be careful."

"I will. Nobody's going to hurt me. Don't you worry."

Another silence.

"Mom?"

"Yeah?"

"I love you."

"Oh, honey. I love you, too."

I gave him a big hug, kissed him good night, and

went down to the long-awaited dinner. Billy brought the pizza to the table. It was tomato with fresh mozzarella and basil, my favorite.

Billy's hair just grazed the shoulders of his purple cashmere sweater, one of his extravagant purchases in the pre-crisis days.

"Dare I ask what's on your agenda for tomorrow?"

"Cletha is first on my list. She doesn't want to talk to me, but if I drop in she'll probably say something."

I watched as Billy cut his pizza with a knife and fork. To set off the purple cashmere, he wore tight black jeans and black leather boots. Sometimes I think I married him for his perfect nose, sometimes for the sexy eyes. I admit I was initially attracted by the wrapping, but it was the poetic soul inside that kept me coming back for more. Since we'd moved to Greymont, we'd begun to take walks again, sometimes with the kids in tow, sometimes after dropping them off at school. Though the subject matter we touched now veered away from certain still-too-sensitive zones, the simple pleasure of sharing our thoughts had begun to reemerge. Yet, I couldn't help but wonder if this new leaf he'd turned over would last. My wounds were pretty raw.

"Morgan invited us for Christmas Eve dinner."

"Cool."

Billy served himself some salad. "He says he hasn't had a real Christmas since his old lady died. He wants to sing carols, have a turkey. We're going to pick out trees together."

"Who's roasting the turkey?"

"All you do is put it in the oven. Morgan and I can handle that. We figure you'll be on duty most of the day."

"I'll try to leave early."

Billy had always been on tour at this time of the year. Last December, we'd still been sorting out our differences. It had been touch and go for quite a while.

His eyes softened and he reached for my hand. Then he fingered my angora sweater. "This is nice," he said. "I don't remember it."

"One of my dad's theater friends gave it to me. She said it suited my eyes." What I left out was that the gift had been to cheer me up shortly after I'd left Billy post-crisis.

Just then the doorbell rang. Mark entered, his imposing stature, at six-foot-two, making the low ceilings of the Cape seem even closer. He stamped snow off his hightops while Billy watched with dismay.

"Brought a six pack," Mark said, handing a carton to Billy. "The good stuff." It was Budweiser.

We settled around the fireplace and Billy tossed on another log. Hardly able to hold my eyes open, I curled up on the couch with my feet under me, determined to keep the meeting short. Mark, oblivious, plopped down beside me. In addition to being taller, he was more muscular and clean-cut than Billy, with short sandy hair compared with Billy's black mane. Looking as if he'd recently showered, he wore a clean sweatshirt and Gap khakis. In the sophisticated and expensive cashmere, with a gold chain round his neck, Billy, though forty-three and fifteen years older than Mark, was slimmer, hipper, sexier. He gave my foot a teasing pat as he eased into the recliner across from the sofa.

Mark leaned over to the coffee table, where he'd dropped the beer, tore open the carton, and popped a tab on a can, handing it to Billy, who, beer snob that he was, held it as if it were medical waste.

Mark took a can for himself. "Want one?" he asked me.

"I'll pass. It'd put me to sleep," I hinted, trying to communicate that he ought to go home soon. Billy found a coaster, put the beer down, picked up his bass, and began fingering runs silently as we talked.

"Do you have any leads on those kids yet?" I asked.

Mark looked at me askance. "They thought the whole thing was a joke," he admitted. "One called himself 'Leonardo,' the other 'Raphael.'"

Billy laughed. "Ninja Turtles."

"Okay. Don't rub it in." Mark concentrated on his Bud. I detected a blush edging his clean-shaven jaw. "I've got another lead," he continued. "This one's right up your alley."

"Yeah?"

"You're not going to like it."

"Why not?"

He stood up, elaborately reaching into the back pocket of his khakis, which were a lot tighter on him than on the celebrities in the Gap ads. Mark liked showing off his well-contoured butt. He handed me three Xeroxed clippings, turning to shoot Billy a just-between-us-guys look.

"Check it out." Mark picked up his beer and took a swig.

One was from two summers earlier. Police blotter item. Phroeng Touch of 28 Normandy Heights arrested for assault. Police had been called to the apartment by neighbors at two A.M. Touch had been in an inebriated condition. His wife, Ly, was taken to the hospital where she was treated for bruises and cuts. His daughter Chram sustained a head wound. She was held in the hospital overnight for observation and released the next day. On the same sheet I noted a follow-up from the Court Calendar section, stating that the case had been dropped because the wife refused to press charges.

I passed the clip to Billy and turned to the next one, a wire story from California that had appeared last year in the *Sheffington Sun*. Why this story had run here was anyone's guess, but the bloodier it was, the more likely the *Sun* was to print it. A Cambodian immigrant in Long Beach had been badly cut up by her parents when she refused to go along with a marriage they had arranged with a Cambodian boy's parents.

The phone rang. Billy picked up.

"Gentle people," Mark said snidely to me.

Billy was speaking quietly into the phone. "No, it's not too late," he was saying. "I hear it's been rainin' out there—"

I looked up. Billy had on his California voice.

He covered the mouthpiece. "Business." He took the cordless to the kitchen. *Business*, I thought. *What's that about?*

"You with me, Szabo?" Mark demanded.

Reluctantly, I turned my attention back to him. "Do you honestly think her own father could have killed her?"

"He beat her."

I tilted my chin, conceding the point. Perhaps the reason Chram wore long johns swimming had not been to be modest but to hide bruises. I wondered why Stephen hadn't mentioned the abuse. He hadn't been reticent about Phroeng's drinking.

Mark tucked the clips back in his pocket. "Let's run down the possible suspects and motives.

"A. Random psycho. A uniformed officer on the scene told me in confidence that she was pretty badly hacked up. Could have been a psycho."

I nodded, nausea hovering like a whiff of distant rot.

"B. Someone she knew. Crime of passion. Her boyfriend. A family member. Maybe this 'Loony Toons.' You wrote that post-traumatic stress story. I've reread it a couple of times. You might want to check with the doctors or nurses which people are suffering the worst."

"C," I interjected. "A political motive. The anti-immigrant crowd, or . . . maybe a vendetta from something that happened a long time ago." Stephen had intimated as much.

"D," Mark added, raising an eyebrow to show that

the political angle hadn't occurred to him. "Money."

"The Cambodians are poverty stricken," I objected.

Again, he went through the ritual of getting a clip out of his pocket. He handed me the paper. It was my own story, about a "Money Tree" festival at a site where they hoped to build a Cambodian Buddhist temple. I had written only two inches because Whit drew the line at being used for fund-raising. None of the Touches were mentioned.

"To be honest, Mark," I said after reviewing the story, "I don't think someone would do that over a minor dispute about money."

"Like you said. Cambodians are poor. A couple hundred dollars might seem like a fortune."

Again I thought about the restaurant plans and made a mental note to see who was collecting funds for the temple and whether anything had been missing.

Aloud, I said, "I'll check it." Billy's laugh echoed from the kitchen.

"Hey," Mark was saying, standing up. "It's eleven."

I stood to escort him to the door, but he was moving in the direction of the TV. "Mind if we catch the news?"

Like a typical male, Mark grabbed the remote and pushed on the power. Channel 4 had Brannigan's press conference, along with shots of the mall. Carolee Clark interviewed a woman who smiled apologetically and explained that she had to find Power Rangers for her son, murder or not: "He'll be so disappointed if they're not under the tree." Cut to coeds being questioned about whether they felt safe. And then Song and her mother, with Eleanor Kerr, standing in front of the Normandy Heights townhouses, surrounded by reporters shouting questions. A police officer was leading the trio to an automobile, trying to hold back the press. A crowd of Cambodians stood around. A teenager waved at the camera.

"Hey!" Mark shouted. "That's my kid!"

By that time the camera had cut away.

Now a somber old Cambodian man stood front and center. He was being interviewed by Carolee, who simpered her appreciation at having found someone who spoke English. He wore a torn, stained wool jacket and looked homeless. Slung over his shoulder was a clear plastic bag full of empty soda cans.

"Sad day for Cambodian people," he kept repeating in a heavy accent.

Carolee asked, "Who would do this terrible thing?"

He shook his head. Despite the incongruous smile that lit his face, tears rolled down his cheeks. His smile broadened and the tears flowed more heavily. The camera moved in close. The man made no attempt to escape its intrusive curiosity. There was a lingering close-up of the wrinkles around the man's eyes, the glistening furrows around his nose, and nearly toothless mouth. And then a jump cut to Carolee, who said, "Carolee Clark reporting from the murder victim's home in Greymont."

We caught the tail end of the Touch story on 25, which ran it after the national news and showed footage of Brannigan describing, with deliberate vagueness, the condition of the body and estimated time of death. There was an aerial shot of the spot where the green Chrysler had been parked.

"I wonder who Brannigan hates more," I remarked, "us or the TV."

"I heard ABC is sending someone up from New York to take over for Carolee."

"Really?"

"It's the Cambodian angle," Mark added. "I was talking to the *Times* guy today. It's hot. A *New Yorker* feature writer is here snooping around. Whit is totally pumped."

"Guard your sources, Mark."

"I'm mum to everyone but you, darlin'."

"Listen, Polanski," I said as Billy reappeared. "I've got an early deadline." I shut off the TV. Billy accompanied me as I walked Mark to the mudroom, where Billy stood, an arm possessively touching my shoulder as we waited for Mark to don his down vest. Mark punched Billy on the elbow and saluted me.

After watching his Mazda skid out the driveway and zoom a bit too quickly down our back street, Billy and I ambled back to the living room. He gingerly picked up the full can of Budweiser with a look of distaste.

"Let me get a real beer." He came back with Noche Buena and a bag of marshmallows. While he stoked the embers, I waited to see if he would say anything about the call.

"Who was it?" I finally asked.

He skewered a marshmallow and sighed. "Oh, lawyers." He seemed upbeat, not his usual demeanor after a talk with the lawyer counseling him on the protracted battle over the royalties of his one song that still got radio play.

11

Early the following morning I drove to the Fair residence. The sprawling farm covered a hundred acres in the rural section north of town. The ride took about fifteen minutes. I passed cows, horses, and hayfields, interspersed with wetlands and woods. Cletha and her husband, a cardiologist who'd died a decade ago, were part of a dedicated core of Quakers. She had grown up here and her legendary activism was tolerated. Most of the native inhabitants were moderately liberal, in a stiff-jawed, frugal New England way, and they accepted Cletha as a fixture. Even Gaffney's crowd—newer inhabitants, small-business owners, and developers—treated her with a begrudging respect. For the last few years all her energy had gone into bringing as many refugees as possible from the crowded camps that lined the Thai-Cambodian border into the US and helping them settle in and around Greymont.

I parked my Civic near the weathered red barn. As I got out, Cletha's Irish setter, Ginger, bounded out from behind the garage, a converted carriage house topped by a cupola with a weather vane in the form of a galloping horse.

Ginger and I were pals, though we hadn't seen each other for a while. I tossed a stick for her and ran to the porch. Today I'd dressed practically—at least on the outer layer. I was wearing boots with reasonable heels and the down jacket Billy had bought me. Underneath I sported skinny black velveteen jeans and a tight, glittery pink sweater.

Ginger beat me to the porch. I tossed the stick again, watched her catch it in midair and settle down to gnaw at it while I rang the bell.

The weather had taken a turn for the worse. Clouds had massed into a wall of unbroken white that hung oppressively low, and the wind had acquired a sharp edge. The thermostat, which had dropped steeply overnight, hovered around fifteen degrees. Despite the practical outerwear, my knees were frozen. And I'd forgotten to bring gloves.

I'd just withdrawn my bare hand from my pocket to press the bell again when the door opened. From the look on Cletha's face I could tell she wasn't overjoyed to see me.

"I was just driving by," I lied, ashamed to pull this bullshit on an old friend, "and I thought I'd stop in."

In her mid-sixties, Cletha was a rugged, large-boned woman with steady eyes and gray hair cropped short. Her clothes were vintage L.L. Bean. Today, in loose gray corduroy slacks and a sky-blue cabled sweater, she looked as if she were ready for a vigorous hike. For a long moment we faced each other. Her uneasiness showed in the furrow between her eyes.

"Would you like some tea?" she finally asked.

I breathed with relief. She was letting me in.

I stamped the snow off my boots, glad that hers was a house where I could leave my shoes on, especially since she kept the thermostat at sixty degrees.

"Could I trouble you for coffee? I didn't have time to fix any this morning."

"No trouble. Come in."

Elated that I'd managed to cross the threshold, I followed her into the bright kitchen of her rambling farmhouse. Every time I saw this room, I felt a twitch of envy. A large pantry opened off one side, leading to a back porch. Tall windows on the south and west let in volumes of light, even on a gray day like this. Above the blue-tiled counters were tall, old-fashioned wood cabinets with glass fronts. Against the north wall stood an antique cherry hutch.

On the other side of the room, an archway opened onto an alcove that Cletha used as an office. It held a cluttered cherry desk, old black phone, and a manual Royal typewriter. A shelf lined with phone books from all over the country was wedged into a corner. Next to the desk were two tall file cabinets stacked with folders.

Cletha opened the door of the potbellied wood stove set in the open brick hearth that dominated the room. Bright coals blazed orange. She jabbed at the embers with an iron poker, took a log from a rack on the brick floor, and tossed it in. As usual an iron kettle was already steaming on top of the stove. She measured fresh coffee beans into a hand grinder attached to the wall and cranked away for a minute. The pungent aroma stung my nostrils and began to wake me up. Her movements were methodical. Carefully she unscrewed the cup from the grinder and measured out the rich brown powder into a filter holder.

"How are Smokie and Keith?"

"They've just recovered from Hanukkah, and now they're looking forward to Christmas," I told her. "How's Prith?"

She responded without resistance, but her offhand tone wasn't completely convincing. "We're coming along slowly but surely. Time's the best cure. That and faith."

Prith had lost his entire family in Cambodia. I didn't know the details, because Cletha guarded his privacy, but I'd gathered he'd been through a harrowing ordeal.

She handed me a mug of coffee and took herbal tea for herself. I breathed in the heady scent of the steaming brew.

"Milk?" she asked.

"Your coffee's too good to adulterate."

"I can take one cup in the morning. That's all. When I was your age, I used to drink it all day. I still love the smell."

I blew on the liquid and took a quick sip.

"Before I forget," she continued, going to a basket near her desk. She returned with two small packages wrapped in foil. "For the kids."

"Oh, Cletha. You didn't have to."

"I bought them months ago. Nothing special."

"Thank you." I tucked the packages into my pocket, guilt crushing the words in my throat.

"How's Billy?"

"Good."

"I ran into him at the supermarket last week. He seemed to have his hands full with your two little ragamuffins." She smiled.

I sipped coffee. "Yeah, kind of like The Keystone Kops meets Our Gang."

"You know, Keith reminds me more and more of your father."

"Think so?"

"Especially around the eyes. There's that depth. Big things are going on in that little mind."

"Keith's so quiet," I demurred. "My father was such a ham."

"Oh, he had his serious side. He used his charm to good effect. And don't be too hard on that boy of yours. He'll bloom. You'll see."

I grinned at her, shamefaced.

"So," she said dryly. "You've come to pump me for information."

I nodded. "Something like that."

"When I heard it on the radio yesterday, I simply could not believe it."

I glanced up at her with a twinge of concern. I'd caught her in a lie. "Song told me she called you when the police came."

Her lips drew into a thin line. The fine web of

wrinkles in her soft old cheeks expanded and deepened. I suddenly wished I hadn't come.

"Yes, she did," she said after a moment.

"I need quotes for my story," I said, letting the point pass. "You know, reaction of the community. Do you have anything to say on the record?"

I wanted to get some kind of formal statement from her that I could show Whit and get out of here. I didn't want to know what she was hiding or why. I hoped that she understood this from the way I'd phrased my question.

Cletha's hand, freckled with age, fidgeted with her tea cup. She looked out the window toward the woods.

"Yes," she said, "I suppose I must say something. The words that come to mind are devastation, tragedy, nightmare. Phroeng and Ly have lost several children already to truly gruesome, brutal deaths. How they've survived even marginally intact is a mystery to me, a testament to the strength of the human spirit. To have this violent murder come now . . . It's a terrible blow to the whole community. There are tremendous suspicions. You have no idea, Zoë. No idea. It's a horrible blow," she repeated, "to the supporters as well as the refugees."

I jotted down the entire quote in my shorthand. "And Song?"

"Song?"

"Do you think she's in danger?"

"Song in danger?" Cletha was disbelieving.

"From the person who killed Chram."

"It never occurred to me. Is that what the police are saying? Someone is after the Touch family?" She seemed genuinely alarmed. "My God!"

"Can you tell me something about Chram's personality? I'm collecting personal anecdotes. The Cambodians," I explained, to appeal to her activist instincts, "have been subject to so much criticism lately. This is going to make the climate more hostile. I think the response is going to be that they're bringing trouble with them. I'd love to add a human dimension to the story of Chram's death."

Cletha warmed her hands on the tea cup and gazed into the stream. "This has really unsettled me," she admitted. "You need personal details." She sighed, avoiding my eyes. "The problem is that Chram was a bit upstaged by her sister. Though I don't know exactly what she went through during those five years under Pol Pot and the Khmer Rouge, I always had the feeling she had a great deal to overcome.

"Even in families where there is tragedy, as with the Touches, there are still things like sibling rivalry, some children favored above others. Chram was less favored. You could see it in her eyes, her shyness. She hardly ever spoke until she met Stephen. Have you talked to him? He probably knows her better than anyone."

"Yes, I did." I smiled. "When did you first meet her?"

Cletha returned my smile. "The Touches came here five years ago. I'd met them twice during my trips to the refugee camps in Thailand. The first time was shortly after the fall of the Khmer Rouge. Bou Vuthy had come from New York, driven, in fact, by Prince Sihanouk's chauffeur. Sihanouk was at the UN at the time, trying to garner support for his people. Peter had arranged for Bou Vuthy to speak to a group of us from charitable religious organizations from all over the Northeast. Catholics, Lutherans, and Quakers, primarily. A few of us decided to try to get people out of the camps and bring them to the US. We raised money for six months and finally in the middle of the summer, we left with Bou Vuthy as our guide.

"I'll never forget driving into the camp, Site II, at the Thai-Cambodian border, seeing it for the first time. The camp was a village teeming with people dressed in the brightest of colors: the traditional Khmer fabrics, mixed with hand-me-downs from the Red Cross, old Mickey Mouse T-shirts, and jeans. I noticed Song the moment I arrived. I suppose she was only five or six, a little sprite of a thing, but she had those bright, dark eyes. Riveting. A very self-possessed child. I think Chram was with her, but I can't honestly remember."

Warmed by her memories, Cletha relaxed. She described the bamboo huts, the thatched roofs, the open sewers, the red mud, the lack of trees and vegetation, and the oppressive, tropical heat. It was a brutal place. There was rampant hunger, anger, signs of violence on children and women. People feared the theft of what possessions they had managed to scrounge. Girls were abducted and raped. People suspected of collaborating with the Khmer Rouge were the cold light reflected off the snow. It was too bad this guy wanted to be an Asian scholar. He would have done well in the movies.

"When did you last see her?"

"Monday."

"The day she was killed?"

"Is that when it happened?" he asked sharply.

"That's what the police say."

He flushed, then put his hand to his forehead. His fingers vibrated terribly. After a moment, he took a breath and exhaled slowly. "A couple of things just got much clearer," he muttered, gazing at me with a great deal less artifice.

"Do you want to talk about your last meeting?"

He closed his eyes. "Somebody was shadowing her. Sending her threatening messages. Calling, then hanging up. Telling her to leave the country, or else. Seems she had finally pinned down this person and was going to have a confrontation."

"Male or female?"

"She wouldn't say. She became withdrawn. Moody. Angry. She insisted on keeping me out of it."

His tension increased, and for the first time I detected grief. The rims of his eyes reddened. He choked slightly. With embarrassment or emotion, he turned away. I felt for him, but at the same time I wanted more detail. Whit's words, "Get a picture," echoed in my mind.

"What happened?" I asked when it seemed possible for him to go on. "On Monday, when you last saw her?"

beaten or killed. The Thai police turned a blind eye to thugs who ruled the camps, but bullied ordinary people and had to be paid off for the simplest of things, like sending a letter to a relative.

"If I go back in my memory, I visualize Chram in the tutoring shed—an open-air school with no books, just a board and chalk if you were lucky. Again, I mostly remember Song. I don't know how she'd managed, but her English was far and away the best in the class, and she chattered like a little bird in Khmer.

"I hate to say it, but Chram was slow. She had terrible trouble pronouncing the phrase, 'Today it is sunny. Yesterday it rained.' I remember thinking, 'There's one who won't make it.' I have to confess, Song was my primary interest. Once I'd seen her, I made a vow not to rest until I got the family out. We gathered names of people we wanted to bring to Greymont, collected sponsors, one for each family. The local Lutheran church as a group sponsored the Touches. Peter Albright was an invaluable help with red tape. He has connections in Washington. You should talk to him."

"He's on my list."

"Well, the entire process was fraught with difficulty. We had to deal with a terribly slow-moving bureaucracy on the US side and a patently corrupt one on the Thai side. I became adept at passing a bribe. It's amazing how many we managed to rescue. Now you can't get anyone out, except unaccompanied minors like Prith. And even that's growing more difficult."

"What was Chram like after she arrived?"

"Quiet. Eleanor Kerr tutored her. She might be a good person to talk to."

I jotted down the name, which had come up several times already. Cletha continued. "And then she met Stephen. That caused quite an uproar. Everyone was shocked when he proposed. To be honest, I hadn't thought he was serious. He pushed her to educate herself and she blossomed. She was doing quite well at the University."

"What can you tell me about her parents?" I asked.

Cletha's eyebrows moved up noncommittally. "What do you want to know?"

"Well, for a start, how do they make their living?"

"Public assistance. There are special programs for political refugees, although there have been cutbacks. For a short time Ly had a job cleaning, but she has a number of health problems including an injury that makes it difficult for her to walk. She couldn't handle the physical labor. Chram held menial restaurant jobs. Then she went to work part-time for Peter. Receptionist or typist, something like that. She got bored with it a few months ago and took a job as hostess at the Lord William Inn."

"Yes, Song mentioned she'd just quit that, too."

"Really? I hadn't heard."

"Do you know anything about her plans to open a restaurant?"

"Of her own?"

"Yes."

"I had no idea."

"Do you know anyone she'd asked for a loan—for the restaurant?"

Cletha hesitated. "No, and we're getting into the territory of rumor."

I searched her face for a clue as to whether she knew more than she was letting on. Even though her gaze was unflinching, I thought she might.

"Is there anyone else I should talk to?" I asked, wrapping it up. "Any Cambodians? And can you find me a translator, or volunteer yourself?"

She smiled dryly. "You're not going to rope me into that. Talk to Bou Vuthy. He puts things in a spiritual way, and for the Cambodians that's important."

"If Prith's here," I ventured, as if it were just an afterthought, "I'd love to get a comment from him, you know, as a new arrival."

Cletha stiffened. "Prith has nothing to do with this."

"Cletha," I said softly, "I think it's only fair to tell you that I know you went to the mall and picked him up the night Chram died."

Her cheeks lost color. "Prith and Chram didn't know each other," she whispered forcefully. "They hadn't even met."

"Wasn't he at the wedding?"

Cletha's lips trembled.

I cast my mind back to the wedding, but I couldn't remember much about Prith, except that he had looked odd in the clothes she'd bought for him, scarecrow thin, awkward, and disoriented. It was one of the few times I'd seen him.

She reached across the table. Her fingers clutched my arm tightly. "Zoë, we have to keep Prith out of this. I'm begging for your help." She pronounced "begging" with such an emphasis that I involuntarily shrank back. She tightened her grasp. "I'm trusting you as a friend. As a *mother*."

I didn't know what to say. Although I'd intended to stop before pressing her into any untoward confessions, I'd stumbled into this outburst.

"We're talking about murder," I whispered.

"Prith needs time," she continued, ignoring me. "He spent two years in a Khmer Rouge labor camp separated from his mother and father. From the age of nine, he could visit his parents only a few minutes a week. You have children. Can you imagine what that must have been like? He witnessed tortures, beatings, killings, starvation."

Her hand went from my arm back to her empty cup. She tapped it a few times with her fingernails, in an effort to suppress her emotion.

"Some people," she said, "can go through things like that and come out whole. But others can't: the sensitive, the intelligent, the artistic. They keep reliving the past, trying to make sense of the senseless."

She put her hand over my notes, her skin papery, the age spots pronounced, the nails thick but carefully manicured.

"I want to tell you something that is absolutely not for publication. Something never to be repeated. Not to anyone. Not even Billy."

I shook my head. "For God's sakes, Cletha. I'm a

reporter, and this is my biggest story. Don't pass confidential information to me. Even though I may honor an off-the-record commitment, if I need those facts, I'll find someone else who'll tell me the same thing on the record, and it will be printed."

Cletha's jaw firmed. The wrinkled skin and hawkish nose took on her true toughness.

"Prith has been through a severe trauma," she said over my objections. "And I'm going to tell you about it. Keep it in mind as you go on collecting your brownie points and your news. Half the Cambodians in this community have had experiences as bad or worse, and it's about time someone began showing some mercy."

12

"At the age of eleven," Cletha began, "Prith, with his entire family, his friends, grandparents, aunts, and an uncle, cousins, children from infants to teenagers, were lined up along a ditch by the Khmer Rouge and shot. They were suspected of some minor insubordination and made an example of, the entire group from his village.

"Prith was hit in the shoulder. All the rest were killed. He was buried alive in the pit under the corpses that fell on top of him.

"By some miracle, he managed to crawl from under the mass of bodies, dig his way out of the thin layer of clay that had been shoveled over them, and, under cover of night, disappear across a barren rice field that had been planted with land mines. He escaped into the jungle. He climbed trees and slept in the branches. He hid from the soldiers that way, foraging for food when he could. He nursed his wound with herbs he'd learned about as a young child from his uncle. He ate roots, fruit from coconut and mango trees, small birds, rodents, and snakes.

"After several months, he came down with malaria. He lay near death by a stream, when he was found by Khmer Rouge soldiers, who nursed him back to health. After the fall of the regime to the Vietnamese, he accompanied the escaping soldiers to the Thai border. They eventually made their way to Site B, hiding their political identity.

"I found him a few years ago on a trip to Site II, where he had been transferred. There are several of these camps along the border, and I'd been trying to get him out ever since. He can't read or write, and a lot of his talk is just gibberish, but he draws exquisite pictures of his childhood village: huts on stilts, roosters and chickens, flowers, water buffalo, wooden carts, and children playing marbles in the dirt under the canopy of trees.

"When we first met, I was teaching English at the camp. He drew a picture of his mother, the bodies there in the grave. Together we held hands and silently wept."

Cletha regarded me solemnly, her watery, washed-out blue eyes conveying the depth of her feelings.

"The psychologist at the health center has been working with us. Peter Albright put me in touch with her. Peter has been a godsend. A small group of us truly care. But all the caring in the world can't undo being buried alive in a ditch with the corpses of almost every person you know. What courage it must have taken to get up and walk away from that grave."

She circled the rim of her tea cup with the fingers of her left hand. "It's a failing in me," she said. "I was proud. I thought I could make a difference."

"And you couldn't?"

She shook her head. "Some days, there's a glimmer of hope. Other days"—her gaze was direct and intense—"it's *hard*. And I'm tired."

"Post-traumatic stress."

"When you called me with that story idea, I thought you had found out from the psychologist or a nurse. Yes, we've been to the hospital, another terrible place. He's better off here, tramping around in the woods. I couldn't bear to have him exposed and taunted. There's a lot of beautiful feeling and generosity among the refugees, but there's also cruelty and distrust, especially with people who aren't very strong."

"How do you document someone's identity when you're trying to get him admitted to the United States?"

"Papers are made out when they arrive at the camps. Almost no one arrives with anything. Sometimes they come with money or valuables. Never with papers."

"Prith came as an unaccompanied minor?" I'd done some mental arithmetic. The Khmer Rouge had fallen over a decade ago. Prith had to be in his mid-twenties.

"We lied about his age. Officially he's eighteen."

Cletha regarded me with a steely gaze, no longer distracted. "You'd be amazed what can be accomplished with a bribe or two. It's a way of life over there."

"Where is Prith now?"

"That's the trouble. I don't know!"

I tried to conceal my concern. "Have you seen him since the murder?"

"I brought him home from the arcade Monday. I made him tea and rice, but he wouldn't eat. He was in a state . . . and he ran off. I think he's living out there in the woods." She motioned toward the back window. I looked out to the fence and the snowy hills beyond. "I come downstairs in the morning and food is missing. I leave it out in the pantry."

We sat in silence for a few moments. Cletha's mouth puckered, her eyes wistful and faded. "Do you want more coffee?" she asked after a while.

"No." I stood up. "I have to go back to the office and finish a story."

She regarded me wanly, as if she wondered whether I would include anything on Prith.

I felt shaky. I'd learned this lesson before: If you don't want to know, you shouldn't ask in the first place. Once people started talking, they blurted out things they'd hide from their own friends and spouses. It's the nature of an interview to keep probing, expressing no opinion or judgment, akin to methods psychologists use. That's why when people read what you've transcribed word-for-word from a tape, they honestly believe you've misquoted.

However, Cletha had so much experience with the press that, despite her emotion, I wondered whether this outpouring had been entirely accidental. Perhaps she feared she might not have the strength to tell the truth when it became necessary. She'd lied already to the authorities for Prith, and I sensed she didn't trust herself not to do it again.

"Cletha," I assured her, "I won't write about Prith unless his name comes up in the police investigation."

The moment I spoke, I regretted making the promise. All this was very murky, in terms of ethics. I'd been compromised in some way. I should have gone to Whit with this information, but I was afraid he'd make me tell the police. And I just couldn't put Cletha through that.

Ginger greeted me eagerly as I stepped onto the porch. Gray clouds swirled over the trees, and a light flurry of snow danced down through the branches and whirled about in an eddying gust. Wanting to play, the dog held the stick in her mouth and followed me, whining. When I reached my car, she dropped the stick at my feet, barked, and bowed her head. Then she leaped into the air, barking again and wagging her tail.

I picked up the stick and heaved it toward the barn. I threw it twice. Each time she cajoled me into throwing it again, with her bowing and wagging. Enjoying the exercise myself after the intensity of my conversation with Cletha, I ran after Ginger. I didn't relish the idea of going back to the computer, facing the ethical dilemma, interviewing more people with secrets they might suddenly drop in my lap.

I tossed the stick. Ginger caught it on the fly and bounded about, tossing it up, chewing it, taunting me, daring me to try to snatch it away. I dodged at her, faking her out. She ran at me, dropped the stick, and gave a whining, happy bark.

I whisked it away, throwing it high into the trees. She jumped and leaped into the woods. I watched her receding figure, the muscles stretched at a full run. She seemed to need the exercise. Cletha must have temporarily stopped the brisk walks she usually took at sunrise with the dog. Ginger was overjoyed to be moving at full speed.

As I waited for her to return, my mind went over what I'd culled in the last two days. A common thread seemed to be Site II. Chram had lived at the refugee camp until five years ago. Prith had been found there by Cletha within the last few years. It was possible they'd met there. The other thread was the Khmer Rouge. Chram's brother had been a member of the radical group. Prith's family had been murdered by them; he'd also been saved by Khmer Rouge soldiers and brought with them to Thailand.

I realized I'd been waiting quite a long time for Ginger's return. She was usually a prompt retriever. I whistled. When I got no response, I called her.

Nothing.

I wanted to see the reassuring wag of her orange tail and her panting snout, so I took a minute to trudge through the snow into the wooded area behind the barn where I'd thrown the stick. I left the clearing and entered the woods. Her tracks seemed to go in several directions, and then they became confused with other prints. I bent down to examine them. There appeared to be boot prints mixed in with the dog and animal tracks. They seemed to come from the rim of hemlocks near the back of the barn and recede into the trees, mostly hemlocks and oaks broken by a few stands of birch. The trail went straight into the woods and up the hill where the trees grew old and tall.

About a hundred yards in, I stopped. A maze of trails seemed to cross and mix once again. There was a large area of compressed snow where an animal had rolled around on the ground, probably Ginger. I had just decided to turn and go back when I heard a soft, muffled sound.

"Ginger?"

All around were hemlocks and tall pines, the evergreen branches outlined with snow. I began to turn slowly in a circle. I walked around a few times and came to a stop. In the shadows several feet away, through a network of saplings, I saw a face.

He stood as if petrified, gaunt, dark skin flawed by pock marks. His eyes, black as midnight, were huge in that emaciated face. They stared emotionlessly, taking me in. His skeletal frame was dwarfed by the oversized wool jacket that hung off his shoulders like the shirt on a wooden scarecrow.

Letting my eyes skim along the trees as I continued turning around in a circle, I pretended not to see him. I was sure he'd been watching me since I'd left Cletha's porch with the dog.

Ginger let out a slight bark. I glanced down. There she was, right beside Prith, whose dangling hand grazed her head. I allowed my eyes to meet his.

"Hi," I said casually.

"Hi," he answered, not moving.

He wore a thin mustache of silky dark hair on his upper lip. When he nodded, his head seemed too heavy for his body, like a huge sunflower threatening to bend the slender stem that held it. The hand that touched the dog was bare, fingers as bony and thin as a chicken's toes.

"Prith?" I tried pronouncing the name in the Cambodian fashion.

He studied me as if I were a hallucination on the verge of disappearing.

I went on with bravado. "I'm a reporter from the newspaper," I said in a chatter of English. "Do you mind if I ask you some questions?"

He nodded with apparent rationality, his long neck unable to bear the weight of his head. "I hear," he said. Or more likely that's what I imagined he said. His pronunciation was so accented that the words could easily have been Khmer.

"You must be shocked about the murder," I plowed on in my direct manner. By the look on his face, I could tell he had no idea what I was saying.

"You name?" he asked. This was clearly an attempt at English. There, I thought to myself, feeling proud, we've made contact.

"Zoë," I said slowly, so he could hear the American sounds.

"Ss-oaw-eey," he repeated.

"Prith, do you know . . . Chram . . . Touch?" I pronounced Chram's name in my best Khmer accent, which I'd learned from Song. I remembered the way she'd ridiculed Brannigan's mangling of the name.

As if the goddess of ice had touched him with a magic wand, venom seemed to seep into his body, gather and pool into those enormous black eyes. His bony fingers clutched at Ginger's scruffy neck.

I don't know how long we stood on the spot, staring. The wind picked up. Through the trees, the sky darkened.

Prith took a step toward me. A sharp fear, unlike anything I'd ever experienced before, suddenly shot through me, as acute and piercing as a blade. I forgot the time. I forgot how cold my knees and hands were. I forgot my confusion. My one thought was of escape.

I wrenched my gaze from the magnetic force of the hatred that poured from his eyes and looked around to see which was the fastest route back to my car.

The dog growled. Then she started barking.

Prith whispered something. My eyes followed down to his left hand, which grasped a long, heavy stick. Letting go of Ginger, he shifted the stick, raising it horizontally in front of his body, with a fist at each end, as if warding me off. A stream of words tumbled from him in an unintelligible flow.

"Kmaoao!" he shouted several times. *"Kmaoao! Kmaoao!"*

Suddenly, he jabbed at me with the stick, and then, with great force, shoved it forward, as if trying to knock me down. I jumped away.

Almost under my nose, he pushed the stick forward again and snapped it in two. At the sound of the loud *crack*, I turned, raising my arm to protect my face. I let out a shriek.

Prith shouted and threw the two halves of the stick at me. Ginger bounded up barking wildly. I fell under the weight of the dog into a pillow of snow.

Ginger whined and barked. She crouched on top of me and licked my face. I struggled to push her off so I could get up and run for my life.

"Down, girl. Down."

She kept barking, thinking it was a game. Finally, I shoved her with all my might and stumbled to my knees. My pants were wet and caked with snow, my knees frozen and raw, my jacket covered, snow in the tops of my boots, a crunchy wet ball trickling icily down the back of my neck. I rose to my feet, steadying myself against the dog.

Prith had disappeared into the woods. There was no trace of him, except a scattering of prints heading deeper into the trees.

Ginger shook the snow off her thick fur and barked in the direction Prith had fled, as if to say, 'What are you waiting for? Let's go!'

"Can't do it, old girl," I said aloud. My voice quavered. My knees, despite their numbness, were so weak I could barely stand. My hands trembled, and the frigid cold chewed at the wet patches on my velveteen jeans.

I jogged back to the Honda, grasping the dog's collar to keep her with me for protection. As I opened the car door, I saw Cletha come out onto the porch.

I waved and walked toward her.

"Zoë. What's going on?"

How much Cletha knew of Prith's whereabouts and mental state, I couldn't be sure. After a moment of indecision, I finally said, "I saw Prith out there in the woods."

A long moment passed. The wind whispered through the trees, and the clouds darkened. Cletha's pale blue eyes met mine. "Zoë, I'm counting on your sense of honor."

I nodded shakily. She seemed so strong, and in comparison I felt so uncertain. What was the right thing to do?

As I drove into town, I wondered how long I could keep my promise.

13

A light snow had begun to fall by the time I reached the office. My worries about Cletha and Prith receded when I collected my messages and learned with dismay that Cecily Chen had canceled our appointment.

After several tries, I reached the elusive professor. "Could we meet later this afternoon?"

"I'm afraid that's impossible. I have a terribly full day."

"That's too bad," I said, letting my voice fall with disappointment. "I guess I won't be able to do the story on the Asian Women's Night Walk."

"Actually we're meeting this evening to discuss it."

I pounced. "If I could do a quick interview before your meeting, the story could run tomorrow."

I could hear the wheels turning, and then: "Yes. We do want publicity." Pause. "How about seven?"

"At the university?"

"No, my home." She gave me her address, a luxury

condominium not too far from the *Eagle*'s Victorian, and hung up.

Relieved, I called Albright and arranged to see him right after lunch, which gave me about an hour. I was too keyed up to think about eating, so I sat at my desk, leaned back in my chair, and closed my eyes. My thoughts turned to the worry of the day: Was Prith guilty? How far could my loyalty to Cletha go? I pulled out a scrap of paper and wrote down my evidence.

On the pro side were:

1. His fight with the woman at the mall witnessed by the Cambodian teenagers.

2. His strangeness. Obviously he suffered from post-traumatic stress. Cletha had admitted as much.

3. He was linked in some way with the Khmer Rouge. Perhaps Chram had known and threatened to expose him.

Opportunity and motive, wasn't that the formula prosecutors were always trying to prove?

On the con side:

1. Cletha picked him up around nine, according to the security guard. If he'd had blood on his clothes, surely Dennison Brown would have noticed. The police had set the possible time of death anytime between six-thirty and midnight. That gave him a partial alibi. After Cletha got him home it would have been difficult, though not impossible, for him to have returned to the mall.

2. So far I had no evidence that he had even met Chram. In fact, Song seemed to think not.

3. Chram had several known conflicts: Rok and Saw were unhappy about her marriage. Stephen said she had broken off their engagement the day she was killed. And her father had been arrested for beating her and her mother.

4. Chram had just leased a space for her restaurant. That meant she expected an influx of money. Prith, being penniless, could have had nothing to do with this.

I was still going around in circles when I heard the familiar, "*Qué pasó*, Szabo?"

I slid the list under my keyboard. "Hey, Mark."

"Want to do lunch? I'll bring you up to date on Brannigan."

I'd considered contacting Brannigan's office to see if any mention of Prith had been made. Maybe Mark would let something slip.

"Good idea," I said. "I was just on my way out."

I grabbed my jacket, and we went up the block to a cheap Italian serve-yourself place. I ordered a salad and a Coke. Mark had minestrone and two huge calzones.

After he'd wolfed down half his soup, Mark confided magnanimously, "My secret source in the police station says they're investigating the sex crime angle. They've got reams of reports coming from the FBI, checking out similar victim profiles."

"Isn't that routine procedure?"

He tilted his head defensively. "They seem to be pretty serious about it." He took a mouthful of calzone.

"Have they found any physical evidence like fingerprints, skin under her fingernails, or stray hairs on the seat or carpet?"

"They can't say. Some of those tests take a really long time. The full autopsy report still hasn't come in." His muscle-bound shoulders relaxed. "How about you? Any new items?"

"Not really."

"Come on, you can level with me." Mark's gaze met mine, all sweetness and sincerity. I could take lessons from this guy.

I grinned sardonically. "I always level with you, dear."

" 'Dear?' I must be doing something right."

"Don't take it personally. I come from a showbiz clan."

"Show business, huh?" He scrutinized me for a few moments.

"Yup," I said. "I was a regular backstage brat."

He snorted. "Yeah, it fits."

"What's that supposed to mean?"

"Just . . . you know." He flushed slightly, covering it with a laugh. "No offense."

I cast him a quizzical look, but let it drop. Sipping my Coke, I thought about trying to squeeze in another visit to Stephen. I wondered what he knew about Prith.

Mark leaned forward, his expression growing crafty. "Planning to do the GFC press conference this afternoon?"

"Yes."

"Brannigan and his people are going to be part of it, and I'm on the police angle."

I let it sit in the air a while, kind of allowing the words to seep in. "So you're saying you want to cover it."

"Well, sure."

Suddenly, I felt a strong desire to hold on to the GFC side, whereas moments ago, it had been low on my list of priorities. But if I attached too much importance to it, Mark would fight even harder to grab it. And if my interviews went the way I hoped, I'd have more than enough to write by tomorrow morning. My mind wandered back to my family. Already I was committed to meet Professor Chen at seven. If I got home at eight and spent an hour with the kids before they went to bed, I could be writing by nine, and it would probably be midnight or one A.M. before I finished.

"Why don't we share the byline," I suggested by way of compromise.

Mark extended a paw. "Deal."

I regarded him suspiciously. Sharing was one of those skills I hadn't learned in kindergarten. I wanted the whole thing to myself, I realized with irritation, wondering how I could shake this nemesis. My stomach knotted with tension. Mark lowered his clean-cut head and slurped his soda.

Finally, I stood up, gathering my stuff. "Sorry to cut out," I said. "I've got an appointment."

"See ya at the press conference, Szabo," he answered with a smarmy grin.

* * *

The Anselm P. Botwick Science and Arts Building was located on the north end of the sprawling State University campus. The imposing two-block-long brick structure looked as institutional and forbidding as a prison. The maze-like building held the Geography Department which, for reasons that were unclear to me, included the Asian Studies Program.

As I approached the open door of Peter Albright's narrow, tunnel-like office, I caught sight of the large, barrel-chested man standing by his desk, filing papers in one of the four tall cabinets crammed into the small space.

"Zoë," Albright boomed warmly, coming to the door, square face topped by a thatch of white hair. He found me a seat by removing a pile of books from a chair near the window, which overlooked a parking lot four stories down. His expressive eyebrows presided over friendly gray eyes and a mouth that was generous with laughter. Since he was usually good for a quote, often a zinger that could be used as a lead, my spirits lifted as I entered the room.

"Terrible thing," he muttered sadly as he returned to his desk. He closed a folder and swiveled the desk chair around to face me. "How can I help?"

"I'm doing a roundup of responses from people who helped the refugees settle in Greymont."

"Tragic. What a shock."

"Maybe that's a good place to start, with your personal feelings. Mind if I turn on the tape?" He nodded an assent and I pressed the record button.

He took a few moments to measure his thoughts, gazing at the microcassette recorder as if it were a lecture hall full of students. "As you know," he began, "I've worked tirelessly for over a decade to get as many people out of those wretched camps as possible. I take this murder very personally. Chram was engaged to my student, Stephen, and was the daughter of good friends, Ly and Phroeng, so it's like a death in the family. I feel shock, outrage . . . and sadness. How could such a thing happen here, of all places?"

A death in the family would make a good lead, I reflected with relief. He inhaled loudly, as if reading my mind. His beefy face was raw, eyes bloodshot and deeply exhausted. It wasn't empty rhetoric. Like Cletha he really felt the pain of Chram's loss.

"But this murder goes beyond the personal," he added with vigor, the professor reemerging. "It could well destroy the first fragile tendrils of trust that have begun to build among the refugees. With the Jews who survived the Holocaust, a similar phenomenon occurred. An inability to trust one's fellow man. With the Cambodians the problem is worse. Because they weren't murdered by a different race, but by their own."

Touched by the reference to the Holocaust, I asked for an example.

He demurred. "It isn't so much what people say, but what they don't do. There is silence. There is stunned shock. I spent part of the day yesterday at the Touch house. They have many relatives, but only two were there."

"Rok and Saw."

He nodded. "Friends and acquaintances who would have been there in the case of an ordinary death didn't come. Do you remember the Money Tree Festival last fall? None of the Cambodians trusted each other to hold the money." He tilted his square head. "They didn't trust Cecily because she's Vietnamese. There's an age-old enmity between the two nationalities. Eleanor Kerr finally volunteered to be treasurer."

"How much was raised?"

"Quite a lot."

"A few hundred? A thousand?"

"Oh, more than that. You'd have to ask Eleanor. She knows to the penny. Should have been an accountant."

Peter and I both grinned at the thought of the upper-class matron as a CPA, and I noted again how Eleanor's name continued to pop up. I'd better call her.

Switching gears, I asked, "Do you think there's any possibility this could have been a hate crime?"

Albright's thick eyebrows lifted. "I don't know. It's a possibility I hadn't considered, but it's certainly worth checking. Do you have any indication?"

"No. Your remarks about Holocaust victims triggered the question. There's a lot of anti-immigrant sentiment in town."

"I agree." He frowned, as if reaching back in his memory. "There have been incidents, too."

"Really?"

"A campus group held a rally. It appeared to die

out, but you never know. And the GFC has been toeing a militantly anti-refugee line."

"They're holding a press conference this afternoon."

He sighed heavily and waited for me to continue. I glanced at my notes.

"Assuming there was a personal motive, were you aware of any problems Chram might have had lately? Did she seem upset or moody?"

He considered it. "Can't say that I noticed. Chram was not what I would call 'bubbly.' She was a serious young woman, quiet, ambitious."

"She intended to open a restaurant."

"I tried to tell her that you don't start out by jumping in and investing money. She didn't want to wait. Stephen was good for her, kept her on a steady keel. He insisted she get her degree."

"Did you play any part in their meeting?"

He laughed. "Oh, no. Stephen managed that all by himself. He told you, I suppose, about Auntie Saw's séance?"

He glanced at the machine. "Don't quote me but, actually, I did play Dutch uncle. I told him to marry the girl or leave her alone. They were a bit reckless. For Cambodians, courting is a family affair."

"Did you notice that they were having any problems in the last few weeks?"

"I've been frightfully busy. I wouldn't have known. Had they been having problems?" His eyes searched mine.

I was noncommittal. "I've heard conflicting opinions."

"To be honest," he admitted, "Chram had a bit of a temper. Stephen, too. They had spats, but what couple doesn't?"

"When did you meet Chram?"

Peter Albright put his hands behind his head and stretched back. "On one of the many trips to the Thai border camps. Cletha became enamored of Song. To get her out, we had to take the whole family. I hate to say it, but Chram was just part of the package."

"She worked for you, didn't she?"

"Yes, part-time, for a year or so. She was reliable, prompt, quick to learn."

"Why did she leave?"

"She wanted more money. As I said, she was impatient to get her restaurant going. She found a job waitressing at the Lord William Inn. It's the most expensive restaurant in the area and tips were high. She did much better there."

"When did she change jobs?"

"October, I think."

"How far along were her restaurant plans? Had she actually started to look for a space?"

He shrugged. "I wouldn't know if she had. I didn't see much of her after she got the new job."

"How would you characterize the family?"

"Struggling. A bit shell-shocked. Phroeng's had a bad time."

"How so?"

"He was tortured by the Khmer Rouge. Pretty rough stuff. Too ugly to repeat."

"Is that why he beat his wife?" I handed him the police blotter item.

The gray eyes lost their humor, the exhaustion returning.

"Do you think he could have killed Chram?" I pressed.

Albright gaped at me, mouth half open. "Is that thing on?"

I turned off the recorder and slipped the machine back in my pocket.

"Who killed her is anyone's guess," he continued. "I don't think it was Phroeng. Don't quote me, but they did have loud arguments. There was physical violence. If you report that I said this, I'll deny it. As I said before, Chram had a temper. The abuse went both ways."

"She hit her father?"

He paused, then nodded. "She hated his drinking."

"How about Rok?"

"Rok is a thug. Again, this is not for attribution to me."

"I won't quote you. If I get independent corroboration, Whit might go to print with an anonymous source."

He listened as if I were explaining the terms of a contract. "My name won't show up anywhere?"

I shook my head. "What's the story on Rok?"

"He ran a black market in Site II. Didn't waste much time when he got here. He started a floating gambling operation the minute he arrived. The Cambodians are terrible gamblers. Especially the women, who traditionally manage the money. I've seen families torn apart when the losses are heavy."

"Do you think he killed her?"

"No."

"Why not?"

"She's family. Rok and Saw cling to traditional values, and family loyalty supersedes all. The Khmer Rouge did their best to smash family ties, because that was the easiest way to take control. They destroyed people's two mainstays of support: religion and family. Without those, Cambodians are lost."

"Then who killed her?"

"It could have been a crazy drifter. It happens." He paused, considering whether to continue, and decided in favor. "And you can't rule out the Khmer Rouge."

"Why would they kill Chram?"

"Any number of reasons," he said, his eyebrows lifting as he met my gaze. "Top of the list? To escape detection and possible deportation. Another—revenge."

"Revenge for what?"

Albright leaned forward again. His eyes were confiding, brow wrinkled. I'd seen the look on interview subjects before, even rock reporting. They wanted me to know something, but didn't want to tell me themselves. He whispered one word: "Betrayal."

"How could the Khmer Rouge reach all the way from Southeast Asia?"

"My dear," he said after a moment. "They're here."

"But immigration policy—"

"People lie to immigration every day."

"But they're not an organized group here."

He raised an eyebrow.

"Do you know who they are?" I asked.

"I know someone who might."

"Who is it?"

Albright's lips spread in a mysterious grin. He took a deep breath and stood up. "I'll give you a call in a day or so, if he's agreeable."

"What's his name?"

"For now," he said, "let's call him Grandfather."

I went straight to the office and added a few of Albright's on-the-record statements to my piece on Stephen, which hadn't run. I called Brannigan to make sure Stephen wasn't about to be arrested. The secretary informed me no arrest was imminent. The phone rang as I hung up. As soon as I heard the voice, I kicked myself for answering. It was Gaffney.

"I have an item for you: More than seventy-five percent of the Cambodians in Greymont are on welfare."

Too busy to hang up, I transcribed my notes while Gaffney raved.

"A political refugee grant, Hal."

"It boils down to welfare—"

With the phone at my ear, I tuned him out. He continued speaking while I drafted my article on the community response, leading with a quote from Albright on the fragile tendrils of trust and the Jews and the

Holocaust. I riffled through my notes on my conversation with Cletha and found a quote of hers for the second paragraph. This way, I'd have less work to do after the conversation with Chen this evening. The drone of Gaffney's voice had a hypnotic effect, helping me focus. He was almost as good as my Walkman. Although a far cry from the intentional irony of David Byrne, Gaffney's rapid fire of "items" and "facts" reminded me of the Talking Heads. I wondered idly if he had any stake in the situation and why he'd called when he had a press conference in less than an hour.

"Hal," I said, cutting him short, "do you have relevant information? Like, do you know who killed her?"

"Just checking to make sure you'll be at the press conference. We changed the time to two-thirty at the Community Center conference room. The television networks are setting up as we speak!"

My line lit up. "I'll be there. Oops, got to go."

It was Song.

"How's it going?" I asked cheerily.

"I told Bou Vuthy your idea about having the funeral on Sunday. Maybe we'll do it."

"Are reporters still swarming?"

"Yes, but not as bad as yesterday." Her voice sounded weary.

"There's a press conference in about half an hour, so the reporters will probably disappear for a while." That gave me an idea. "If you want, I can stop by and pick you up. We can disguise you and go to the press conference together."

"I wouldn't be in the way?"

"No, you can help provide balance. I'll pick you up in fifteen minutes. Okay?"

"All right." She seemed relieved at the opportunity to get out of the house. "Thank you."

Within seconds my line had lit up again. It was Whit, pressing as usual.

"How are you doing?"

"I've made a couple of changes in the Stephen piece. Can we go with it? Brannigan assures me he's not about to pounce. I spoke to Cletha and Peter. Chen's meeting me tonight. What do you think," I added, "about looking for a Khmer Rouge connection? Several sources have brought up the subject."

"Who?"

"Practically everyone I've spoken to. Someone offered to find me a Cambodian elder to talk on the record."

Whit hesitated. "Zoë, this is the kind of poking around I'd rather have you do with a partner."

"There is no way I can get people to talk with Mark there."

Whit sighed. "I want to be told where you're going, who you're talking to, and when you expect to be back."

"Okay," I promised, trying not to reveal my jubilation. "One last thing. How about a companion piece to the supporter article, the Asian community's reaction? I could fit in Cecily Chen's march, plus Bou Vuthy." And, I thought to myself, I could nose around even more.

Whit was silent for a moment. I heard his pencil tapping the phone. "You've got a lot on your plate."

"Yeah, but it's all under control," I lied.

"Mark says he wants to write the press conference piece."

"We agreed to share the byline. Gaffney's been pestering me to come. I just got off the phone with him."

"Okay," Whit said reluctantly, "but if you're pressed for time, I'm going to throw the GFC to Mark."

"It's my beat," I objected.

"This is a big story, Zoë. You can't do it alone."

Before I could respond, Whit hung up. I was about to call back when my line rang again. The University Press Office was calling to complain that the piece we'd run in today's paper was incorrect. The memorial service for Chram had been rescheduled. It would be held on Saturday.

"Christmas Eve?" I asked in disbelief. With the Memorial on Saturday and Chram's funeral on Sunday, I was going to miss part of Christmas Eve and Christmas afternoon as well. My stomach gnawed as I remembered my promise to have an old-fashioned holiday. Noting the time, I realized I had to put my guilt on hold. I was running late. Mark hadn't shown his face since I'd arrived back in the newsroom after the meeting with Peter. What was he up to now?

As I was packing up my disk and notes, not wanting to leave anything where a snooping eye might find it, my phone lit up yet again. This time it was the

University Women Students Association, announcing that they would take part in the Asian Women's Night Walk. After jotting down this information, I grabbed some microcassettes and a pack of spare batteries and ran out the door.

14

Song opened the door, her somber seventeen-year-old face brightening when she saw me.

"Ready?" I asked, scrutinizing her clothes. Her brown wool coat wouldn't attract attention. Still, reporters might recognize her as the murdered woman's sister. I took a pair of Jackie O. sunglasses from my pocket and slipped them onto her nose. "Let's go," I said. "I'm in a rush."

When we got into my Honda, I scrounged through the mess of stuff in the backseat and dug out a big floppy hat that Billy's mother had given Smokie for dress-up.

"Try this," I said, tossing it to her and starting the car.

She twisted her long black locks into a braid and pushed it under the brim of the silly hat.

"I'm a fashionable lady," she primped, "like you."

"Cut it and dye it pink. That would give your folks a heart attack."

She giggled. "No. I like it long."

"Here." I handed her a camera borrowed from the newspaper. "If any reporters come close, just hold this up and start snapping pictures."

"With sunglasses on?"

"No one will notice, believe me."

When we finally burst into the press conference, a local representative stood at the podium, delivering what seemed like a long, dull speech. The huge room was packed. I recognized people from local media and stringers from the bigger papers, who were beginning to become familiar. Many of the other people in the room were in Gaffney's coalition. But in a bunch on the far end, I spotted the pro-refugee crowd. Cletha was among them, next to Peter Albright and his wife, a tall woman with majestic red hair. Directly in front of them Cecily Chen, elegant as always, sat with Eleanor Kerr and a smattering of Cambodians, including Bou Vuthy in his orange robes. I didn't see Stephen. On the other side of Cletha were a group of African-American students. One young man wore dreadlocks. I wondered what all of these opponents of the GFC crowd were doing here.

I gestured to a spot behind some TV equipment, where I thought we'd be well-hidden. I didn't want any of the reporters bothering Song. Down near the front I caught sight of Mark in his sheepskin vest, flirting with Kate, whose long braid dangled down her back to her waist. She sidestepped his attentions and clicked away with her favorite old Nikon.

Down in a corner, I recognized someone else.

"Don't look now," I whispered to Song, "but your uncle Rok is here."

Rok quietly scrutinized the crowd, as if trying to memorize every face. His features were hard, the scar ugly, even from a distance. Near him stood a couple of young Cambodian men in suits with baggy pants and spiked hair. One glanced toward me and nudged Rok.

The speaker finished her remarks and gave the floor to Gaffney, who slicked down a stubborn strand on his balding head. He made his way to the mike and adjusted it, then stood quietly while the cameras flashed and TV cameras rolled, savoring the limelight. The purple capillaries on his cheek appeared to have been softened with makeup. Clearing his throat, he unveiled a chart and picked up a pointer.

What he said boiled down to this: Immigration was the major source of America's problems. His chart indicated that the number of refugees on assistance had shot up over the last two decades.

"As you can see, hundreds of thousands of dollars are being spent with no end in sight. Seventy-five percent of the Southeast Asian immigrants here in Heritage County are on some form of aid."

He cleared his throat again and shrugged his shoulders as if his jacket constricted his movement. He unbuttoned the navy blazer and tugged at his sleeves. An American flag tie tack stood out prominently on his wide maroon tie.

"That's just the beginning," he said, going on to

cite costs for ESL and tutoring in the schools, police and social services, Head Start, Medicaid, and Medicare. He pulled out a sheet and read off a long list of police blotter items, including the arrest of Phroeng for battery against Chram and Ly. The room buzzed. I glanced toward Mark, wondering if Gaffney had done the research himself or if he'd been helped. Mark seemed so absorbed with Kate, suggesting camera angles, that he didn't appear to be listening. However, at one point, he signaled me with a wink and a thumbs-up sign.

Almost done, Gaffney stuck out his belly and put one of his hands in his jacket pocket, his face beaming with satisfaction as he surveyed the large audience. He joked that the best language program for the schools would be for native Khmer speakers to go back to Cambodia where they could understand everything that was said. His supporters laughed coarsely.

Then he grew serious and talked about his POW days. "The Communists are gone," he concluded. "It's time to stop accepting hundreds of thousands of refugees. They're draining our resources. This has nothing to do with politics. It's pure economics. Years ago, me and my buddies fought side-by-side. Some of us died, some still can't get jobs. I don't see anybody talking about helping the vets. What happened to America? Why can't we take care of our own first?"

GFC supporters applauded and Gaffney took questions. In addition to reporters, there were hands raised in the middle rows where Cletha's group clustered. Cletha rose to her feet. Gaffney ignored her, pointing to someone else. After several questions, the noise was pierced by Cletha's loud voice.

"Excuse me," she bellowed.

Gaffney steadfastly refused to look in her direction, nodding instead to a stringer from the *Globe*.

With a nod toward Cletha, the reporter said, "I'd like to hear what this lady has to say."

Gaffney reddened. "She can call her own press conference if she wants. This is a GFC event."

Shouts rose from Cletha's crowd. Several stood up.

"Young man," Cletha boomed, despite the fact that she had no microphone. She was addressing Gaffney. "I cannot allow your statements to go unchallenged. It's time for a bit of truth!"

There were shouts and applause.

Song clasped my arm. "She is so brave."

"Nothing scares her," I whispered, rooting for Cletha.

She gave her usual spiel about redressing the wrongs that had been done against the Cambodian people, starting with Nixon and Kissinger.

Then Cecily Chen stood up and made a similar statement. "I recognize several Cambodians here," she added. "Why don't we let them speak for themselves?"

There was applause.

"Hey!" Gaffney shouted. "Hey!" He was losing control. The television lights had turned from his to Cletha's group. Reporters flocked around her, and Carolee Clark, bless her, was holding a Channel 25 mike in her face.

Suddenly lights shone in my eyes. A reporter from the local cable channel had spotted Song, who seemed terrified. I grasped her arm and forced my head in front of the camera. "No comment," I shouted.

"Let's get out of here," I told Song.

The African-American student in dreadlocks was standing up, speaking in a voice that projected like an actor's. "Sir," he said, "may I ask where your ancestors came from?"

The capillaries on Gaffney's cheek had begun to darken. "I'm Irish and proud of it!" he exclaimed.

"Your ancestors came from Ireland to escape a famine. Mine were dragged here in chains. We are all immigrants!"

A chant started among the students.

One of the selectmen stood at Hal Gaffney's side, waving, trying to get the room to come to order. Peter, his wife, Eleanor, Cletha, and the whole Quaker crowd started reciting a Buddhist prayer led by Bou Vuthy, while the blacks and a few Latino students kept repeating: "We are all immigrants." It was the closest thing to theater we'd had in Greymont since I'd arrived, and if Song hadn't been so upset, I would have stayed to the end.

As we cut through the side door, we ran headlong into Brannigan and two burly detectives. Brannigan led with his chin, running on caffeine and adrenaline. I hadn't seen him since the night the body had been found and I was surprised at how tired he appeared. His dour face, nicked from a recent shave, was about ten inches from mine.

Glaring at me as if I were a monster that persisted in following him, he was momentarily distracted by the sight of Song, who'd lost her hat in the rush to escape the melee. She held up the camera, snapped a photo, and the flash lit his face as he snarled, "Out of the way."

"Any new suspects, Detective?" I asked.

He squinted at Song suspiciously. "Who's your friend?"

"Have you found the murder weapon? I've heard rumors—"

He cut me off. "We go on fact, not rumor, Ms. Szabo, and I suggest you do the same."

"Was it an Asian weapon?" I persisted.

He scowled and elbowed his way past me, followed by his entourage.

Song and I strolled down Stanhope Street, past one of the many Chinese restaurants in town, on the walkway that led toward Jamieson's ice cream parlor.

"You said Chram had found a space for her restaurant."

"Yes."

"You mind if we take a look at it?"

Song shrugged a reluctant okay, shaking out her hair. When we finally reached the storefront I had examined the night before, Song confirmed it was the spot Chram had wanted, but when I asked if Chram had made any moves to rent it, Song shook her head wearily.

"I'm so tired of talking about this."

"Do you know if she'd contacted the realtor?"

Her face drew into a tight mask of resistance. "You're like the police, asking the same questions over and over."

Song's eyes were puffy. It occurred to me that she probably hadn't slept at all since her family had learned of the murder. I wavered, ashamed of my own insensitivity.

"Tell you what," I whispered conspiratorially, "let's not say another word about—*it*."

Her eyes brightened slightly, but worry still etched lines into her brow. My maternal instincts began to take over. I wanted to ease that stress, if only for a short while.

I took her arm and turned toward Jamieson's. "You like American ice cream?"

Her face lit up childishly. "Yes, Zoë, I do."

Over double strawberry cones, I guided the conversation to things that had nothing to do with the murder: her school, her dreams and ambitions, my rock 'n' roll writing, Billy's taste of stardom. We compared favorite bands. I told her funny things my kids said, which she matched with stories about her young cousins.

As we were finishing, the idea hit. I couldn't, no matter how much I tried to repress it, make it go away. The devil on my shoulder whispered in my ear, and I heard myself saying, against my better angel, "Would you like to do some research for me?"

She tilted her head, her dark eyes growing leery. "About Chram?"

"Yes."

"What would I do?"

"Point me in the right direction, ask a few questions, translate."

Even though I didn't want to use the girl, I kept remembering that the murderer was at large, probably somewhere in town.

"I'm not going to lie," I blurted at last. "Yes. I'd like to get the story before anyone else. But I also want to make sure the murderer is caught."

Her long, dark lashes fluttered down as she studied her hands. "Sometimes," she said, not looking at me, "I think it would be better if no one found out."

"Song, this is hard for me to ask, and you don't have to answer. Do you think someone in your family might have done it?"

A shadow passed across her face, the clouds covering the sun that had been shining through Jamieson's windows. Her large black eyes stared straight into mine.

"It's possible, yes."

The cloud moved away and the low afternoon sun shone in our faces.

"Do you want to help?" I asked.

She shook her head, long locks rippling like waves on a dark sea. "No. Zoë, I can't."

15

It was about four-thirty when I pulled into the driveway of our cozy Cape, looking forward to spending a couple of hours with my family. Finding no one home, I followed the well-traveled footpath through the snow across our yard to ask Morgan if he had any clue as to the whereabouts of my husband and kids.

After knocking loudly and getting no answer, I tried the door. Sounds of men's voices echoed in the entrance hall. I let myself in and went into the parlor, where I found Morgan and Billy in the midst of a heated discussion about how to assemble an antique tree stand.

Billy, in a blue-green sweater, leather pants, and Italian boots, sat cross-legged on the maple floor in the U-shaped alcove of the south-facing bay window, fitting together several pieces of black wrought-iron, while Morgan issued incoherent instructions punctuated by exclamations of dismay.

"Not that one. Here, let me."

"Hold on, big guy, I got it." Billy twisted a few pieces of metal together and pushed the stand into the center of the bay. The six-legged pot stood on its own. Billy rose, proud of his handiwork.

Morgan still objected. "The legs are on backwards."

"Nah, this is how it's supposed to go."

"The tree is going to fall over."

"Let's try it. Hey, stranger," Billy said with a smile when he noticed me in the doorway.

"Hi, guys," I said. "Where are the kids?"

Billy gave me a quick kiss. "Outside. Everything's cool. Right, Professor?"

"Absolutely." Morgan greeted me. "Come see what we found."

On the back porch, they showed off the two firs they'd spent the morning selecting and cutting at a tree farm out in the country halfway to the Vermont border. The evergreens, tied up with twine, were propped near the kitchen door with their trunks in black buckets of water.

A whoop came suddenly from the snow fort in the middle of the backyard. The shouts were accompanied by a volley of snowballs. Two yellow and blue puffballs ran out from behind the wall.

Keith charged me. A soft plop of icy wetness hit my chin. I ran after him. Shrieking playfully, he ran away and ducked into his fort.

"Mommy, I'll help you," shouted Smokie.

She chased Keith, throwing snowballs and missing by miles. I caught up with my son, swooped him into my arms, and kissed him all over while he wriggled like mad.

"No fair!" he giggled. "No fair!"

Smokie jumped on me and we all fell in a pile of snow.

"Let's put up the trees," I suggested.

Cheering, the kids scrambled to their feet and ran to the porch.

We all helped Billy remove the twine and shake out the branches, but when Billy, Morgan, and I attempted to set the tall fir in the stand, we realized we should have waited. The boughs were so bushy that we had trouble holding the trunk to lift it. Billy sawed off a few lower branches that were interfering with the fit of the holder, and Morgan gave them to Keith and Smokie, who busied themselves attempting to fashion the cut boughs into a wreath. I crawled under the tree and tightened the screws while Billy held up the trunk and Morgan directed.

After about twenty minutes, we finally managed to get the tree to stand on its own without tipping. The grand balsam fir rose majestically almost the full height of his twelve-foot ceiling and completely filled the bay window. We spent a reverent moment admiring the dark green branches, which filled the entire room with a pungent, piney scent.

In the meantime, Smokie and Keith had begun bickering over some ribbons Morgan had given them to adorn their "wreath."

"Hey," Billy said, kneeling down on the floor between them. He settled the argument quickly with a soft voice and careful attention to each one's explanation. Smokie's dark eyes took in everything he said with an eagerness and trust that touched me to the core. Her tiny fingers crept toward his hand and curled around his thumb.

"Ready to set up our tree?" he asked, standing.

"I came home to make you dinner, so the kids can go to bed at a reasonable time. I hate to tell you this, but I have to work tonight."

"Oh, jeez, Zoë."

"I was so busy. I kept meaning to call, but—"

Billy glanced toward Morgan. "Babe," he said, "I didn't get to call you either, but I've got something I have to do tonight, too."

"What?"

"Harley's band needs a backup bass on a demo. I'm supposed to be at the studio in Sheffington at eight."

My face fell. "Oh." I scanned my mental address book, trying to figure out who I could call at the last minute to sit.

"Don't give it a second thought," Morgan volunteered. "I'll watch them." He looked so old and tired that, despite his eagerness to help, I worried the kids might be too much for him to manage.

"I feel guilty about having Morgan baby-sit," I murmured to Billy as we were helping the kids into their snowsuits.

"Makes him feel useful," Billy whispered. "Can you give me a lift to Sheffington later? Here, Keith, my man, let's pull on the boots. Umph. Feet are growin'."

"Drop me at the office and take the car. I can walk

home." Cecily Chen's condo, a few blocks from the office, was only a mile and a half from our house.

"One of the guys might be able to pick me up."

"No. The exercise will do me good."

Billy turned his chocolate eyes on me. "You're sure?"

"Yeah. Have dinner with us?" I asked Morgan. "Linguine alla Szabo, my dad's recipe."

We traipsed through the snow over to our Cape, which was so much smaller than Morgan's Victorian that it seemed as if we were entering a dwelling belonging to hobbits rather than humans. Morgan and Billy took up the argument over where to put the tree they'd dragged over, while I started dinner. Smokie went straight to the MIDI keyboard, making up tunes in a setting called "Open Wide," which mimicked the whine of a dentist's drill. She alternated this with the sounds of explosions. Keith helped make the salad and set the table.

My father had spent time in Italy on his flight from Communist Hungary and had learned how to cook *alla panna*. Basically, he put cream in a pan, brought it to a boil, threw in whatever vegetables he had, and then tossed in pasta. I diced a shallot, sautéed it in butter with portobello mushrooms and peas, added cream, and let the whole thing simmer while I brought water to a boil. When the linguine was done I combined it with the sauce and fresh-grated parmesan in a large bowl and called everyone to the table. With a big salad and fresh bread, it made a great meal, if a little rich. Sometimes, I just tossed vegetables with pasta and left out the cream. The kids loved this stuff, which was lucky, since it was often the only thing I had time to cook.

Unable to convince Smokie and Keith to go to bed before we had to leave, Billy and I said good-bye while they cuddled together on the couch listening, wide-eyed, to Morgan read a retelling of *The Iliad*. With Morgan around, it was a cinch they'd get into Harvard straight from elementary school.

We drove for a few minutes, nearing the Victorian on Main that housed the *Eagle* offices.

"You were so sweet with the kids today," I said.

Saying nothing, Billy let his free hand touch mine. He parked in front of the office. Before I could gather my gear, Billy caught me in his arms. It started as a light peck, but quickly escalated into a soulful French kiss. Perhaps he had been as affected as I by the contrast between this Christmas and the last.

I gazed into his eyes, stroking his hair. "It's good here, isn't it?"

Billy's face clouded. He took my hands in his and nuzzled my fingertips.

"I should be back around nine," I said, preparing to leave.

"Don't wait up. You know how these sessions are. Might go all night."

The magic of his kiss dissolved into shadowy apprehension.

"Now, don't get that look," he chided softly.

Without warning, tears rolled down my cheeks.

He put his hand at the back of my neck and kneaded my shoulder. "This is what I do."

I took a few breaths, recovering control. "I know."

"Have I given you a hard time about your work?"

"No."

"You've got to be fair, Zoë. It goes both ways."

"I can't help thinking that when you're out at the studio, recording, someone's going to take out some smoke or some . . ."

"Don't condemn me before anything happens. If I screw up, you can yell."

"Billy, if you screw up . . . it may break my heart, but it will really be the end."

He drew back his shoulders, then leaned into me, pulling my whole body to his, embracing me so hard I could barely breathe. He kissed my neck, my breast, my mouth passionately, deeper than before. For a few minutes, we necked like teenagers, and the windshield steamed up with our heat.

"I've got to go."

"Me, too."

We rested our heads together. I put my hands under his soft blue sweater and felt his silky skin.

"Later," he whispered, taking my hands and releasing himself from my touch.

I left the car and watched as he drove off, the little blue Civic skidding slightly on the icy road as it raced to make the light.

On my way into the newsroom, I met Mark coming out the door at a near run. He slowed down when he saw me.

"*Qué pasó*, Szabo?"

"Same old. How about you?"

He looked at me a little funny. "I, uh, did the GFC piece."

"I might want to make some additions. I've got half an hour before my next interview."

"Yeah? With who?"

"It's about the Asian Women's Night Walk."

He grinned slyly. "Your lipstick's smeared."

I inadvertently put a finger to my lower lip.

"Leave your copy on my desk," he added. "I'll enter it when I get back."

"Where are you going?"

He rolled his eyes toward the ceiling. "The master calls."

"Well, don't let me keep you."

I ducked into the bathroom and checked my makeup, which, between the tears and the necking, had suffered some damage. I rinsed my face in cold water, combed through my short hair. I refreshed my mascara and put on a new coat of Starlight Tango lip creme. I'm a sucker for exotic names; anything related to music is irresistible. The glittery color went well with my metallic pink sweater.

I spent another precious moment admiring myself. My left ear had four holes. The top three held studs, all given to me by Billy during the deluxe years: a tiny pearl, a ruby—the real thing—and a sapphire. In the lowest hole I wore a dangling silver dog, picked up in Mexico after much haggling in turista Spanish. On my right ear, there was a small gold crescent moon and a silver star, given to me by my dad when

I'd first pierced my ears, and on the lowest hole, a dangling silver bone—for the dog. The kids just adored these earrings.

Despite the fact that it was a bit out there for a mom, not to mention a reporter-mom living in Greymont, I really liked my punk-glam style. The only people in town who dressed anything like me were high-school girls imitating their favorite rock heroines. Keith's kindergarten teacher nearly keeled over when she first laid eyes on me, but she was cool enough not to say anything. Someday I supposed I would change, but right now things like makeup, jewelry, and clothes seemed to be the only tie to my former lifestyle. I could identify with the Cambodian elders, clinging to outward symbols of their lost culture, despite the scorn of their more adaptable children.

I spent so much time in the bathroom that I had only a few minutes to lay out my treatment of the GFC story. I led with Cletha's demonstration, because it seemed so much more exciting than Gaffney's tired old line—talk about dogs and bones. When I was done, I printed out the draft and left it on Mark's desk with a note, asking him to add my material to his story. I'd check the final copy in the morning, if I had time.

Half an hour later I sat in the dining alcove of Cecily Chen's impeccably furnished home, admiring my elegant surroundings: upholstery in subdued shades of sand and stone and walls decorated with tastefully framed Chinese ink paintings. A magnificent peony-embroidered kimono with bright pinks, yellows, and purples adorned the wall above the black-frame couch. A cathedral ceiling angled upward to a skylight. Over the mantle of the stone fireplace hung a Japanese screen of mountains and a waterfall.

Across from me sat Professor Chen, an Indonesian graduate student named Sradanny Irda, Malis Soppah, a Cambodian sophomore at the State University, and Eleanor Kerr, Chram's English tutor. In the center of the ebony table were scattered take-out containers of rice, chicken in black bean sauce, green beans with ginger, lo mein noodles, and tofu in spicy Szechwan sauce. Even though I wasn't really hungry, having just had dinner, to be polite I took some green beans and tea, a fragrant jasmine blend.

"We have Chinese restaurants in Vietnam, too," Cecily told me when I commented on the food. "I'm ethnic Chinese, though my family lived in Vietnam for several generations."

Sradanny and Malis murmured that they loved Chinese food and we broke the ice discussing the differences between Chinese restaurant food in their various countries.

"That was quite a demonstration this afternoon," I commented after we had gotten the preliminaries over with.

Sradanny smiled wryly, but Eleanor Kerr, matronly in her green wool jersey dress and frosted hair in a stiff salon flip, took the comment at face value. "The GFC does much more harm than many of us are willing to admit. The state cuts to refugee services this year have been devastating."

I asked her to explain, and she spoke about people with psychiatric and medical needs that were going unmet and children in abusive situations who couldn't get help.

"There is a lot of abuse in the refugee community," I agreed. "Can you estimate how prevalent it is?"

Eleanor flushed. "I don't have figures, but people are under a great deal of stress."

Cecily supported her. Sradanny, trying to steer the conversation to the march, made some general statements about violence against women. "Wife beating in some Southeast Asian countries," she added, "is commonly accepted."

I mentioned Chram's family and asked if any of them knew about the abuse she had suffered. Although Eleanor furrowed her brow, no one volunteered any information.

"Okay," I ventured, deciding to take another tack. "Can you describe when you last saw Chram?" Neither Cecily nor Sradanny had seen her in weeks. Malis said she'd spoken to her briefly several times during the previous week.

"And you?" I asked Eleanor.

Her deep-set eyes gazed at me sadly. "I saw her the day she died."

A hush fell over the room.

"I hadn't seen her," Eleanor continued, "since her citizenship interview in October. So I was surprised at the change that had come over her."

Eleanor sighed, looking toward Professor Chen, and seemed to make up her mind to go on.

"You see," Eleanor began, "in the four years that I knew Chram, she'd already gone through a tremendous change. When she arrived from Site II the family was in a state of near starvation, suffering from all the illnesses that come from malnutrition and severe psychological trauma. Chram had been at a very impressionable age during the Pol Pot rule. These were her adolescent years.

"She had been brutalized. Beaten. Raped repeatedly. She'd witnessed the cold-blooded murder of one sister and the slow death and torture of a second, as well as the deaths of innumerable extended family members and close acquaintances."

As Eleanor spoke, in deliberate and painstaking detail, I felt both concern for her and a sense of elation knowing that this was on the record, and that the interview, despite Cecily's initial resistance, was going to range far afield from the specifics of the Night Walk tomorrow night. I scrutinized Cecily momentarily, wondering whether she'd set it up this way on purpose. Her expression was hard to read. She focused all her attention on Eleanor Kerr, taking in what she said as if she were hearing it for the first time.

"So when I first tutored Chram at the library," Eleanor continued, "she was very quiet. As the English lessons progressed, she began to come out of her shell and express herself.

"The first breakthrough came one afternoon several months into our sessions when we were working on terms for kinship relations. Mother, father, we'd already done. Sister, brother, aunt, uncle, niece, nephew, cousin. I said she had one sister, meaning, of course, Song. She held up her fingers to show three sisters. Three, she insisted. I was silent, guessing, I suppose, what she had in her heart. Three sisters, she said. Then she folded down two of the fingers with her other hand and held them down.

"'Brother,' she said, holding up the other hand. She held up a finger and folded it down.

"'All dead,' she said, touching the folded fingers to her chest. We sat in silence for the rest of the session, ten, maybe fifteen minutes. There was nothing that could be said."

I wondered if Chram in her grief had been lying about the death of the brother, the one Song had told me was Khmer Rouge and was possibly still alive.

Malis, the young Cambodian woman who had so far said nothing, frowned as Eleanor spoke. "It has been very bad for us," she said. She was pretty in a blowzy way, with rouged cheeks and big, permed hair. Her plump body was clothed in a long brown skirt, which was too tight, and a gold-embroidered vest over a pink turtleneck. "It's been the same for me. I lost my mother and brother. My father and I got out together."

"But Chram seemed to be doing so well. Stephen has been wonderful for her," Eleanor added, with an engaging, hopeful smile.

Malis's eyelids fluttered slightly.

"You disagree?" I asked.

"Stephen was very good to Chram and to her father and mother. And her mother has a deep sadness and does not get well." On the surface what she said about Stephen seemed positive, yet her expression indicated she'd left much unsaid.

"But?" I prompted.

She shrugged. "I never really liked him."

"Why not?"

"Probably just a personal thing."

I'd talk to her later when there weren't so many people around. To Eleanor I said, "What change did you notice on the day she died?"

Eleanor looked to Malis, who seemed ready to speak, but Malis politely indicated that Eleanor go first.

"She was moody, sharp-tongued, which she'd never been before. And fatalistic. Only a few months ago, she'd seemed excited and enthusiastic, full of hopes and plans. When I saw her last week, she was down, expecting the worst. Suddenly, she was seized with anxiety about her citizenship, thinking it might not go through. She asked me all the ways it could be stopped, which was absurd. Her notice of final hearing still hasn't come in, but it should any day. She felt desperate about the restaurant and getting a loan even though the plan was for her to finish school first. And she told me the oddest thing."

"What?"

"I considered it mildly suicidal, but I was so busy what with Christmas coming up—Lord, it's in three days—well, she said there was no future, only the past. That they were like a circle, like a snake biting its tail. She said that the snake had swallowed the lotus and in a few days the mouth would swallow the tail. I've told this to the police, but they seem to dismiss everything I say."

So that's why I'm here, I thought, suddenly understanding why, despite her initial reluctance, Cecily Chen had set up this meeting. They wanted to get the attention of the police. Crime reporting wasn't all that different from rock journalism—you kept running into people looking for publicity. Only with a murder, their angles were a little harder to figure.

"She talked about a snake," Malis jumped in. "She mentioned it many times, especially in the last few months. Ever since she became engaged to Stephen. I wonder if there was something strange with him sexually?"

"Did she mention phone calls?"

"She didn't talk about it specifically, but something was bothering her," Malis said. "She talked about receiving bad messages. I thought she meant from ancestors, but it could have been phone calls."

"I got the distinct impression," said Eleanor, "that she was having psychotic episodes, that something had happened recently to spur horrific memories or that she'd literally been contacted by someone out of her past."

"Do you know anything about her brother?" I asked.

Malis and Eleanor regarded each other uneasily.

"I've heard," I continued, "that he might not really be dead."

"There's a rumor," said Malis, "that he's still alive in Cambodia. Well, I guess everybody will be talking about it soon enough . . . and that he was Khmer Rouge."

"And," added Eleanor dryly, "that was how he kept Song, Chram, Phroeng, and Ly alive."

"Phroeng was taken to be killed for stealing a pumpkin to feed Ly and Song. They were both sick," Malis said. "Her brother stopped it."

"I think the brother helped them get across the border to Thailand," said Eleanor. "Because of his Khmer Rouge connections he couldn't qualify for refugee status."

"There is another rumor," said Malis, "that he is in the US."

Eleanor looked surprised.

"Would she have something to fear from this brother?" I asked.

Malis shrugged. "Maybe there was something her brother did that he didn't want anyone to know. Maybe she knew, maybe she threatened to tell."

"For money?" I asked.

Eleanor's lips parted. "She'd leased a space for her restaurant."

"Really? When?"

"In the last few weeks. A place on Stanhope. She asked me for a loan, which she insisted she'd be able to pay back in six months, right after she graduated."

"Did you lend her money?"

Eleanor flushed. "I wrote her a check for a hundred dollars. She was so agitated, I couldn't say no."

"Did she ask anyone else for money?"

Eleanor looked as if she were telling tales out of school. She seemed terribly troubled.

"Now that you mention it," said Cecily, "she asked me and several others in my department. I dismissed it as a wild fantasy. Chram was given to daydreaming and making impossible plans. She said Stephen had promised to back her as soon as she got the restaurant degree and her citizenship papers. He has money, you know."

"I wonder why she wasn't willing to wait for his help?"

"Pride, maybe," said Cecily. "She wanted to prove she could do it herself."

"She asked a lot of people," Eleanor added. "She went to the Chamber of Commerce. Hal Gaffney told her to go to the SBA."

"She asked Gaffney for money?" I repeated with disbelief.

Eleanor nodded. "She went to everyone."

"But Gaffney?"

Eleanor sighed. "He'd been her employer."

I scrutinized Eleanor. "What made her think Gaffney would lend her money?"

Eleanor became flustered. "She seemed truly desperate." She took a deep breath and added, "We can't rule out another possibility—that some traumatic memory, very deeply buried, had been brought out by some recent event. I hate to say this, but when I saw her she seemed very bitter toward Stephen."

"I've never trusted him," Malis said.

"Why not?" I asked.

"He's a flirt," Malis confessed, looking uncomfortable.

"He is," said Sradanny. "He asked me out several times. He seems to be one of those guys who has a thing about Asian women."

I thought about the moment I'd witnessed last fall at the wedding: Stephen in his beautiful silk jacket, holding Chram's arm as she wobbled in her high heels. The look on her face. The sensuality, the tension had struck me then. Now I wondered if it had been a look of anger. Or fear.

16

It was a little after nine-thirty when I left Cecily Chen's and began the trek home through downtown Greymont. My pace kept slowing as I mulled over what Eleanor had said in response to one of my final questions about Prith's behavior at the wedding.

"Why, yes," she'd replied. "It's funny you should mention it. I'd forgotten."

"Forgotten what?"

"Not only was Prith there, but he appeared to be fixated on Chram. He'd only arrived a week or so before the wedding. I remember Cletha's eagerness to have him meet other people his age, native Khmer speakers. But it didn't work out as she hoped."

Malis was more dramatic. "When Prith's eyes first fell on Chram he turned white. He seemed terrified."

"Did she notice?"

"Yes," said Malis, ignoring Eleanor's suddenly anxious expression. "I was watching her. She was in a group pose with her cousin. They were supposed to stay perfectly still while the monk went on and on."

I vaguely remembered the moment. I'd been watching the monk and listening to Song's translation. I hadn't paid any attention to Chram.

"She happened to glance at the crowd standing just outside the window. Prith was there, staring at her in the most . . . *evil* way. As if he could . . . Well, with hatred. She rocked back on her heels and almost fell, as if she'd seen a ghost. I thought she might faint or run. Her hands trembled and her face drained of color. She never looked Prith's way again. He tried to approach her several times, but she always gave him the slip. He shouted at her once and she ran away. Stephen followed right behind her, then afterward he went to Prith and told him to leave her alone."

My thoughts were interrupted by the sound of a car. I had just turned off the busily traveled Main onto High, a quiet residential street. Glancing back, I saw the black hulk of an automobile creeping up the block with headlights off. I turned at the next cross street and stepped behind a hedge. Like a shark silently slipping through still, deep waters, the shadow drifted by. I held my breath, pressing my body against the shrubbery as it passed. At the next corner, the car halted, the engine droning on. No one got out. The lights remained shut off.

The surreal aura I'd experienced when viewing the corpse enveloped me again. For several minutes, the car hovered motionlessly. Then, as imperceptibly as it had loomed out of the night, the apparition glided around the corner and vanished.

I held my pose by the privet hedge and waited. After several minutes, when the car did not reappear, I stepped out from my hiding place. Chiding myself for letting my imagination run wild, I turned and jogged home.

Morgan was watching the news when I let myself in the back door. "They went to bed early," he assured me, packing up his laptop when I arrived. "Any new developments?"

"Not that I know of. What did the news say?"

"Just a lot of garbage about Gaffney." Morgan shook his head disapprovingly. "Oh, Billy got a call. There's a message on the counter. Hope you can read it."

I saw him to the side door and watched as he walked across the path to his place and let himself inside. Morgan's light went out. I locked all the doors and windows, checked on the kids, who were sleeping soundly, and went into the living room to decompress.

When Billy came home, I was curled up on the sofa watching MTV, wrapping gifts, and drinking chamomile tea to calm my nerves.

"How'd it go?" he asked.

"Productive. You?"

He held out his hand. "Steady as a rock. Can I go out again tomorrow, teacher?"

"Was I right about the dope? It was there, wasn't it?"

"No comment. All you need to know is I didn't touch the stuff." He bent down and kissed me. I smelled nothing more incriminating than tobacco smoke.

"This guy you are playing with—his name is Harley?"

"Yeah?"

"Funny. That's not someone I remember."

"I played with him last summer. Guitarist who thinks he's hot shit."

"So, is he?"

"Johnny Winter by way of Milli Vanilli."

I laughed. "That I have to hear."

"You'll get your chance. Any calls?"

"Morgan took a message. LA area code. You've been getting a lot of California calls lately." I followed him into the kitchen.

Billy shoved the note into his back pocket and went to the pantry. He returned with a box of Special K, which he poured into a huge bowl. He sliced a banana, splashed in milk, went to the refrigerator, and traded the milk carton for a Bass Ale. I sat with him at the table, sipping my tea.

"So?" I asked.

He looked up blankly.

"What's the deal?"

He took more cereal. "Just more legal crap."

"Like what?"

"Nothing I care to go into right now. Are you any closer to figuring out who murdered Chram?"

Deciding I didn't really want to rehash more legal

and financial fallout from the crisis, I told him what I'd found out from Eleanor Kerr and Malis Soppah.

"I don't know what to think," I concluded, eager to expound on my theories. "Was it the restaurant and money? Or was it something to do with Prith and the Khmer Rouge? I haven't ruled out Stephen. He's involved on some level. You know he's a flirt, if not worse? Malis blushed so hard when they started talking about him. I cornered her alone when we were leaving and she admitted he'd made a pass. Sradanny said he'd asked her out, although she's like the Ice Queen. I can't imagine Don Juan making a pass at her."

"For some guys flirting is like breathing."

"Speaking from experience?"

"Maybe," Billy teased. "This Stephen is a good-looking guy, right?"

"Yeah."

"If he's just reasonably polite, it might seem like a come-on."

"But he seems so calculating. He hinted pointedly about the Khmer Rouge. And he volunteered that he and Chram argued on Monday before she was killed. He says she broke off the engagement."

"Just like that?"

"Yeah. It seemed odd that he should have told me."

"If he did make passes at all these women, maybe she found out and read him his rights."

"There's something missing or out of place. With a jigsaw puzzle, if you twist the piece, sometimes you suddenly see where it fits." I thought about that for a second, trying to twist Stephen around to see how else he could fit into the picture that was beginning to emerge. "I called him today, and his housemate said he was down at the police station. This is the second time he's been questioned. I wonder if he's hired a lawyer."

"What was he doing at the time of the murder?"

I dug out my notes of the interview with Stephen. "Here it is. He was so upset after their argument, which was late afternoon, that he started driving to Vermont. In Brattleboro, he decided to turn around and drive back. He called Chram's house around eight. Song answered and told him she'd been gone for several hours. She says Chram got a call soon after returning from her meeting with Stephen. Chram told Song—and I quote—she was 'going to visit an old friend.' That was the last time anyone saw her."

"So Stephen had the opportunity," Billy said. He'd finished the cereal and was rocking on the back legs of his chair.

"I guess so. He talked to Song at eight. Chram was killed anywhere between six-seventeen P.M., the time on the receipt, and midnight."

"Does Stephen appear spooked?"

"Yeah. But if I were stabbed to death and the police were interrogating you, wouldn't you be? Especially if we'd just broken up?"

"What motive could he have?"

"Anger at being rejected."

"So the scenario goes something like this: She gets

a call and goes out Monday night before six."

"At the mall she argues with someone who looks like Prith."

"Who is later picked up by Cletha after the security guard is called because he's making a nuisance of himself at the arcade. What time?"

"Dennison Brown says the woman came around nine." Prith disappeared shortly after he arrived home. Cletha's place was several miles from the mall. Unless he hitchhiked it would have been at least an hour before he could get back.

"And at eight Stephen calls and Song answers the phone," Billy mused.

"Yeah. And I recall her saying she'd been surprised because she had the impression that Chram was with him."

"So he calls just before she's killed?"

We stared at each other. Ghosts began to fill the room.

"He could have accidentally run into her," Billy suggested.

"He could have seen something or someone that would give him a motive for murder. A motive we're not yet aware of."

"Or," said Billy, "someone who might give him a clue as to who the murderer is."

"If he was there, which he says he wasn't. He says he was driving around in his car." A new thought occurred to me. "But there is one person whose presence has been established—and that's Prith."

"So either Prith is the killer . . ."

"Or he knows who is," I finished the sentence. "Maybe that's why he's so freaked."

"Yeah," said Billy. "Maybe he witnessed the murder."

"Before Cletha picked him up. Maybe that's why he was so wild in the video arcade."

I began to consider whether to bring Prith's name up to Brannigan.

"Let's say Stephen killed her," said Billy, getting into it. "Try to imagine what happened. Let's say they ran into each other accidentally at the mall. It's late. She doesn't want to have anything to do with him. He demands an explanation. He's mad. She breaks away, he follows. She shops, he tags along, pleading. She keeps giving him the brush-off. Finally, he says, let's go sit down and talk someplace quiet. They go back to the car. She tells him flat out the engagement is off. He gets furious. 'You can't do this to me,' he's yelling. She shouts something back. He loses it. Something snaps. He has a knife. Where does he get the knife?"

"From his collection of ancient weapons."

"You're kidding."

I shook my head. "They're hanging all over his living room wall."

"He wouldn't be that stupid, would he?"

"Probably not. But you can't know for sure."

"Well, for argument's sake," Billy proposed, "let's say she has the knife. Keeps it on her for protection."

"That makes sense. She's been through a lot. I'll bet she'd carry something for self-defense."

"Say she picks up the knife and tells him to get out."

"He starts out defending himself, loses it, and kills her."

We stared at each other for a second. It was plausible.

Billy poured the rest of his ale into his pint glass and took a sip.

"She had some gruesome wounds. Whoever killed her was totally out of control. He must have been stabbing and stabbing until he came back to his senses."

"The killer must have been covered with blood."

"The car wasn't too bloody," I said, remembering the brown stains on the tan terry cloth seat covers, the blackened flesh of the dead woman, her dark eyes as blank as a doll's, staring into the distance.

"Let's say the motive was jealousy," I went on. "Somebody has just got into town. A former lover of Chram's. Maybe somebody who has a hold on her. Someone she owes something to—"

"From the past . . ."

"Yeah, from the past. Here we are back to Prith."

"Chram and Prith," Billy mused.

"One thing doesn't make sense."

"What?"

"When she went to the Khmer Rouge labor camp she was about twelve or thirteen."

"How old was Prith back then?"

"He's in his mid-twenties now, even though he looks eighteen. Back at the beginning of the regime—

year zero they called it—he couldn't have been more than nine or ten. A ten-year-old boy and a twelve-year-old girl?" I asked dubiously.

"When the regime fell," Billy said suggestively, "you've got a fourteen-year-old boy and a sixteen-year-old girl. That's a hot combination."

"Cambodians don't have sex out of wedlock."

"Sure, and elephants fly. Everyone has sex out of wedlock. Some people just don't talk about it."

"Malis said he gave Chram some look at the wedding. He gave me a fright, too, when he went at me with the stick."

He frowned. "You didn't tell me about that."

I explained what had happened at Cletha's, wondering for a split second if I should mention the car that might have been following me tonight. But he looked so concerned about the attack with the stick that I didn't want to give him additional grounds for worry. "It was so strange," I concluded. "I could have sworn I was totally alone, and then, presto, he was right in front of me."

"He's pretty good in the jungle, huh?"

"Cletha says he climbed trees and slept in the limbs, so he wouldn't be eaten by tigers. I'll bet he was up in one of those trees." I sipped more tea. "He couldn't be her brother, could he?"

Billy shook his head. "The whole family would know it. Besides, wasn't the brother older?"

"I don't know, Billy. I just don't think it was sex. The way Malis described his look at the wedding—it was horror or fear or hatred. Not passion."

"Maybe she had something on him—something so damaging it was worth killing to keep her from telling."

I stood up and put away my notes. "For Cletha's sake, I hope we're wrong."

But I had a sick feeling in the pit of my stomach that we were on the right track.

17

I stared with disbelief at the monitor as I read the final copy for this afternoon's paper. It was ten A.M., just past deadline. The headline trumpeted "Immigrants Drain Local Coffers." Although I could find a few paragraphs from the article I'd left on Mark's desk last night, most of it appeared to have been written by Mark. Way down in the last inch I found a passing mention of the protests by Cletha's group. A photo of Hal Gaffney with his chart and pointer accompanied the piece, next to a long sidebar bearing my byline on physical abuse in Cambodian families. It had been lifted from the end of the story I'd written on the Asian Women's Night Walk to be held today. That piece, to my absolute outrage, had not made it into the paper. On the phone, Whit was explaining testily that he'd slotted it for tomorrow to run alongside photos that Kate would take at the march tonight.

"The article on the press conference," I told Whit angrily, "is unrecognizable."

"The byline is shared with Mark," Whit replied. "I'm busy. We'll talk later."

I slammed down the phone and went looking for Mark. I found him in the kitchen engaged in a game of wastebasket napkin-ball with Kate. She was winning, swishing two shots in a row.

"Szabo, *qué pasó*?" He backhanded a pass and I caught it.

"I'll tell you *qué pasa*, you jerk. Why'd you screw up my piece? Why'd you give Gaffney all that space to blow off his big mouth? Why didn't you at least ask for my approval?"

Though his body remained at ease, his eyes seemed to shine with subdued triumph. "Don't get bent out of shape. I incorporated the copy you left on my desk last night."

I wasn't going to back down. "Next time get an okay from me on the final draft."

"You weren't here, as you ought to recall."

Stung, I realized that Mark, the sneak, had bided his time, waiting to strike when I wasn't there to defend my position.

"Then don't put my name on your story."

He shook his shoulders the way a large animal might shiver to loosen its muscles. "You know, we're supposed to be partners on this story. You seem to think you've got sole jurisdiction."

Kate spoke up. "He has a point, Zoë."

"Thanks, Kate. Next time he encroaches on your beat, don't come complaining to me."

Mark cleared his throat. "Zoë. This is not your beat. It's *ours*."

I shot him the most hostile glare I could summon and turned my back on them. This was a mistake I vowed not to make again. No more shared bylines, no more pretense of collaboration. No one was going to wrench any facts out of me until I was ready to publish. I decided to go after the police side, noting that I'd started the whole story with my interview of Brannigan. I wondered if I could get him or someone in his office to talk off the record. If I made headway where Mark had hit a blank wall, that might prove to Whit that I should call the shots.

I was still steamed when Whit called an impromptu meeting over coffee to plan the next stage of our coverage. Even though the paper had only been on the stands for an hour, already refugee supporters had phoned to complain about the coverage. The support story had run under the fold, with the Gaffney piece above, and it had been considerably shortened.

"Eleanor Kerr called. She was near tears," I complained. "I didn't know what to say, considering I gave her the impression her information would be handled in a different manner." Some of what she'd told me about family abuse had run in the sidebar. "She felt used. You should have asked me about the changes."

Whit's patrician face betrayed as much emotion as the sphinx. "If you're not willing to be a team player, Zoë, go back to Hollywood."

"I've always considered teamwork to be a two-way street. You deliberately twisted my input to make Gaffney look good."

Whit stared me down. "Everyone has a right to a hearing, whether you agree or not." While I fumed silently, Whit wrapped it up. "Zoë, what's on your agenda for this afternoon?"

"I'm going to see Stephen to find out if he's managed to get a speaking slot at the memorial service." Several people had lobbied to prevent Stephen from speaking.

"Can't you do that by phone?"

"Not really."

Whit glanced toward Mark. "How about you?"

Mark grinned cockily. "I could call the university about the memorial."

Whit motioned to me. "Need a sidekick?"

"What? To talk to Stephen?" I made a face.

Mark feigned a wounded sigh, then glanced at Whit, as if to say, "See what I have to put up with?"

"Oh, *please*!" I muttered.

Mark's ex-jock grin taunted me silently.

Anger flashed in Whit's eyes. "Go see Stephen, if you insist, but take Mark along. It's a precaution."

"Fine," I said, standing up. Whit frowned, signaling Mark to follow me.

"Kate," Whit said. "Get shots of kids playing in snow."

She was furious and didn't hesitate to express it. "With a murderer loose you're going to put *cute* on the front page. Don't you need pictures of Stephen?"

"Oh, if I need photos, I'm sure Mark can take them," I told Kate with a catty smile.

Mark and I left Kate arguing heatedly with Whit, knowing, of course, that she'd lose. No one ever managed to talk him out of an assignment. Some of us persisted, going on the theory that, while you might not affect this particular call, you might get the benefit of the doubt on the next one.

I stopped at my desk to dial Stephen, but as soon as I heard his line begin to ring, the light on my line lit. I switched over.

"Zoë?" It was Song.

"Yes."

"I've been thinking about what you said yesterday. Can we meet?"

"Sure. Could you hold? My line's ringing. Yeah?" It was Billy. "Babe, I can't talk. I'm in the middle of an important call. I'll get right back. Song? Where do you want to meet and when?"

"How about Jamieson's in half an hour?"

"I'll pick you up."

"No. Don't come here." She got off in a hurry, and I dialed home.

"Zoë," Billy said, "I've got a problem."

"What?"

"I have to go to Boston tonight."

"Why?"

"This guy, Harley, he booked a last-minute gig and, uh, asked if I'd fill in on bass."

"The guy from last night?"

"Yeah."

"Funny. You never mentioned this guy before yesterday, and suddenly you're like a member of his band. When did you have time to learn his stuff?"

"Ever hear of charts?"

"But this is so last-minute."

"Yeah, I'm sorry. The guy's counting on me."

"I want to cover the Night Walk, and this will be like the third night this week we've asked Morgan to sit."

"I arranged to take the kids. I can leave them at my folks' while I do the gig, come back tomorrow. You'd be free to follow your leads. I could pick up the car in a couple of hours, you get a ride home with someone or walk."

The memory of the dark automobile emerged from the compartment to which I'd consigned it. "I guess that makes sense, but—I don't know—I guess I'm being selfish. I'd really like someone to come home to."

"Now that you mention it, I'm getting a little lonely here, too. For some adult company. You haven't been around much."

I was about to object, but turned and saw Mark at his desk over near the water cooler. He was watching me with a faint grin— eavesdropping, I'd lay odds. I heard the kids romping in the background.

"Kate," I called as she walked by, her braided ponytail swinging moodily, signaling defeat. "Are you going out to the sledding hill?" She gave me a glum nod. "How about picking up Billy and my kids?"

"Oh, sure, why not?"

"Billy? Kate's going to photograph kids sledding. Do you want to tag along with her? I can meet you there after my interview and you can take the car." Billy jumped at the chance to get out of the house. "She'll be there in twenty minutes."

I gave Stephen a call and he agreed to see me later that afternoon. I was just sneaking out to meet Song when Mark caught up with me.

"We're partners. Remember?"

"I'm going to lunch."

"Hey." He clapped an arm over my shoulder. "I'll join you."

We walked along through the icy streets. The sun shone on the snow, melting it to slush, which was less difficult to navigate now that I'd adapted my style to the needs of a reporter on the go. New England had begun to win out over California. I wore the Bean jacket and jeans and my already messed-up black leather boots, which I'd spent part of last night treating with mink oil so they'd ward off water. I'd compensated for the outer camouflage with silvery blue lipstick, chartreuse eye shadow, and a green silk chemise with a skimpy black cardigan.

Jamieson's, despite the intersession, was crowded. The ice cream shop, which also sold burritos and soup, was a popular place for a cheap, quick lunch. The booths by the windows were filled, so Mark and I took seats at one of the small tables bunched together in the middle.

I took a quick look around and failed to spot Song.

"When do we see Stephen?" Mark asked, unwrapping his jumbo burrito.

"Later," I muttered. Having to drag Mark around felt like having an albatross around my neck.

"You're in a mood, Szabo."

"If I rewrote your piece, you'd be in one, too."

He sucked at his teeth. "Whit liked it."

We glowered at each other. Then, with a self-satisfied shrug, he turned his attention to his burrito. I was angry at him, dismayed at the prospect of Billy taking the kids and the car to Boston, abandoning me, and worried about how to shake Mark if Song showed up. So my stomach knotted and I couldn't bear to look at the burrito I'd bought. I picked at it and pushed it aside.

It took Mark all of four bites to finish, then he pushed his chair back and stretched his long legs, gazing at me with a little smirk.

"An apology might be in order," I said coldly.

He turned his head, as if searching for someone at an adjacent table, then gave me a slow sidelong glance. "Listen, we had a deal."

"That we'd *share* the byline, not that you'd take it totally."

He waited a moment, then leaned forward, resting an elbow on the table as if he were going to propose arm wrestling to settle the matter. "Sometimes, Szabo, you have to pass to the player who has a clear shot."

"A teammate, darling, doesn't stomp all over you in order to score."

He laughed. "No? If you keep hogging the ball, he might."

"I'm the one who left *my* copy on *your* desk. I don't consider that hogging. If you couldn't include a portion of my version, why couldn't you just ask me to read it over? There is a difference, Mark, between consultation and usurpation."

He leveled his gaze at me, almost gloating, but a tinge of pink began to creep around his ears. "Okay," he said, as if making a huge concession. "I'm *sorry*." His mouth opened in a half smile. "Your turn, Szabo."

"I'm touched, Mark. I really am. That was so heartfelt."

He grinned down at me with mock gentility and glanced at my plate. "You going to eat that?"

I pushed it forward. "Be my guest."

"Where you going?"

"To the rest room. Want to join me?"

He blushed. "That's okay. You go on."

"Thanks."

When I returned, I caught sight of him on line for an ice cream. While he chatted with the counter girl, I slipped out the door, tremendously pleased with how cinchy it had been to escape. I walked to the gas station, scouring the street for Song, who was about ten minutes late. I had just put a quarter in the pay phone and dialed her number when I caught sight of her long brown coat as she stepped off a bus that had just pulled to a stop across the street. I slammed down the receiver and ran toward her.

"Zoë," she whispered. A dark blue patterned scarf covered her head. I threw my arm around her and gave her a quick squeeze.

"Come," I said, looking around. I saw no sign of Mark or his red Miata. "Let's go sledding."

Song was seated in my Honda, her coat wrapped around her. Though the worn garment looked as if it had been acquired from the bins of donations to Quaker Rescue, the blue scarf with a lavender weave livened it up. Despite limited resources, Song had a good sense of style. I drove down Stanhope Street, past the *Eagle* offices and the Commons toward the spires of the Greymont College campus. The hill where Kate and Billy would be was about a mile down the road.

"After your article today," Song said, "Uncle Rok forbade me to talk to you."

"He read it?" I pictured his reaction to the abuse story and a tremor of uneasiness sifted through me.

"He and Saw have eyes like tigers. They see everything, even in darkness. He finds boys who help him. They tell him what's in the newspaper."

"I've heard rumors that Rok runs gambling games."

Song was silent.

"Do you think I could go see the gambling?"

Song suppressed a smile. "Are you crazy? How are you going to see gambling?"

"You could take me."

"Rok would have my head! Yours, too."

So, I thought, he did run a game. "Have you seen it?" I asked her.

She gave a barely perceptible nod.

I stopped at a red light. A sleek blue Ford drew up behind me. "What do people do?"

"Oh, it's stupid. They have tiles and dice. They throw them down on a table and if it's one thing they win. Another, they lose. I've seen it once and then I didn't go anymore. I don't like it. It's for old ladies."

"Did Chram gamble?"

Song laughed. "She wanted to be an American business woman. She wouldn't throw money away."

"Who plays? Your mother?"

"Sometimes."

I was about to take a left into the campus when I checked the rearview mirror. The blue Ford, a few lengths behind me, had also pulled into the turn lane.

I suddenly pressed the gas pedal to the floor. The Civic did my bidding and jumped ahead, leaving the blue Ford behind.

Song looked at me with surprise, but said nothing.

"Sorry," I said.

I drove recklessly, turning onto side streets and up alleys until I finally came to a stop not far from the college. The Ford was nowhere to be seen. I drove quickly back to the ivy-covered brick buildings, taking side roads and coming in from the south part of campus.

A steep slope beyond the lot, where I finally came to a stop, went unbroken for about a hundred yards until it leveled in a long flat expanse, which receded to a row of tennis courts, set off in the snow by tall fences. Behind the courts playing fields stretched toward a perimeter of woods. In the far distance rose bluish mountains against a background of gray swirling clouds.

"You drive well," said Song.

"Sometimes."

Neither of us spoke about the Ford. I wondered whether she knew, but didn't want to worry her if she hadn't realized why I'd taken the sudden detour. My pulse throbbed; otherwise I maintained a surface calm. "I'm going to park behind those vans. Maybe we won't be spotted."

All along the panoramic hillside, spots of color clustered and moved up and down the slopes. Kids in snow jackets dotted the landscape. They walked uphill and slid down on wooden sleds, blue and pink coasters, and black and lavender tubes that spun as they descended. Some sat on the seat of their pants on plastic bags. The air rang with the laughter and shouting of sledders hurtling out of control, warning those climbing back uphill to move out of the way.

We sat in the car and watched. Finally, seeing that Song was shivering, I suggested we get out and walk. "I've seen this," Song said as we climbed up the slope, watching the sleds speed past us, "but I never tried it."

"Not with your friends?"

"I skate. Roller-skate too. But no sledding."

"That's right, you're an athlete. You ski?"

She shook her head. "My mother won't let me. The first winter we were here, my best American friend broke her leg skiing. After that, my mother said, 'No way. Nothing will hurt my daughter.' You wouldn't believe, Zoë, how she protects me. She tells me about the pain when she gave birth. About making sure I had food when I was a baby. I was very tiny. They thought I wouldn't live. In fact, they said some kind of words in case I would die. Then Aunt Saw took hairs from my head and put them in a special place to fool the evil spirits. They would take those hairs instead, thinking it was me. My mother says that's why I'm still here."

I thought of the story told the previous night of the punishment Phroeng had suffered for stealing food so that she and her mother could eat.

"She wouldn't like you to be here now," I said. "Talking to me."

"In her deepest heart, she wants Chram's killer punished. But I lied about where I was going. I told her I'd be at the library, working on a paper. Maybe she asked Rok to check."

"Are you afraid of him?"

"He tries to do what's best for the family." Her black eyes skimmed over the fields and hills covered with snow. She smiled suddenly and pointed. "Look!"

I followed her arm over to the far side of the sledding area where a familiar man was playing with two children. A woman in a navy parka snapped pictures.

"That might be Kate."

We picked up the pace, walking around the edge to avoid getting plowed down by sledders. Kate's braid became visible as we closed the distance. She was engrossed in photographing Billy, Smokie, and Keith, and didn't see us approach.

Smokie started shouting. Billy held the rope of the sled and began pulling, the kids trying to get him to give them a ride.

I gave Smokie a big hug, then embraced Keith. "Come on, Billy," I challenged, making a muscle. "Let's pull these kids up the hill."

The four of us, Song, Billy, Kate, and I, grabbed the rope and dragged the sled to the top, with Smokie yelling, "Giddyap! Giddyap!"

Kate slid down with the kids first, then Song took a turn. Billy and I stood holding each other, sharing a moment of quiet contentment. Song rolled off into the snow and the kids jumped after her, shouting. The three of them pulled the sled. Kate went off after photos.

"Been here long?" I asked Billy.

"Yeah, I was beginning to think you weren't going to show."

"Song took forever to meet me. And then she was spooked. I figured this was as good a hiding place as any. She has something she seems to want to tell me. I'm not sure what. I'm letting her take it slow."

Although we were out in the open, anyone searching for Song or me wasn't likely to look here. When you don't want to be seen sometimes it's best to hide in full view. Song's body language betrayed that she was ill-at-ease. I wondered how much trouble she'd had getting away from home and whether the blue Ford had been following her or me. The kids were running after her, and she approached with a shower of giggles.

"My turn," I called and ran to the sled. I lay down with Keith on my back. It was a wonderful ride, a thrill. The sled moved faster than I expected, recklessly bumping over the swift snow. I was disappointed when we abruptly slowed down not far from the tennis court fence. I'd wanted the ride to go on forever. I'd never before appreciated how much I loved speed and the fear that went with it.

At last we'd had our fill. The clouds darkened, the wind blew colder. Billy wanted to leave; both kids had begun to shiver. I wanted to drop Song off at her apartment complex, but, growing anxious, she drew me aside.

"I can't go near my house in your car. The other day someone saw you pick me up."

"Who?" I scrutinized her anxious eyes.

"Rok," she admitted after a hesitation. "He was very angry."

I explained to Billy that I had to stay and talk to Song. We decided to meet at the office in half an hour. Even though I'd promised to trade cars here, he agreed to hitch back with Kate and wait for me.

After helping pack the kids into Kate's Subaru, Song and I ambled along watching the last of the sledders. Two parties of boisterous teens collided at the middle of the slope with a loud smacking crash. I drew in my breath. One boy rolled over spread-eagled and still. The others stood up and finally noticed. One ran over to the body.

"Hey, he's hurt!"

The still one suddenly jumped up, calling, "Gotcha!" They laughed and punched each other. Boys playing rough.

"Zoë," Song said softly in my ear. "I have something to tell you."

"Let's keep walking. No one can hear us."

"The afternoon before Chram died. That Monday. Something happened that I didn't tell anyone about. Rok says not to tell. So please don't let anyone know I said it. Chram and Rok had a very bad fight. He ate lunch at our house. Chram said somebody was trying to keep her from getting her citizenship papers, and she blamed Rok."

"Wouldn't she qualify for citizenship more quickly after she married Stephen?"

"I'm not sure, but Stephen made it a condition that they wait until she got her papers. His parents insisted."

"Why would Rok keep her from getting the papers?"

"Because he wanted her to marry a Cambodian. He and Saw have friends in Lowell who have a son, much older than Chram. They arranged for her to marry him—without even telling her."

I was beginning to get a picture of a woman trapped. I felt a pang of empathy for Chram, to be so close to her dream and yet so held back.

"Rok hit her. He said she was . . . He said a name. I don't know why he wanted her to marry his friend if she was so bad as he says. He was in a rage. He made a threat. If she didn't marry this man and break off with Stephen, he would beat her . . . or worse.

"Chram said, 'Do what you like. I would rather be dead.' She said she was going away and that we wouldn't have to worry about her anymore. And she took me outside. She was crying. She gave me this. She told me to hold it for her. That it might help her some day."

Song glanced around, stealthily. A few sledders were still on the hill. A bright streak of orange-gold lit up the gathering clouds. In the distance the hills were snowy and a peak or two glittered in the reflected light of the low winter sun. No one was anywhere near.

She dug into her pocket and pulled out something wrapped in a square of pink silk. She unwrapped the fabric to reveal a small silver box ornately embossed with elephants, tigers, palms, vines, and flowers. Hiding within the vines was a cobra poised to strike.

She pressed a hidden spring and pulled a pin. I expected the top to come up, but it didn't. Instead a drawer lined in velvet popped out from the side.

In this pocket was a tiny pouch. Song rolled something out of the pouch onto the silk. It was linked gold mesh, about three inches long, a web in the shape of a vine, with a gold lotus blossom bearing a large, rosy pearl at its center. It appeared to be part of a necklace or bracelet.

For a few moments I gazed at the gold links, the vine, the lotus blossom, the pearl, with amazement. Finally, I asked, "Did Chram say what this is or why she was giving it to you?"

"For safekeeping. She said she could never explain.

She said, 'Be a good little sister. Hold this for me.' She gave it to me after she got that phone call I told you about before. I didn't tell you about the fight with Rok because . . . I was afraid."

Her voice trailed off in a whisper.

"Do you think he killed her?"

Song cast her dark eyes down toward the dirty snow under our feet. "I pray every night that he didn't. But I can't sleep. I wake up. Chram's ghost is upon me, suffocating me. Telling me things. They seem so clear while I'm dreaming, but I wake up and I can't remember. Zoë, I'm scared. My mother. She cries. She screams. She walks in her sleep. My father has been drunk ever since Chram died. He falls on his face at the foot of the stairs and I have to drag him up to the bed. I don't know what to do."

"Have you talked to Bou Vuthy?"

She shook her head, the dark locks tossed over her coat, falling down her back. "I can't. He frightens me, too. I don't even know the proper words, the way you're supposed to talk to a monk. There are special words I never learned. It's so much easier to be an American. I can understand why Chram wanted it so. I wish she were back. Even though she was mean sometimes, at least she had hope."

"You should stay with Eleanor Kerr."

Song shook her head. "My mother needs me."

"Song, I know this is going to upset you, but please hear me out before you object. Will you listen and not run away? I promise I won't make you do anything you don't want."

She nodded with trust in her eyes. I didn't feel worthy of that trust, but she so desperately needed someone that I became determined to dig inside and try somehow to find the strength to rise to the challenge.

"I know your first instinct will be to say no, but just listen. We should show these things to Detective Brannigan. You should tell him what happened the last day Chram was alive—everything in detail. I'll stay with you if you want."

"Can you do it, Zoë?"

"Me?"

"I don't want to talk to the police. They scare me. You know we have to have them at the funeral? My mother says she won't go if they're there, and Uncle Rok and Aunt Saw say it will be a scandal if the child's mother doesn't appear at the funeral. They all say I have to shave my head. I don't want to cut off my hair."

Her round face turned toward the sun, which was shooting beams through the clouds. The snow, packed and gouged from rough use, glowed golden in the winter light.

"I'm tired of the dead," she added, gazing at the sky. "They rule us. They won't let us go. As soon as we begin to loosen their grip, the minute we begin to escape and breathe and see the sun and the light, they come at us with their bone fingers and dig into our skins and whisper in our ears. And another one dies. And another. So there are more to do the work of haunting and hunting us. Until we give up and die ourselves."

For a few moments we watched the sleds glide down the shimmering slope.

"Let's go to the police right now," I said at last. "We'll get it over with quickly."

"You go. I don't want to see them." She closed up the box with the broken strands of necklace and put the package wrapped in pink silk in my hands.

"If I go to the police with this alone," I told her slowly, letting each word sink in, "they will ask me where I got it. I have to tell them the truth. When they find out you gave it to me, they will come to you and ask questions anyway. It's much easier if you come now, yourself. Then they won't suspect you of hiding something."

She relented with a sigh, as if I were a parent insisting she do her homework before watching TV.

"It won't be as bad as all that," I said, giving her a friendly nudge toward the car. The wind came up in a cold gust and pushed with more urgency.

18

A half-hour later we were in the police station with Detective Brannigan. We had literally bumped into him as we maneuvered through the narrow hallway of the cramped station in the basement of Town Hall. Brannigan had been carrying a Styrofoam cup full of coffee and it spilled on his tweed jacket, which looked as if it came from the same Salvation Army store where many of the Cambodians bought their clothes. Though his eyes were tired, his cheeks were reddish and raw. He pulled a torn tissue from his pocket and offered it to Song, who accepted it so tentatively that Brannigan finally took it back and wiped the coffee drip from Song's coat himself.

"Detective," I said.

In the midst of dabbing at his own jacket, he looked up dourly.

"Song Touch has something to show you."

He paused awkwardly, glanced at Song, and did something of a double take, recognizing her at last.

"There's an empty office down the hall."

We followed him through a rabbit warren of offices and hallways until, finally, he opened a wooden door with a glass window inscribed E–3. Brannigan ushered Song inside. As I was about to follow, he turned and barred the way like an over-aged adolescent. I'd promised Song not to leave her alone and I was determined not to disappoint her. She'd endured enough betrayals in her short life.

"I gave my word that I'd stay," I protested. "Can't you see how terrified she is?"

Song did look alarmed. So much so that Brannigan relented, dropping his arm. He was one of those short, wiry, aggressive men who were always trying to prove their superiority to make up for lack of height.

"We're off the record as of right now," he muttered and then focused on Song. "What's this about?"

Song placed the silver box on the gray metal desk that took up most of the small office. We stood because there were only two chairs, both shoved under the desk.

"Ms. Touch, why don't you have a seat." He clumsily pulled a chair from the desk and beckoned to Song. Meekly, she eased herself into it.

"Chram gave it to me," she began. "Just before she left on Monday afternoon. That was the last time I saw her."

"Had you seen it before?"

She shook her head.

Brannigan approached the desk and examined the

box without touching it. Song cringed as he bent close to her.

"Who's seen it?"

"Zoë."

"Not your parents?"

"No."

"Aunt, uncle, other relatives, friends?"

She shook her head.

"Why did she give it to you?"

Song briefly outlined the events that occurred on the last afternoon of Chram's life: the fight with Rok, the phone call, the hurried exchange of the box for safekeeping until she returned. "Be a good little sister," Song said, repeating Chram's parting words.

"That's all she said?"

A nod.

"Have you told anyone about it?"

"No. Only Zoë and you. Chram was afraid."

"She gave you no hints about what was frightening her?"

She described the fight over citizenship with Rok and Chram's bitterness and despair over Stephen.

"Did you look inside?"

Song took the box, undid the secret latch, and the pocket drawer popped open. She picked up the pouch and let the broken links of the necklace fall onto the silk cloth.

Brannigan grunted. "You've never seen this particular jewelry before?"

"Not before I opened this box."

"Do you have any idea where Chram got it?"

"No," said Song. "But I think this is why she was killed."

"Why?"

"Just a feeling. A deep secret. She didn't want to give it to me. It was for safety."

"I'd like to keep this for a while," said Brannigan. "To test it for fingerprints and other evidence. Do you understand?"

Song nodded.

"I'll have to have you sign a form. All right?"

Again she nodded. Within a few moments, a uniformed female officer entered the room, which now felt rather crowded. Song signed a release and took the receipt. We were held up temporarily by the fact that she was, at seventeen, a minor, but they decided to have me sign as a witness.

"For the time being," Brannigan said, "let's keep this a secret just among us. Szabo?"

I nodded. "How about Whit?"

Brannigan scowled but okayed it. "Nobody else. Not a word in the paper. We don't want—" He broke off and asked Song, "Do you feel comfortable going home? I can put you in protective custody, but I'd rather not."

"I want to go home. My mother needs me."

"Eleanor Kerr might be willing to take in Song and her mother," I suggested.

"No!" Song insisted. And we acquiesced, not without misgivings.

In a little while, Song and I were standing outside at the Valley Transit bus shelter. She didn't want me to drive her home, so I waited with her until the diesel bus rumbled along after twenty minutes. When Song got on, she gave a delicate wave good-bye. I watched her face in the window as the bus pulled away from the curb and moved down the wide street. The lamps cast pink circles of light on the snow, and the wind blew. The twinkling strands of fairy lights in the trees on the Commons danced madly.

Racing back to the *Eagle* offices across the street, I found Billy conversing with Mark and Kate, while Keith, perched on Mark's chair, played Tetris on Mark's computer.

"There she is," called Smokie. "We're going to Boston! Can you come?"

"Sorry, sweets, Mommy has to work." I knelt down and she climbed onto my lap. With feelings of regret, I nibbled her fingers and stroked her silky brown curls. "You come back tomorrow and we'll decorate the tree."

My line lit up.

"Szabo here."

"Is your Asian story done?" Whit asked.

"I'm going to update it after the march tonight. I can work late."

Smokie, eavesdropping, gave a Shirley Temple pout and shook her head vigorously, sticking her fingers in my mouth. I pried them out and kissed her ear. "What?"

"I said what else have you got cooking? I have a hole to plug in tomorrow's paper."

I thought of Brannigan and the jewels. "There's new evidence," I said, lowering my voice. Mark was still conversing with Kate and Billy—about the rock club in Sheffington, which was rumored about to be sold.

"I've been at the police station most of the afternoon, but I've been asked to hold off filing a story."

"Come up and we'll talk," said Whit.

"Can it wait? I've, uh"—I hesitated, not wanting to bring up the kids—"my family's here and I'm—"

"Fine, get rid of them and come up." Whit slammed down the phone. I found that irritatingly abrupt.

"Mommy," Smokie began.

"Yes, sweets."

"Are you sad?"

"No, I'm just busy. Sorry."

Her eyes, as soulful as her dad's, peered into mine. She put her fingers on my face and pushed at the corners of my mouth. "I can make you smile."

I stretched my mouth into a toothy grin and she giggled. Billy ambled over. "You took your sweet time."

The smile I'd made for Smokie faded. "So you're off to Boston?"

He coughed, seeming fidgety, on edge. His bass and an amp were stacked in a corner, near my desk, along with a duffel-type overnight suitcase.

"You have something for the kids to snack on during the drive?"

"Jeez, Zoë, it's only an hour and a half."

"More like two."

Mark laughed. "Male versus female time."

Billy smiled bloodlessly, annoyed at the interference.

"Is something eating you?" I asked.

"I'm eager to get going. Ready, kids?"

"Billy?"

"Listen, I've got to go over my set, get the kids settled, and hightail it over to Bonhomie's by eight. It didn't help that you're nearly an hour late. So just cool it."

"Don't bite my head off," I demurred, noting that Bonhomie's was a pretty big club for a nowhere band like Harley's to be playing. "Sweetie," I said to Smokie, not wanting to force the issue in front of the kids, let alone Mark and the rest of the newspaper staff. "Let's put your coat on."

"I can do it all by myself!" she boasted. She ran to the chair where her and Keith's jackets were piled, pulled hers out, and flipped it over her head the way she'd learned in preschool. Billy grabbed the bass and amp. I took the overnight bag and walked them out to the Civic, which Billy loaded while I secured the kids in their car seats.

"You be careful," he said, as he paused at the door.

"You too."

His hand at the back of my neck drew me close. We kissed lightly. "We should be back mid-afternoon. I assume you're working tomorrow."

"I'm going to leave early. How about Morgan? Does he need help?"

"We're all set. Mom's baking a pie to send back for our dinner, so if the turkey blows up, we won't starve."

"So tomorrow night, we'll party."

"Yeah."

"Hope your gig goes well," I said as he got in. He gave me a little look.

"Yeah."

I found it depressing to say good-bye to my kids. Smokie and Keith twisted around in their car seats and waved like crazy out the back window as the Civic choked before speeding off toward the highway. I was all alone, and even though I'd been eager for the freedom that that offered, I felt miserable.

Back at the office, my loneliness was quickly buried in the pile of things that had to be done. I climbed the stairs to Whit's office and reported most of my conversation with Song. As soon as he heard about the necklace links in the silver box, he put in a call to Brannigan and left a message saying we would hold the story for twenty-four hours, but after that, unless Brannigan gave him a very good reason, we were going to print.

"Write it before you go home. And," he added, as I headed toward the door, "go to the Night Walk and finish that Asian response piece. If you need a translator, let me know, we'll try to dig someone up."

I thanked him, went down to my computer, put on my Walkman with an old Springsteen tape, and started writing. Feeling that the Asian piece suffered from not having a broad enough array of sources, I remembered Peter Albright's promise to set me up with Grandfather. The force was with me: He answered on the first ring.

"Oh, yes. I was about to call you," he said heartily. "He's agreed to meet you."

"Great. Tonight?"

"Oh, no. It's too late to arrange anything. It has to be on the hush. He's willing to talk, but he wants some protection."

"Whit prefers sources to be named."

"Why don't you hear what he has to say and then you can make up your mind about whether to use it."

"Okay. When can we get together?"

"Tomorrow morning?"

"What time?"

"Eleven."

"During the memorial service?"

"Yes. That way he won't be seen talking with a reporter."

"Will I need a translator?"

"I'm speaking at the service, but I can get you started. He has a bit of English."

I put my hand over the phone and called to Mark across the room. "Are you covering the memorial?" He nodded affirmatively. I agreed to meet Albright in his office in the morning. If I could get something definitive on the Khmer Rouge, it would be a coup.

The Asian Women's Night Walk was scheduled to start at the university near the Campus Center at eight. I suddenly remembered Stephen. I was supposed to meet him at five and here it was after six. I punched in his number and let the phone ring. No answer. I decided to run over to his place to see if I could catch him. I stole a glance at Mark, who was talking on the phone and tapping his keyboard. No need to bother him with this little errand.

Slipping out unnoticed, I felt a mild surge of triumph, which was instantly dampened by the sight of the blue Ford, idling under the lamplight on Main a few doors up from the *Eagle*. Standing beside it was Rok Boeng. I eased back behind the door and watched through the glass. A few minutes later, a car came by and double-parked next to the Ford. The passenger window went down and someone leaned out, asking if they intended to give up the parking space. Rok lit a cigarette and puffed on it, twisting sideways, and waved the car on.

I summoned my courage, zipped my parka, left the building, and headed up the sidewalk. Rok tossed the cigarette onto the street. As always, he wore better clothes than most of the Cambodians. In a dark topcoat and leather gloves, he moved with quick steps in my direction. As he approached, I nodded to him politely.

"Jum reap sua," I said, using the greeting I'd memorized for Bou Vuthy, leaving off the "honored monk." It was all the Khmer I knew.

He scowled.

My gaze took in the blue Ford, out of which descended a tough-looking Cambodian youth with a baggy suit and spiked hair. By American standards, he wasn't especially big, but he looked strong enough. He leaned against the fender and regarded me sullenly.

"You understan' my Engli'?" Rok asked suddenly. He dropped almost every final consonant and clipped his vowels short, but I understood well enough. I nodded, having a bit of trouble finding my voice.

He moved closer than was comfortable. I smelled his breath, which was ever so slightly sour.

"No understan'?"

"Yes. I understand. What do you want?"

"I ha' proble'. Maybe you help." He smiled, but it wasn't the typical smile of a foreigner. There was nothing beseeching or helpless about it.

I waited. He stepped even closer. I stepped back.

Rok's face puckered. He took another step toward me.

Stepping back again, I glanced around. The street was empty. The traffic light changed and two cars drove by. Across the great intersection near the Commons a couple emerged from an automobile but turned in the opposite direction toward the old cinema.

"Maybe you help," he said again.

"Tell me what you want."

"Song. She don' lissen."

His exaggerated Khmer features widened into a dark leer. I heard something that sounded like someone's audio system being played with the bass cranked up all the way, a throbbing, thudding pulse that seemed to shake the very streets, and then I realized it was my own blood pounding in my ears.

"I tell don' talk reporter. What she do?"

He glanced over at the spiky-headed youth, who moved forward.

I took another step back, edging, despite my desire to break free, toward the buildings lining Main. There was an alley there, leading back to a deserted parking lot.

The two of them pushed toward me. The youth shoved me roughly. I tried to skirt around him, but Rok blocked my path. I pushed him with my forearm and he forced his body into mine. I had to step backward to avoid being knocked down.

Both men continued to walk into me.

"Leave me alone," I said sharply. The police station was almost directly across the street. Surely someone would hear.

Rok put a hand out to keep the youth from shoving me harder. "You lee' Song? Okay?"

I was about to speak when I heard footsteps. "Zoë?"

The two men glanced up. I turned to see Mark jogging toward us. In half a second, he drew up beside me, putting a hand out toward Rok.

Rok slid his malevolent gaze toward Mark. I felt overwhelming relief. Mark towered over the stocky Cambodian. Even the punky youth seemed somewhat cowed.

Rok's attention turned back to me. He jutted out his lower jaw and said something abrupt and guttural that I didn't understand. The tearlike scar stood out in hideous relief, accentuated by the lamplight.

I attempted to speak, but words wouldn't come.

"Hey, buddy," said Mark in an easy tone. He took a step in front of me.

Rok signaled to the younger man. I could see now why Peter Albright had called Rok a thug. With a bully's obstinacy, he stood his ground and fixed a recalcitrant gaze on Mark. After a moment or two, he abruptly broke the connection and nodded to his companion. The two slowly backed off, ambled almost lazily to the blue Ford, and climbed into it. We watched the sleek sedan as it paused at the light, then turned left and rolled down past the Commons.

When it had disappeared, Mark turned to me and said, "What was that about?"

"Nothing."

Mark's skeptical stare seemed to penetrate my very skin. "Pretty intense bit of nothing."

"Listen. I'm glad you came by, but I'm fine now, and I want to go on alone." I felt a prickly shame at my inability to defend myself.

"I can't figure you, Szabo."

"Then don't try." I pulled away from him and moved down Main toward Stanhope.

"Where you going?"

"To see Stephen."

"I better tag along, don't you think?"

The air inside my lungs seemed to quiver as I released my breath in a puff of icy fog. "When are you going to get it into your thick head," I sputtered, "that I don't want your help?"

He said nothing. Just stood motionless. Then: "You think you're so smart, but you make some pretty dumb moves."

Despite the thudding bass drumming in my ears, my anger flared. "Why don't you go find sources of your own instead of trying to horn in on mine?"

Mark surveyed me for another few seconds. "Okay," he muttered after a tense moment, "have it your way."

Then he sauntered back toward the office. I watched him take the front steps two at a time and disappear inside the old building. I swallowed back the thickness that crept up from my gut.

At Stephen's house, the same disheveled woman I'd met the first occasion opened the door again, with the same indifference when I asked for Stephen. She barely glanced at me before moving back to her desk, covered with books and papers in the front parlor.

"What are you working on?" I asked.

"My thesis," she said mournfully.

"What's it about?"

"Spectacle in Hawthorne," she answered bleakly.

"*The Scarlet Letter*. Read it in high school."

"Try *The Marble Faun*."

"Sure thing." I didn't volunteer that Hunter Thompson was more my speed. "Is Stephen here?"

She nodded toward the stairs. "I think he's in his room. First door on the left."

After kicking off my boots, I climbed the maple staircase to a wide hallway lined with a faded oriental runner. The first door on the left was ajar and a light shone from within. I rapped on the door. Silence. I called softly, "Hello? Stephen?"

I heard a radio playing low.

I knocked again with no response. The force of my knocking pushed the door open slightly. I peeked in, seeing the edge of a wooden desk and a computer.

"Stephen?" I opened the door a bit wider. The room was empty. A navy and sky blue patchwork quilt covered the double bed. Windows stretched around the room on two sides, with bamboo shades rolled down. A green banker's lamp angled over a sheet of copy near the computer and flying toasters flitted across the screen. I went in, deciding to wait, figuring Stephen had gone to get a snack or something and would return. I perused the books on his shelves. You could learn a lot about a person this way, I'd discovered from my years of interviewing rock musicians, who inevitably had their own bios on their shelves.

Most of the books here were on Asian history. Some were on art. A volume on the psychology of rape victims stood on a shelf near the bed, along with essays on Japanese culture. One of the shelves was entirely filled with books on Buddhism. On the wall hung photos of Stephen and what appeared to be his family. There was a large photograph of Chram. Her dark eyes seemed to be weighted by sad knowing. Her generous mouth curved in an ambiguous half-smile, like the Mona Lisa. I had begun to feel as if she were a close friend.

"What am I overlooking?" I asked. Chram's eyes were somberly cast down. I followed their trajectory toward the desk and noticed the papers clipped to the wooden copy holder under the lamp. Checking the hallway and seeing no one, I went back in and quickly skimmed the pages. A glance told me that they seemed to be related to his thesis. I looked through them again. Nothing. For a few moments, I stared hard at the photo of Chram. Her eyes seemed fixed on the lamp. As I rummaged through a pile of books near the keyboard, my hand accidentally pushed the mouse. The toasters on the screen stopped flying and a checking account ledger appeared. Stephen, it seemed, had been in the midst of reconciling his bank statement when something had called him away. Feeling a bit guilty for perusing his financial records, I nonetheless glanced through the most recent transactions.

He was well-organized. Memos neatly indicated what each check was for: rent, phone, student fees, groceries. I found a check made out to Chram for fifty dollars. Not a huge sum. It had been written in November. If he'd been in the middle of reconciling, the check register should be around somewhere. Just when I was debating whether to peek in the top of the desk drawer, I spotted it. The edge of paper poking out of the heavy book on the desk. I couldn't read the title because it was in a foreign script, possibly Khmer. I opened the book and found an uncanceled check with no notation as to purpose. It was in the amount of $1,450 and was made out to Delstar, Inc.

The date on the check was December 19, the day Chram was murdered. The check appeared to have been crumpled and smoothed out. After studying it, I tucked it back in the thick book.

Still no sign of Stephen. I was investigating the collection of polished stones on his bureau when I inadvertently caught sight of the snapshot stuck in the mirror frame. The picture had been taken outdoors on a wide plaza in some large city. There were five people. Two were women—both Asian. Two of the men were white. One was tall and lanky with short brown hair. He looked familiar but I couldn't place him. The other was shorter and wore a military uniform. The third man was Asian, probably Cambodian. He wore a suit. Neither of the women were Chram. They both appeared young—in their early twenties I guessed. One had Chinese features that were vaguely reminiscent of Cecily Chen's. The other was extremely pretty. A man might have said beautiful. She appeared to be Cambodian, slim, delicate, and she was wearing lots of jewelry and an elegant sarong. I turned the picture over. There was no date.

I heard footsteps coming up the stairs, so I slipped the snapshot back in its place. When Stephen entered, I was in the middle of the room, facing the door. A glance at the computer informed me that the screen saver had reactivated, so that there was no trace of my snooping. "Oh, there you are!" I said. "Your roommate told me to wait for you here."

Stephen wore royal blue sweatpants, a gray Henley shirt, and a moss fleece vest. A muscle twitched in his cheek though his translucent eyes took me in amiably. "You're late," he said quietly. "I thought you'd changed your mind."

"I got tied up in an interview. I called, but there was no answer so I just took a chance and came over."

He closed his eyes and pinched his nose with two fingers, then sat down on his bed.

"Have a chair," he said.

"I just have a few loose ends to clear up. First, are you going to speak at the memorial service?"

"Yes."

"I heard some people objected to your participating."

"You heard right, but I'm speaking."

"How did that come about?"

"They can't stop me. Is that all?"

"How many times have you been questioned by the police?"

He winced. "Three."

"Have you hired a lawyer?"

"No."

I wanted to ask about the check, but I didn't have the nerve. "When was that picture of Chram taken?" I asked instead, indicating the one on the wall over the computer.

He sighed. "Last year."

"She had a very special quality."

He looked at the photo. Now his hand went to his forehead. "You finished?"

"She was worried about getting citizenship papers."

He said nothing.

I repeated the statement.

"What do you care about her citizenship?"

"You refused to marry her without those papers," I pressed, moving closer.

"What the—"

"You refused to marry her," I said, right in his face.

His jaw trembled and his fist clenched at his side.

"Why?" I asked.

His gaze went from me to the floor, then wandered, sadly I thought, toward the picture of Chram on the wall. He bowed his head, his hands creeping to his forehead again.

"So," I said, "you let Rok and Saw get their way. You let them break up the marriage."

He closed his eyes. I could hear his faint breath quaver. In a barely audible sigh, he whispered, "Yes."

"Rok broke up your marriage." I repeated, feeling as if the pieces were finally falling into place, but not understanding where it all was leading. "How? Did he threaten Chram?"

He spoke with self-loathing. "I did it," he finally said. "I broke it off."

"Why?"

Bitterness glittered in his beautiful eyes as they bored into me.

"Rok threatened *you*?"

He shook his head suddenly, maybe remembering he was talking to a reporter. I followed his gaze, which flicked inadvertently toward the little photo stuck in the edge of the mirror frame.

"Or was it something else?"

He shifted his gaze back to me with a hint of surprise.

"A little extracurricular activity?" I asked.

He caught my drift and sneered. "You're way off base."

"Am I really?"

A narcissistic light was kindled in the turquoise eyes, despite the hostility in his tightening muscles. "You reporters are always looking for smut."

"You know what they say, where there's smoke—"

"Look—"

"Perhaps your taste ran to older women. Always exotic, always Asian. Weren't they, Stephen? Was it Chram you wanted or just access to women through her?" I turned toward the mirror and pointed. "One of them?" I asked with a rush of insight. I took a step toward the bureau, but before I could reach the snapshot, he grabbed me by the arm and jerked me around.

I yanked free of his grasp. "Did she *beg*," I demanded, "or *threaten*? Was it a lover's quarrel that went too far?"

He put a trembling hand on my shoulder, clutching my sweater. "Get out," he whispered. "Get the hell out."

19

Though it didn't generate much news, I found the Night Walk moving. A few hundred women of all ages carried white banners and flashlights and wore white clothes. The ghostly throngs paraded along the dark streets, winding up from the Campus Center through the university grounds to East Street and down Stanhope into Greymont Center. I felt a tug, wanting to be with them, yet I was consigned to the role of impartial observer. The women were shouting out their right to walk alone safely, and after today I had no trouble relating to that sentiment.

I stood at the side of the road, the street lamps illuminating the snowbanks. The tiny flashlight beams bobbed against the black. When the march reached the Commons and Town Hall, I reluctantly tore myself away, crossing the street to the office, where I added some color to the Asian women story and flagged it for Whit. Mark, also working late, steadfastly ignored me. Now, with Song's secret discovery,

I held a key clue to the police investigation, which Mark knew nothing about. This fact should have given me a sense of triumph, but I felt strangely subdued. We worked without speaking. I needed quiet, I thought. It would be good to have a few hours at home alone to think things through.

I didn't relish walking home alone, not with the possibility of the blue Ford lurking under cover of night. However, I simply couldn't swallow my pride and ask Mark for a lift. Instead, I packed up my gear, shut down my computer, and ventured a breezy, "I'm out of here!"

"Night," Mark replied with professional distance.

I stopped for a long moment at the front door of the building, scanning the street outside for signs of idling automobiles or murky figures near lampposts, half expecting Mark to sidle up behind me and offer a ride, but he didn't. After a few seconds of indecision, I turned back. I hesitated by the pocket doors leading to the office shared by the reporters, then I resolutely continued down the hall and left by the rear.

At home, too restless to sleep, I turned on the television and watched the news, then music videos on MTV while I wrapped Christmas presents: the art supplies, pirate puzzle, Play-Doh extruder, and stamps for Keith; bunny puppet, baby doll, doctor kit, and bouncy ball for Smokie. Then I admired the soft sweater from the upscale men's shop. Deep blue wools were knit in an intricate pattern with streaks of wine mohair: Billy's colors. It had cost more than we'd agreed to spend, but I couldn't stand not giving him something extravagant. He so loved luxury. When I finished, the gifts, decorated in bright paper, metallic ribbon, and tiny ornaments from Wingate's, gleamed like precious jewels. I placed the two Cletha had given me for Smokie and Keith with all the rest under the fragrant tree.

Then, anxious about tomorrow's interview with Grandfather, I wrote out a short list of questions, but found myself fighting the impulse to call Billy's folks and check on the kids. Finally, I shut off the television. Still keyed up, I turned on the stereo and listened to "Fire." The song was on a Rhino CD I'd picked up in the $4.95 bin when I'd bought the B.B. King album for Billy, which I'd just wrapped.

I hadn't been able to get the old hit out of my head since hearing it on the radio the night I'd found the body. As soon as the drums and cymbal began that insinuating *chink a-chink a-chink*, I was transported back to my youth again. Seventeen and a rebel. That had been the year I'd shaved my head, cutting off what had been long golden hair. I'd also had the butterfly tattooed on my left buttock. I'd been Song's age. It had been the same year that the Khmer Rouge was overthrown by the Vietnamese and the reign of terror had come to an end. Even though my parents had opposed the war and I had no excuse for my ignorance, Cambodia hadn't registered high on my radar. I'd been more interested in driving my folks crazy, especially my mother, and in boys.

I had three boyfriends that year, all obsessively self-centered, which, to be fair, I was as well. None of them had a car, although one had a motorcycle, and we zoomed through the Manhattan canyons wearing snotty rich-kid attitudes even more outrageous than our S&M-style clothes. Another was a sensitive kid, who probably was gay but either didn't know or wasn't ready to admit it at the time. We'd talked about the theater and music, my two consuming passions. The last boyfriend, and the one who led to my complete estrangement from my mother, was a delinquent who'd dabbled in drugs. Probably he'd been an addict, although I'd been too naive to realize it. A virgin at the beginning of the year, I'd slept with them all by the end. I probably got less of a kick from the actual sex than from the idea that I was being slutty, which I thought was terrifically cool. The one with the motorcycle, who'd looked a little like Springsteen, had been a fairly good, if inexperienced, lover. Wanting to prove how bad I was, though, I spent a lot more time with the guy who did drugs and whose idea of good sex was having me do a striptease and go down on him. My mother was absolutely beside herself, especially when I moved into my friend's loft. And then she got sick. Liver cancer. It moved fast. We were into speed, violence, slam dancing, noise. Funny, how we sought out those things.

"I say I don't love you
But you know, I'm a liar
'Cause when we kiss
Oo—ooh—Fire."

I imagined Chram and Stephen. The attraction for her must have been the way the song described it, desire and fear. Or had she been like me? Using Stephen as a way to escape her family, especially her mother. Ly, Rok, and Saw must have been oppressively overbearing. I remembered what Peter Albright had said about Chram, that she had a temper, that the abuse went both ways. I could see her beating up Phroeng, even Ly. I tried to imagine the anger that being the victim of repeated abuse, rape, torture might have created. What did that do to a person? Especially when mixed with the normal teenage impulse to rebel?

I dozed off, the music playing over and over. Perhaps I dreamt. I don't know. I woke up groggy and exhausted, feeling horribly alone. I'd spent enough nights in the last few years without Billy that I was used to being without him, but my kids—I'd literally never spent an entire night away from them before.

I showered, dressed, and had a leisurely breakfast. I wanted to call Billy, but I didn't relish talking with his mom, who still hadn't forgiven me for leaving him last year and threatening divorce. Anyway, I told myself, he probably hadn't gotten in before four; he'd be asleep until noon.

I decided against jeans, since my schedule would be light. All I really had to do was the Grandfather interview, and Whit would put the paper to bed early. I wore a straight black skirt with a slit and a snug cream jersey with a shirred collar, taking extra time with my makeup, toning it down because I didn't want to scare off Grandfather. I threw my favorite teal coat over me, and then, realizing I had to walk all day, put on my boots rather than the screaming stiletto heels I wanted to wear. As a precaution, I left by the kitchen door and cut through the backyard to the next street so I wouldn't be seen.

Professor Albright, looking more rested in a handsome gray suit, his white hair combed and his complexion much rosier than the last time I'd seen him, greeted me at the door of his narrow office and followed me into the tight space.

Seated in the green vinyl armchair was a very old man with deep tan skin and thick steel-gray hair. Age lines ran from his nostrils to the corners of his wrinkled mouth. Despite deep bags, his eyes were round and astute. Around his neck, over threadbare shirt and pants, he wore a brocade Cambodian scarf, woven in shades of green, black, and gold.

As I studied him, I began to recognize him as the man I'd seen weeping on television, the one interviewed by Carolee Clark, who'd carried the bag of soda cans slung over his shoulder and whom I'd assumed was homeless. In this setting, his back to the window which overlooked the sprawling State University campus, he seemed more dignified.

He stood when I entered and put his palms together in a *sompeah*. I echoed the gesture. Then he gripped the arms of the chair, easing his body into it. Once seated he pushed his stiff leg down and I realized it was an artificial limb.

Catching me staring at the leg, he gave a shrug of gentle acquiescence to the will of the gods, revealing a scar on the inside of his palm.

"This is Grandfather," Albright said heartily, hovering over us. "The Khmer term is *Tah*. Tah Krem, Zoë Szabo, the reporter. Can I get you coffee or tea, Zoë?"

"No, thank you." I sat down and smiled at the old man. "Thank you for agreeing to speak to me. If it's all right, I'll start asking questions."

"Fine," said Tah Krem, nodding patiently.

Albright lingered by the file cabinets and sipped coffee.

"Mr. Krem, how long have you lived in Greymont?"

Albright chuckled. "*Tah*, Zoë. It's a form of address, instead of 'mister.'"

"I get it," I said with a quick smile. Tah Krem smiled also, seeming to understand.

"I been here one year." He grinned even more widely, his face becoming a tawny wreath of wrinkles. Behind the smile, his eyes scrutinized me carefully, sizing me up.

"Your English is very good," I said.

"Thank you."

"Where did you learn it?"

"I learn many language. I was waiter twenty year. In Phnom Penh. Best hotel. Many foreigner."

We both nodded and smiled. Albright took a sip of coffee and shuffled through his notes for his memorial service speech.

I asked Tah Krem how to spell his name. He told me.

"How long have you known the Touch family?"

"Long time," he said. He was missing two bottom teeth. The others were crooked and discolored. "In village before war. And at Site II, border camp. Bad people there."

Albright had already warned me, no tape. The man's accent was so thick, I couldn't have understood a recording anyway. When I had trouble deciphering his speech, I repeated what I thought he'd told me, and he would nod or correct me.

"The Khmer Rouge?" I asked.

"Today Khmer Rouge," he said with a shrewd grin, "tomorrow Khmer Blanche."

I smiled, and he saw that I understood.

"*Français*?" he asked. "You speak?"

"*Un peu*," I said. "A little."

He laughed, nodding eagerly. "*Moi aussi. Un peu.*"

I instantly liked the man. We connected. "We're going to get along fine," I told Albright.

"Good." Albright patted me on the shoulder encouragingly, whispering. "He's a character." To both of us he said, "I'm on in fifteen minutes, so if you'll excuse me." He made a *sompeah* to Tah Krem, who bowed. They spoke a few words in Khmer. Then Albright left, requesting me to pull the door shut when we left.

I asked about the Touches. Tah Krem described their early years as rice farmers in his home village.

"Did you know Prith Prahn?"

"Yes. In the camp. *Il était Khmer Rouge,*" he said, slipping into French. "*Tous le monde ne le savait que les Americains.*" He was Khmer Rouge. Everyone knew except the Americans.

So far that fact, though I'd suspected it, had eluded me. It had also escaped the notice of twenty or more journalists, the social welfare agencies, the police and immigration officials, Cletha Fair, and Detective Brannigan. Perhaps that was the reason Peter Albright had wanted Tah Krem to tell me. He couldn't bear to betray Cletha.

"How do you know Prith was Khmer Rouge? Wasn't he too young?" I asked in my bad high school French, when he was unable to understand my English. From that point on the conversation was mostly in French, with English counterpoint for clarification.

"No. Bad men in camp leave Prith alone. *Comprenez-vous?*"

I nodded.

"Hear rumors. Prith has friend. Big man Khmer Rouge. They leave him alone. Steal from others."

"Is it possible," I asked, "that the rumors weren't true?"

"*Oui, c'est possible,*" he admitted, and added philosophically, "What is possible? What is impossible? The only impossible thing is to tell the difference between the two."

I laughed in agreement when I deciphered the statement, which was delivered in French a good deal more comfortable than mine.

"Prith seems very unhappy," I said. "Maybe crazy?"

"Many people seem unhappy who are happy. Many seem insane who are sane."

"Are you saying Prith's craziness is an act?"

"No. I cannot judge who is sane and who is not." His broken teeth showed, jagged and discolored.

"Did Prith meet the Touches in Site II?"

"Maybe. I am not sure."

"Do you know anything about the one Touch brother who was Khmer Rouge?" I asked at last.

"Touch brother was Khmer Rouge?" He shrugged. "Yes, that is what some people say."

"Chram's older brother, who some say is dead, some say is alive."

Tah Krem blinked. *"Il y a un frére. Il y a une Khmer Rouge. Ce n'est pas la même chose."*

His voice was old and fuzzy, his words slurred, endings missing, with a Cambodian accent laid atop his French. Added to that was my untutored ear for the language. I asked three times, and he repeated the same phrase slowly, his hoarse voice growing louder each time.

"Une?" I asked at last, emphasizing the feminine ending.

"Oui. Une." One female.

"Une était Khmer Rouge."

He nodded quietly, his eyes watching me carefully.

"Not Song."

He shook his head.

"One of the daughters who died."

Again he shook his head.

"Chram?"

He nodded.

"How do you know?"

"People tell things to an old man. They seek comfort from the monk, but they come to me to confess."

"Were you in Phnom Penh when the Communists took over?"

"No," he said. "I fled to the mountains. I hid for two years. I lived with peasants farming rice. If anyone heard me speak French, I would be killed like that." He snapped his fingers, laughing so his discolored teeth showed, and he drew his index finger across his throat. "To tell the truth, in a way every Cambodian who survived was Khmer Rouge. We went along. It's like your witches in Salem. Only proof of innocence is death."

"Horrible," I murmured.

His eyes closed halfway. "The true horrors," he countered, "are the things for which no words exist."

"What did Chram tell you about her activities with the Khmer Rouge?"

"She collaborated. Many her age did. She lived with other teenagers, indoctrinated in the Communist philosophy. Angkor this, Angkor that. They wanted to recreate the great civilization of Angkor Wat, and to do it they believed they had to kill everything new."

All modern learning had to be wiped out, he explained, all technology. They wanted to go back to the old ways. But they destroyed the old ways, too.

One of Chram's sisters died because Chram caught her eating raw cabbage in a field. Chram went to the camp commander and told. Chram's sister was punished by being tied to stakes outside. No one was allowed to help her and she died. Chram pretended that someone else had told. She'd lied to her own family. When this happened, she saw the cruelty and mindlessness of those in control.

"Is it possible," I asked, "that someone here killed Chram to get revenge?"

Tah Krem nodded perceptively. "Revenge," he said. "We Cambodians call it *kum*. It's a disease for us, *kum*. One *kum* leads to another and another. A never-ending story. Like a poisonous snake biting its own tail."

It was the phrase Chram had used in her last meeting with Eleanor Kerr. I closed my notepad and studied the old man. Our eyes met and, across continents, time, and the extreme remoteness of his experience, we shared a moment of communion.

"One more story, Chram told me," he added gravely. "She herself committed murder."

I had just stood up and was preparing to leave when he said this.

"There was a woman. She found out something about this woman that would have resulted in an instant death. The woman gave her a necklace to keep her silent, but someone overheard and told. Chram's choice was to put the woman to death by her own hand or die herself."

I felt the blood drain from my face.

"You are shocked? This is nothing. *Il y a beaucoup de secrets ici.*" The bags below his eyes seemed to darken.

"Many secrets. Some are better forgotten. You understand? We Khmer people have made our way on rafts of dreadful secrets drifting down a river of death. It is our fate. We are survivors." He paused, his mouth stretching into a grimace.

"Have you told the police?"

"No police."

Our gazes linked.

"I have crossed many rivers. Rivers where the bones of my friends, lovers, children, and parents float thicker than fish in the rainy season. Let the dead keep their secrets."

"Don't you want Chram's murderer to be punished?"

"Life is punishment enough."

"The killer could strike again."

"One more death. *Ça ne fait rien*. This means nothing." He paused, grinning, his teeth gapped and black. He concluded in heavily accented English: "A drop in the bucket."

20

When I got back to the office, I sat thinking for a long time. Finally, I went upstairs and told Whit I had new information about the Khmer Rouge, the necklace, and a possible motive for Chram's murder.

"I'm worried about two things," I told him as I sat across his antique desk. "I can't vouch for the trustworthiness of my source. And if we publish anything about the necklace, it might endanger Song."

Whit stroked his lower lip with the back of his thumb. He stared out the bay window at the Town Hall across the street. "Call the Immigration and Naturalization Service. Find out the status of Chram's citizenship application."

"It's going to have to wait until Monday," I said, wondering if he'd forgotten it was Christmas Eve.

He looked up questioningly, then the realization came and he allowed his thin lips to approximate a smile.

"I'm leaving early," I continued. "Has there been

any word from the police about the murder weapon?"

"No, but we're very close to having enough to go to press with these new facts."

"According to people I've spoken with over the last couple of days, there are Khmer Rouge sympathizers here. Especially among the young. They think the terror has been exaggerated, and many of them blame the Vietnamese, who took over after Pol Pot."

"That's good. Can you write it by Monday? We'll give Brannigan some extra time with the necklace."

I hadn't told him about my visit to Stephen or the blue Ford. There were still a lot of loose ends I had to examine. I had to talk to the broker managing the property Chram had wanted to lease. I also intended to poke around during the funeral to find out what I could about Rok. Maybe I'd be able to sneak a glance at his papers. There might be something that would give me a hint as to the identity of the people in the snapshot I'd found at Stephen's or the significance of Delstar, Inc. Prith's name had not yet come up in my discussions with Whit, and I intended to hold it back until I had incontrovertible proof. I owed that much to Cletha.

"So, is Billy cooking the turkey?" Whit asked, making small talk as I gathered my notes.

"If he gets back from Boston in time. If not, he's promised his Mom's apple pie."

"You're lucky in love." There seemed to be a wistful undertone in Whit's voice. Aside from the fact that he was unmarried, I knew nothing about his personal life.

"We've had our ups and downs. Say," I added after a moment's pause, "you're welcome to have dinner with us. At least come by and have a drink when you finish here."

Whit seemed pleased at first, then enveloped himself in a blanket of New England reserve. "Oh, no. I have plans, but thank you."

"Rain check?"

He flushed, then said gruffly, "Well, all right."

"Whit?" I scolded. "This isn't the army. You're allowed to fraternize with the troops."

He actually chuckled. "You go home to that family of yours."

"Merry Christmas," I said.

"Same to you."

As I left I caught a glimpse of him tapping at his keyboard. Then he turned and stared out the window at the gray sky and dark clouds.

Keith tugged my arm after I hung up my coat. "Mommy, come decorate the tree."

Billy stood stage center before the fir that I'd left bare that morning, now dripping with tinsel and lights. The scent of evergreen, fresh popcorn, chestnuts, and wood smoke filled the air. Billy calmly issued instructions to Smokie, who teetered on tiptoe on a chair as she hung a glass bulb precariously close to the tip of a thin branch. She took her time, quite businesslike for her three years.

Keith's eyes danced with the season's magic. I felt a twinge of regret that my mother couldn't know these wonderful grandchildren. At seventeen, the life I was living now had been worlds away, as completely unimaginable for either me or my mother as life on an alien planet. I wondered for the first time what she would have thought. Of course, she would have been relieved that somehow I'd managed to avoid the worst pitfalls that just before her death I'd seemed headed for; yet, I remembered with a remnant of the old bitterness how impossible her expectations had been. She'd been the worst kind of artistic snob. Not long before she died, we'd had a surreal conversation about the men we'd each been involved with, and she bragged that every one of her lovers—and there'd been several before she'd met my father—had been at the top of his field. A third-rate rock star whose meager fame had been extinguished by changing fashions would not have seemed a worthy husband to her. And my career, the patchwork mishmash of freelancing and rock journalism, she would have found hopelessly low-brow. This latest craze of mine, the effort I was putting into smalltime news, would have merely baffled her.

I remembered again, with a stab of pain, that the day after tomorrow would be the anniversary of her death. I had a load of her artwork, arcane collage boxes on various surreal themes, and huge canvases that were somewhere in the no man's land between pop and abstract expressionism, in storage at a warehouse outside Sheffington. I still couldn't bear to look at them and had rebuffed Billy's suggestion that we hang a few of the boxes, which he actually liked.

As I watched Billy and the kids decorating the tree, I remembered my last moments with her. It had been a difficult death, a difficult time for me. I'd been so rebellious in the year before her illness, and her dying had left me with all that unresolved conflict. I supposed I'd always suffer from remorse that I hadn't been kinder and more generous in that final year of her life. I'd been headstrong and stubborn and I'd felt betrayed by her illness. Abandoned. I remembered the final kiss she'd given me, skeletal and weak in her hospital bed. Her cheeks had been pink from the blood transfusion and an injection of morphine that the nurses had given her so she would be at her best for our visit. Her lips, though, had been cold on mine; it was the only time I could remember her kissing me on the mouth. She'd gazed at me for several minutes, the tears welling up in her eyes, and she'd said, "Good-bye," as if she meant it forever.

When I'd left the hospital, there was a light snow falling on the city, and I fully expected to see her again. But I never did. Later that night, my father called me from her room and told me that a few minutes earlier "the spirit had flown."

"Mom!" Smokie hopped off the chair, jumping into my arms, interrupting my memory.

Keith and Billy moved toward me, Keith trying to climb into my arms and Billy holding me close. The four of us fell into an inclusive embrace.

"Family hug!" shouted Keith, climbing up and kissing my lips so hard that it hurt. "Mom, why are you crying?"

"Am I crying? I guess I'm happy to see you."

Keith wiped my tears with his gentle fingers and I laughed.

"Merry Christmas," Billy said, his eyes searching mine. There was no trace of the annoyance that had colored our moments together before he'd left for Boston. He seemed rested, energetic, almost bubbly. I cast my eyes toward the tree. There were piles of boxes arranged below it. *Oh, please,* I thought, *please let him not have spent too much money.*

We finished with the tree, packed the gifts we'd bought and made for Morgan, and went across the yard. Billy had returned from Boston at noon and the two of them had started the turkey, the aromas of which wafted through the parlor as it cooked. I made cranberry and orange relish and a huge salad. Billy mashed potatoes, Keith and Smokie's favorite food. After dinner I banged out carols on Morgan's old upright piano, with Smokie in my lap, playing the tunes an octave above me with one finger. Keith sang, Billy played lead on his acoustic steel string, and Morgan accompanied on accordion.

"Man," Billy said, "we should take this show on the road."

Morgan beamed blissfully and rapped out a blues riff on his accordion. Even Keith, the least musical one in the family, seemed cheered by the idea.

Finally, after more music and an exchange of gifts, our Christmas party was done. Billy and I packed the two sleepy children in our arms and carried them home. When we'd tucked them into bed, we went downstairs to fill the stockings. Billy's mom had made huge red flannel socks decorated with silver bells and green and white cut-outs, and embroidered the kids' names on them. She'd even sent a bag with candy and trinkets because she didn't trust me to get stocking stuffers. And though she'd been right—I'd forgotten all about that part of Christmas—I still resented her intrusion. A devout Catholic, she had not exactly welcomed the idea of having a half-Jewish daughter-in-law, and she was devastated when I refused to raise the kids in her religion. As a result, she treated me as the family heathen. Setting aside my resentful feelings toward my mother-in-law, I stuck oranges in the toes, and Billy pawed through the trinkets, sorting them for each stocking.

"How was Bonhomie's?"

"Great."

"You didn't have trouble following his charts?"

"Huh?"

"Harley's charts?"

"Oh. No."

"Harley's band must be pretty hot to get that gig."

Billy's chin tilted toward me, the dark eyes shaded. "Uh. Yeah, well, I—"

He wore a scarlet sweater that contrasted nicely with his black hair. I'd changed for the party into a shocking pink retro cocktail dress, low-cut with thin rhinestone straps. Our eyes tangled for a moment and went into a sultry kind of dance, as I became aware of the fact that tonight our colors clashed badly.

"I have a confession to make," he said.

"If you feel so guilty, why don't you take your hand off my knee?"

"Babe. This is good news."

"Yeah? How come you couldn't tell me before?"

"You want me to be honest?"

"Sure, give it a try."

"Because you've been so damn pissed at me, I feel like I'm walking on eggshells."

The remark stung, but I didn't answer it. I waited a couple seconds then said, "So, what's the confession?"

"I sent some songs to Vivi Cairo."

I knew of Cairo, though I'd never met her. She was an old acquaintance of Billy's, a diva with a voice like a heat-seeking missile and a talent for picking hits and influential lovers. She'd toured with the Stones and like them had outlasted most of her contemporaries, although her drug problems were legendary among rock cognoscenti.

"She's forming a new band. They played Bonhomie's last night to work out material. She asked me to sit in for a couple of sets."

I didn't say anything for a few minutes.

"You knew this several nights ago, didn't you?" I glanced down at the packages. "That's how come . . . all those gifts."

"She's cutting an album next month. In New York, not California. A couple of days' session work. She wants to record two of my songs." He paused, like a toreador taking a final tour of the ring before driving in the lance. "And she's asked me to do the tour."

Suddenly, I wished I weren't wearing the seductive pink dress and all the clown makeup. It was hard to muster gravitas while masquerading as a bimbo.

"So," he said. He got up and went to the kitchen and came back with two beers and two glasses—some special Irish brew one of his brothers had given him.

He opened one, poured a glass, making sure to angle it so a head wouldn't form, and pushed it toward me.

"You know, if this works out," he went on, after pouring a beer for himself, "if you still miss the fast lane, we could think about . . ."

"Moving?"

He shrugged and took a sip of his beer.

I picked up Smokie's stocking and listlessly began stuffing it. A tiny rabbit, the fur so soft. I stroked it.

"I thought you wanted to live in the country," I said. "Thought you wanted to get away from . . . the trappings . . . the temptations—"

"I did, *but*. Hell, Zoë, I'm going nuts here."

"Really?"

"It's different for you. You've got the paper, the interviews . . . the murder. All I'm doing is hanging out with the kids. Okay, I've enjoyed the songwriting."

"See. You weren't really writing when we were in LA. You've gotten so much more done here. I mean, isn't it great? You've sold two songs! Who knows, maybe one could be a hit. Somebody else will cover it. That's really exciting. So that's who you've been talking to on the phone."

"Yeah."

"Okay. Well, at least I wasn't paranoid."

He put a hand on my knee again, and I moved away. "Don't be that way," he said.

"How do you want me to be? All smiley and happy?"

"Yeah. That'd be nice."

A calm came over me. Words, sentences, paragraphs, subheadings started filling my mind. I debated whether to give them voice or just let fate have its ruthless way with me. I heard myself speaking.

"I could have stayed in New York with the kids. I had a job offer. You begged me on hands and knees to get back together. We'd go off and live happily ever after in the idyllic country. The rose-covered cottage. Now I've made the career change, got something going here at last . . . and then you come and say, 'Well, I really didn't mean it.' You're going on tour? Remember what happened the last time?"

"That's not going to happen again."

"Yeah, right."

I finished with Smokie's stocking and picked up Keith's. I was damned if I was going to cry. I got a Kleenex and blew my nose, just to ward off the impulse. I stood up and hung the stockings on the hooks Billy had screwed into the mantle.

"The funeral is tomorrow," I said.

"Yeah?"

"I've got to cover it."

"The paper said it was going to be a private family affair."

"They don't want the whole town showing up. The Touches are overwhelmed as it is, but every reporter who's been on this story will be there. I can't miss it."

"What time?"

"Around noon."

"Noon?"

"You have a problem with that?"

His eyes targeted on me slyly. "You're gorgeous."

"What's on your mind? Sex? Personally, I'd rather eat nails."

"I take it that means you don't want me to go on tour."

"No."

"Well, that's clear."

I sat down and put my head in my hands. I knew Christmas was bad luck. My head pounded. My gut felt as if somebody'd reached in and pulled out my insides.

"Listen," Billy said, "let's not make any decisions. I told her I'd sleep on it."

I nodded numbly. I was thinking about the kids. They'd been so happy when Billy had come back, so confident and secure since we'd moved. They were getting settled in here. Keith had friends in kindergarten. The school was wonderful. Smokie loved her preschool. They loved the big yard and their swing set. This was not my rock 'n' roll dream. We were far from the glitter, the stagelights, the glamour. But I had to face reality: The fantasy just hadn't worked. I didn't want to do to my kids what my parents had done to me. I didn't want them to have to grow up in the rarefied atmosphere of fame.

Billy moved to the couch where I was sitting. He turned my face toward his, breath on my lips. His eyes were crinkled, with delicate crows' feet at the corners, a mark of his past. I remembered the first time I'd seen him, in concert before the interview where we'd met. Even then his magnetism was something I couldn't withstand. His fingers worked a subtle magic as he loosened the strap of my dress. He pressed closer with a sudden sob, heedless of my weak attempts to resist.

If Santa and his reindeer had landed on the roof with clattering hooves and commotion, if the red-suited elf had made it down the chimney, somehow managed to avoid the hot embers in the fireplace and left heaps of glimmering gifts nearby under the tree, Billy and I wouldn't have noticed.

The family had gathered downstairs by seven A.M. Enough time, I thought, as I watched Keith and Smokie eagerly picking out and unwrapping presents. Billy was sheepish and loving. Our disagreement had been delayed by the intricate lambada our bodies had performed, but it had not been resolved. I wavered between empathy and resentment, between the joy of being loved and the impossible demands of that love.

We went through the rituals of exclaiming at the gifts, tearing open all the packages that only a few days before had been so carefully wrapped. Grandma and Grandpa Harp's gifts were a hit. Smokie adored the new unmarked doll, dressed in billowing tiers of organdy and lace, and Keith enthusiastically pieced together the Playmobil pirate ship I hadn't been able to buy him myself. Billy put on the B.B. King when he opened the package and seemed almost teary when he unwrapped the extravagant sweater.

I opened his present. "What in the heck?"

"This could save your life." He demonstrated the black cellular flip phone. "Now, if you're late, you can let us know—wherever you are. And if you ever find yourself in a sticky position, you can call for help. I had it activated yesterday."

"We can't afford it," I objected.

"You never know," Billy insisted. "Someday you may be very happy to have this. I got a small one so it can fit in a pocket."

By the time I had to leave, Smokie had settled down with the doctor kit and was gleefully administering a shot to Grandma Harp's fashion doll, under the watchful eye of her father. Keith was spread out all over the floor with his art stuff drawing pictures of squirrels, foxes, and snow sprites. I wondered who would be at the funeral, if the murderer would show, and who it might be. And then my mind wandered back to another funeral that had occurred fourteen years earlier. A wave of pain engulfed me as I remembered the walks my father and I had taken so many times during the last months of my mother's life. We'd stroll across the park from Mt. Sinai on Fifth Avenue to our apartment on Central Park West. One day, near the end, they'd operated. My father and I sat together in the lounge throughout the long, four-hour ordeal, waiting for word. Later, when we began our familiar journey, my father had turned to me and said, "I could have sworn I saw your mother come into the room, look at us, and then turn and walk away." I didn't tell him, but I'd felt exactly the same thing.

That qualified as a ghost. I tried to imagine what Song might be feeling with that altar full of family ghosts, watching, waiting, listening, hearing the secrets of today, and knowing, though not telling, all the secrets of the decades leading to the destruction of their native land. Song and I had more in common that I'd realized: Neither of us could ever go home. We were stuck with having to fashion whatever comfort we could out of broken promises, fragmented memories, and improvised dreams.

21

Uncle Rok's scarred face registered a grim scowl as he opened the door. I made a *sompeah*. He glowered, but finally stepped back and let me enter.

Around the room I saw many Cambodians in white, which was the traditional color for funerals. The women wore sarongs, blouses, and shawls. The men wore shirts, slacks, and thrift-shop sweaters. The room had been emptied of furniture, except for the bureau with the altar. Next to it was a long folding table against the wall. Covered with a white cloth, it was heaped with offerings: plastic flowers, a few real chrysanthemums, fruit, cigarettes, betel chew, paper money for the dead, grains of rice.

In a corner, conspicuous in dark suits and shoes, stood Brannigan and his lieutenant. Song's parents weren't in view, nor was she. A TV crew discussed wiring and lighting, while video lights went on and off. I approached the altar and casually studied the photographs. As far as I could tell, no one in the pictures resembled the people in the snapshot I'd found in Stephen's mirror.

I went upstairs and rapped lightly on Song's open door. In the midst of an argument with Aunt Saw, Song barely nodded hello. About a third of her hair had been chopped off to just below her ears. Saw picked up the scissors with her one hand, the missing arm hidden by a dangling sleeve. Song's hand went up to ward off the shears. Her words were Khmer, short and heavily inflected.

Saw shook her head, speaking fast.

They kept arguing about *soh*, the older woman gesticulating and frowning. Finally, Song turned to me.

"She wants to use the razor on my hair. I just want to cut. She says it will be a disgrace if I don't shave. What do you think I should do, Zoë?"

Saw squinted at me recalcitrantly. In halting English she insisted, "We Cambodian do thi' way." She made a cutting motion with her hand. *"Kat soh."*

The argument continued until Saw finally relented. Song finished cutting off her hair in jagged bunches. When she finally looked in the mirror, she let out a soft moan. She touched her hair tenderly, mourning for the locks that had fallen on the floor below her, while Saw unsentimentally swept them up with a piece of cardboard and a dust brush.

Ly opened the door. Her eyes were ringed by deep circles and her mouth was puckered at the corners. She wore a baggy off-white sarong, a tight bodice, and long tunic. With her shaven head, she looked almost like a man, except for the silver scarf which hung loosely around her neck. She barely noticed me, speaking in brief popping syllables to Song and then to Aunt Saw.

"She says I shouldn't have cut my hair," Song translated. "She says the ghost of Chram won't rest no matter what. My aunt is trying to make her calm."

The two older women exchanged a few words, which were interrupted by a gong ringing through the tiny duplex. Song grabbed her shawl and put it over her head, trying to hide her shorn hair, and we went down to join the services.

A group of musicians sat cross-legged in the dining alcove, playing gongs and drums. Carolee Clark spoke into a microphone, preparing a segment for the evening news. She looked as if her feet were killing her and she wanted to be anywhere but in this dingy apartment. The place had filled with people. I recognized local ministers, a rabbi, some university people, and the helping community. Peter Albright and his wife entered and joined Eleanor Kerr and Cletha, who clustered together in a tight bunch. Prith was not there. So far, neither was Cecily Chen, although I spotted Sradanny and Malis. I tried to catch Cletha's eye, but she steadfastly avoided looking in my direction. Reporters milled through the crowd, trying to find English-speaking Cambodians for interviews. Phroeng was surrounded by a large crew, all with notepads and microphones. A well-dressed Cambodian man translated lucidly.

"Song," I whispered.

She turned. "What?"

"I need your help."

She frowned. "Now?"

I nodded toward the stairway, and she followed me up to the second-floor hall.

"What do you want?" she whispered when we were alone.

"Do you have the key to Rok's place?"

"Don't be crazy."

"I'm serious. I found something the other day at Stephen's. I want to check if any of Rok's records might clarify it."

"What?"

"I'm not sure. There was a picture. There were some Cambodians in it. Maybe I can find something similar at Rok's."

"It's impossible."

"No, it's simple. While everyone's marching to town, I can slip into his place and look around. I'll have plenty of time before anyone gets back. All I need is the key."

She looked up at the ceiling and sighed.

"Do you know where there's a key?"

She thought for a few moments, then gazed at me with foreboding. "My mother keeps one in the kitchen."

"Where?"

"In a drawer."

"Which one?"

"The top one near the stove."

"What number is Rok's apartment?"

"Fourteen. Zoë . . . if he finds you—"

"Let's go down to the kitchen. It will probably be less obvious for you to get the key."

"Yes. I know which one it is."

She went downstairs and I followed a few minutes later.

The talking hushed almost all at once. People pushed back to make way for the monk, Bou Vuthy, small and shriveled in his saffron robe and heavy cloak. The entire party focused on him as he quietly approached a wooden pallet that two men had brought in and placed before him. He circled it three times. A silence fell over the room and the ceremony began.

In single file came a line of Buddhist nuns with shaven heads and long white garments. They sat in a row against the wall. Auntie Saw and a few other women offered them a bit of food. As they moved among the nuns, the women *sompeahed*, even Saw, holding up one hand against an imaginary one.

The family members bowed to Bou Vuthy, and he spoke to each one individually. The video lights shed a harsh white glare upon the ceremony. Phroeng and Ly approached the monk and the three spoke. Ly gave a long cry. Chatter rose among the women coming now to comfort her. Song stood a bit apart.

The litter at the center was lifted by four men in cheap suits. Covered with flowers, the litter displayed a blown-up formal photograph of Chram. Wearing a thin orange sweater and pearls, hair done in long waves down her back, she looked vibrantly alive. The flat, somewhat masculine face struck me differently now than it had a few days ago. In the dark eyes, instead of fear and sadness, I detected defiance tinged with shame. I scoured the room for Stephen Giles, but couldn't find him.

The monks, nuns, and guests chanted. The sad, eerie music—*chlawng kaek* Song called it—rose in volume. The singer shouted plaintively through a mike wired so poorly that the sound kept breaking into static.

Just as the procession moved out into the courtyard of the townhouse complex, I felt a hand on mine. I turned and saw Song. She signaled me not to speak. A small metal object was pressed into my hand. My fingers ran against the sharp outlines of a key. Outside were crowds of Cambodians and other town dwellers. We waited as people put on coats and shoes and drifted out into the frigid Christmas afternoon.

"We're going to walk to the Commons," she murmured to me. "Then we come back for a ceremony at the temple. It will be a long time, but be careful. Rok has spies."

As she blended into the procession, I tried to melt into the crowd of onlookers before leaving the group. When the parade receded out of sight, I pulled behind some shrubs and sneaked back to the building. Number fourteen was at the opposite end of the row of townhouses from Song's apartment. Parked not far from the door was the blue Ford. I didn't see anyone near the car, or near Rok's place, but a group of people were clustered at the end of the drive where the funeral parade had exited onto the street.

I walked slowly toward number fourteen and passed it. I could see no sign of anybody watching. Had all Rok's men gone with the procession? I slowly ambled back toward his door. I rang the bell. No answer. I rang again. When I didn't get an answer the second time, I slipped the key into the lock. The door opened, and I moved quickly inside. It took ten minutes of harried searching before I found a file cabinet in an upstairs room. I pulled at a drawer. Locked. I went to the cheap fiberboard desk near the window and looked in the top drawer for a key. Although I didn't find one, my hand fell on a few legal sheets held together with a large clip. They were handwritten, in Khmer, a frilly alphabet, decorative, and totally illegible. However, buried in the back of the bunch I found a printed form in English. It seemed to be a lease. Two names were typed: Delstar, Inc. and Saw Boeng. I tucked the papers into my coat, holding them against my chest, and closed the drawer.

Downstairs, I examined the family altar. If any of the people pictured were the same as the Cambodians in the old snapshot I'd seen at Stephen's, I certainly couldn't recognize them. Luckily, I happened to glance out the window near the door before leaving. Two Cambodian men, one the youth with the spiked hair, were chatting next to the blue Ford.

Letting myself out the back, I cut through the woods in a circuitous path to my Civic, which I'd parked several blocks away. I jumped into the car, drove to the newspaper office, which was totally deserted, copied the papers, jammed the copies in my desk drawer, and locked it. With my heart racing, the original papers stuffed inside my coat, I drove back to the Normandy apartment complex. The two men still stood guard in front of Rok's apartment. Without a moment's hesitation, I sped out of the complex and parked a few blocks away. Making sure I hadn't been followed, I jogged back through the woods.

I was about to approach the rear of number fourteen when I heard someone come up behind me.

"What brings you here, Ms. Szabo?"

I spun around and caught my breath, finding myself inches from Brannigan. I shoved the key back into my pocket and clasped the papers against my chest.

Brannigan looked as if he could use a good night's sleep. He scrutinized me.

"I was looking for you, Detective."

"Why?"

"I hear you've found the murder weapon."

His face cracked into an irritable frown. "I've got uniformed men sifting every dumpster in the four-county area. I've got frogmen in the river. If it's been disposed of, we'll find it." He glared at me suspiciously. Rok's papers crinkled under my coat as I clamped my arm against my chest to keep them from slipping.

"Do yourself a favor," he added, eyes narrowing.

"What?" I asked, wide-eyed as a Valley Girl.

"You find anything that looks even the slightest bit incriminating, tell us about it."

I pushed out my chin. "In exchange for an exclusive on the arrest?"

"Don't get smart."

"Is that a threat?"

"Call it a friendly suggestion. You find murder investigations interesting? Go to police school. Get yourself a badge. This is not a game, Szabo. You get a shade too close, and next thing you know we'll be scraping your brains off the asphalt in some alley."

His words had the desired effect. "I get the point."

He studied me, not unpleasantly, and said, "Good."

My thoughts were interrupted by the sound of the marchers returning down the main road. They'd arrived at Bou Vuthy's temple when I joined them. I found a spot next to Peter Albright and his wife. Cletha, who was with them, nodded to me curtly.

"I've been following your stories," she said, with a hint of disapproval in her voice.

I felt guilty, knowing that the family violence stories were at the heart of her censuring gaze. Cletha had standards few could live up to, especially a journalist with the obligations to tell both sides of an issue, not simply the side she thought was right.

"How's Prith holding up?" I asked.

She pressed her lips. "That piece on Hal Gaffney was full of inaccuracies. Not your usual careful style."

I didn't say what sprang first to mind, that I'd had to share the byline. If she didn't appreciate what I'd done to spare her foster son, well, there was nothing I could say to raise myself in her eyes. I felt our friendship, based on her relationship with my parents, slipping away. Then I thought of Tah Krem. Of Prith's collaboration with the Khmer Rouge. Of the fragment of necklace. And the dead woman, killed by Chram so long ago in the death camp. I wondered if I'd done the right thing, not telling Whit . . . or Brannigan. The papers rustled against my chest, and I wondered how to get them back.

Peter Albright put his arm around Cletha. "Dear, she's doing her job." He gave me a supportive wink.

We followed the litter around the building three times. It was decorated with a huge Hmong, a bird symbol, which Peter explained symbolized the flight of the soul.

"They believe in reincarnation," Peter said as we squeezed together near the door to the monk's temple room. We watched the family carry in offerings of flowers, fruit, and cigarettes. Song caught my eye momentarily and smiled with relief.

"Mixed in with the Buddhist ritual is traditional folklore and magic," Peter continued. "Sometimes it's hard to separate the two. The point of the ceremony is to make it easier for the spirit to stop wandering, to find a place to rest."

Cletha stood beside us, a frown of concern never entirely leaving her face.

"Song didn't shave her head," she whispered to Peter.

I noticed Brannigan's men posted at the corridor. A voice blared through the boom box, chanting a psalm in Khmer called *smode*, Peter told me, about traveling alone through the jungle of death and rebirth.

A group of young men entered. They wore fashionably baggy pants, short, spiked hair, and loose jackets. Behind them came Stephen Giles. Dressed in a traditional Khmer costume, loose white pants, jacket, and shawl, he seemed as remote as he had the afternoon I'd first interviewed him. His head had been shaved, so the beautiful blond hair was gone, but his turquoise eyes were as icily compelling as ever.

A hush fell over the crowd.

The punky Khmer boys quieted and the boom box music broke into a haze of static. As Stephen strode deliberately into the monk's temple room, reporters rushed about and video cameras pointed toward him.

He approached the golden flowered litter, fell on his knees, and bowed prone before Bou Vuthy. The monk made a tidy, disdainful *sompeah*.

Stephen spoke in Khmer.

The monk responded.

"What's he saying?"

"I can't make it out," said Cletha, who'd softened toward me slightly.

"He's making the traditional show of supplication and gratitude to the monk," Peter informed us. "The monk is blessing him."

Stephen placed a bouquet of pink gladiolus on the bier and again fell at the monk's feet.

A sudden cry rang out.

To the left of the monk, behind the row of white-robed nuns, a struggle ensued. The TV lights illuminated the back corner, where four men held a flailing Phroeng.

"Hai! Hai!" Phroeng shouted, followed by a rush of language.

The men shouted. Ly looked dazedly toward the group.

"He's shouting that a four-legged animal has just entered and must be slaughtered," Peter whispered.

The monk moved toward Phroeng and put a holy hand on him. Behind, Brannigan's men closed around. Phroeng calmed momentarily. But Stephen went to him and said something in Khmer.

"Murderer!" Phroeng shouted in English. His face was bright as a laser, the beads of sweat covering his forehead lit with a drunken flush. "You not welcome at her funeral!"

There were catcalls from the crowd. Phroeng was not taken seriously. Stephen knelt, making a sign of supplication toward Phroeng. People murmured approvingly.

"He's asking Phroeng to accept him as a son and daughter," Peter whispered.

"Why?"

"To calm the old man down."

But Phroeng cried out in anguish and spat on Stephen's freshly shaven scalp.

People shouted.

"They're saying he's bewitched," said Cletha.

"More like 'inhabited by a ghost,'" Peter corrected her.

The monk held out his palms, trying to quiet the crowd. He lectured, and they listened. I heard the teenagers snickering.

"He says the suffering on earth is heavy. The path of *metta* is the only way."

"What's *metta*?"

Peter Albright took a noisy breath, raised a furry white eyebrow, and in his most professorial tone uttered one word: "Forgiveness."

As the crowd dwindled, I hung around waiting to catch Song alone. So far she'd been surrounded by reporters, and either Rok or Saw stood steadfastly beside her. Every time I approached, they would watch me like hawks.

Unable to get close to her, I asked people at the fringes of the crowd about the Khmer Rouge in the US. Once one started, others added their own tales. Two older women told me about a gang of kids who persistently referred to themselves as Khmer Rouge. A man mentioned a newspaper in Lowell that openly advocated their return to power. And the ESL teacher at the high school told me that many kids in his class openly disputed tales of Pol Pot's genocide. "Some of the older people are in a state of denial," he told me. "They don't want to believe that Cambodians could do this to their own people, so they blame the Vietnamese. They push away their memories and substitute comforting lies."

The afternoon faded into twilight. We'd moved to the Touch apartment. Song was still guarded by family, and I wandered about the place, wondering what to do. Finally, I went into the kitchen, having decided to put the key back in the drawer since there seemed to be no way to return the papers. To my dismay, I found Saw at the stove, stirring a huge pot of curry. "Come. Eat. You hungry?"

I nodded. "Thank you."

She ladled curry and rice into a small plastic bowl. "You want beer?"

"Oh, no thanks."

"Soda?"

"All right."

A leaden ball formed in my throat.

"Very sad these things," she said.

Again I nodded. "Yes."

"I get soda," she said.

I reached in my pocket and waited for her to leave the room. In the five seconds she was gone onto the back porch to dig a soda out of the cooler, I slid next to the drawer near the stove, pulled it open a crack, and slipped in the key.

22

I left Song's apartment and drove into town, wishing I could read Khmer, wishing Billy hadn't gotten the tour offer from rock diva Vivi Cairo. With an old Springsteen tape blaring, I drove along, grooving on the smooth baritone, the heavy rock beat, the earnest, depressed lyrics of tawdry working class lives, the poetry of crushed illusions and illicit hungers. Usually, these songs seemed far removed from my own life, but tonight the words mirrored my feelings. I didn't want to go home. I didn't want to face the stormy argument Billy and I were bound to have.

I didn't want to be the one who said no and yet I feared the future might be a repeat of the past: the long months alone with the kids while he toured, the phone calls, the yearning, the things that weren't said, the warning signs, phone calls getting later and more infrequent, the slurred words or the wild, giddy, nervous banter, and then . . . the call from the hospital or a band mate.

Springsteen was singing. Not knowing where else to go, I headed toward the office, driving in the dark to the pounding rhythm of "Born in the USA." The song faded into "Hungry Heart." I listened to the entire side, and then turned the music down and picked up the cell phone. Billy answered on the second ring, his voice full of emotion.

I told him I was on the way to the office to write up the funeral story, then I'd be home.

"Don't stay away too long."

"I won't."

"Because we need to talk."

"Yes," I said after a pause, dreading the words I might feel compelled to say.

I played the Springsteen tape while I wrote. First I tapped out a few inches on the funeral, highlighting the explosive scene between Stephen and Phroeng. Then, inexorably drawn to the mystery of Chram's past, I began a story on the Khmer Rouge. With testimony from the Cambodians at the funeral, Tah Krem, Peter Albright, and Song, there seemed to be enough. I literally lost track of time as the Springsteen tape continuously replayed thanks to autoreverse. My subconscious traced the alternating rhythms of my smoky tango with Billy while my conscious mind attacked the keyboard, writing what I hoped would be one of the last articles on the murder.

As I was putting away my Walkman, the door opened. Whit stood there, in a sweater and tie. He stared at me, quiet and somewhat distracted, like an aimless ghost. Sometimes I wondered if he had any personal life at all. Though I'd known him only the eight months I'd worked at the *Eagle*, it seemed odd that he'd never mentioned friends or even hobbies outside the paper.

"Oh, Zoë. I thought we might have burglars."

"No such luck." I grinned. "Merry Christmas!"

"Did you have a good dinner?"

"Scrumptious. You should have stopped by."

"Yes," he said. "Maybe I should have."

I showed him the stories I'd just logged.

"Do you have a name and address for this Tah Krem?" he asked when he finished reading.

"Yes."

He nodded thoughtfully. "This links the Khmer Rouge with the necklace Song found. I think we're ready to go to print. Call Brannigan and get an official statement."

My mind went immediately to Prith and Cletha. I hadn't included him by name in the story, but I'd referred to someone of his description. I took a breath and tried to organize my thoughts, hoping I could hold him off, even if only for a day. "I have more information, but I haven't had time to go through it."

"Who's your source?"

"Well, I've . . . some papers have been brought to my attention."

"Papers?"

Whit studied me, frowning. For a long while he said nothing, then he picked up the phone.

"Detective Brannigan," he said, then waited, not looking at me. "I'll hold. Tell him it's Whit Smythe at the *Eagle*." After a short exchange with Brannigan, Whit handed me the phone. "Ask him about the Khmer Rouge. We can hold off on the necklace for a day or two."

"What's this all about, Szabo?" Brannigan's voice had a harsh edge.

I read the text that referred to Khmer Rouge activity in the area and possible involvement in the murder. "Do you have any comment?"

"*What*?" he sputtered. "What the hell is this about? Didn't I warn you this afternoon?"

I held onto the desk. "Is there a comment? Whit wants to publish in tomorrow's paper, so if you have any—"

"There's no connection," he spat angrily. "It's absolutely absurd. Off the record, I want you in here with any information you might have. And if you don't come of your own accord, I'm going to slap you with a subpoena for your notes."

He slammed down the phone. I looked at Whit. "He says it's absurd. Off the record, he's going to subpoena my notes."

Whit raised his eyebrows. "Really?"

I nodded shakily. In rock journalism, no one ever threatens to subpoena your notes. I was a long way from Oz, but it didn't feel like Kansas either.

Whit thought about it, then shook his head. "He's bullying you. He won't do it."

I sat down, wondering how I'd allowed myself to

become entangled in all this. What I had to do was get rid of those damned papers of Rok's.

"I've promised so many people I'd protect their identity," I said forlornly.

"Do you have any idea who might have killed her?"

I shook my head, still unwilling to betray Cletha and name Prith, although ever since I'd heard Tah Krem's story I'd become increasingly convinced that Prith must have done it. But then, of course, if Rok knew of Chram's Khmer Rouge connection, he might have blackmailed her. Maybe that was why she'd cut off the engagement to Stephen. What if she'd lured Rok to the parking lot and attempted to kill him?

Whit sighed. "Let's go on the theory that Brannigan's bluffing. We've got a few days before he can do much. We'll print this piece tomorrow. Find out more about the necklace and firm up your sources. I'd like to run that story Tuesday. If we wait too long, someone else is likely to beat us into print."

I nodded.

We went over the story with a fine-tooth comb. He wanted independent confirmation of Chram's collaboration with the Khmer Rouge, which he insisted on including. I called Peter Albright, but couldn't reach him. I tried Cecily Chen, but her line was busy. Finally, I reached Eleanor Kerr.

"Did Chram ever tell you," I asked as delicately as I could, "about things she did in the labor camp that she felt guilty about?"

"Are you thinking of something in particular?"

"I've heard rumors about the Khmer Rouge."

"Like you, I don't want to say anything that might not be true, but I sensed she felt guilt over her sister's death. She died from exposure, and none of them were allowed to go near her while it was happening. And the last time I saw her she really was terrified about her citizenship. Even though at that point it was a fait accompli. All the papers had been sent. She'd passed the test. But she was so anxious."

"Go on."

"She was a strong-willed person. Driven. I did feel there was something she was trying to escape."

"Is there anything more you can tell me about her relationship with Prith?"

"No. I've told you all I can remember." She was quiet for a moment. "You might try Professor Chen. She spent quite a lot of time with Prith this fall, as did Stephen."

"Stephen?"

"Yes. Cletha's had a hard time with Prith. He's had episodes bordering on psychosis. When Cletha couldn't understand his outbursts, at different times Cecily, Peter, and Stephen went to the house and tried to calm him."

I remembered how neatly Cecily Chen had avoided having me interview her alone. She'd refused to answer questions over the phone and when I'd finally pinned her down to the interview, she'd arranged a group meeting where she'd said very little.

"We can go with this," Whit said, perusing the article on screen for the umpteenth time. "We have a few people on the record—the ESL teacher and the Cambodian housewives. Your anonymous sources corroborate each other." He met my gaze. "Of course, if you dig up anything more definite . . ." His eyebrows shot way up.

"I'll see what I can do."

He squinted at me. "Whatever it is, keep it legal."

"Sure thing, boss."

He scribbled on a piece of paper. "If I'm not here, you can reach me at this number."

After Whit went upstairs, I took the copies I'd made of Rok's papers, folded them, and put them in my purse with Whit's private number. Then I went to the kitchen, took an old carton of milk, and rinsed it out. I rolled up the originals, put them in the carton, wrote "Whit" on it, and placed it back in the refrigerator.

The night was dark, the wind had picked up slightly, and the temperature had fallen. My coat, which I'd worn to the funeral, was not heavy, but I decided to walk. I didn't have far to go.

It was about eight when I reached Cecily Chen's apartment. Getting no answer, despite the fact that there was a light in the upstairs window, I rang the bell repeatedly. Finally, thinking she might still be on the phone, I tried the door and found it slightly ajar.

"Professor Chen?" I called. I cracked the door. The

living room was dark, but a light beckoned from the kitchen. Canned TV laughter echoed in faint, intermittent bursts.

"Professor Chen?"

I stepped inside.

"Hello?" I called.

Other than the sitcom, the house was quiet. Maybe she'd gone out to a neighbor's and left the television on. Maybe she was on the computer and didn't hear me knocking. That could account for the busy phone line. I went to the foot of the stairs, where a beautiful red and gold Chinese fan adorned the wall.

"Professor Chen?" I shouted.

I thought I heard a sound toward the back of the house. "Oh, there you are. I'm sorry, the door was open so I—"

I entered the kitchen and looked around. Immaculate, the large room had been done in black and natural wood. Shiny counters, refrigerator, stove, and dishwasher were nearly new, all black, the cabinets smooth and modern in cherry wood. Matte charcoal tile covered the expansive floor. The muted blue-gray walls were decorated with gold-framed posters of calligraphy in black and white. In a corner, specially built to hold it, was a small television with what looked like "America's Funniest Home Videos" showing.

In a chair facing the TV screen sat Cecily Chen. Her head slumped forward, as if she were blind drunk. Her eyes bulged in an unpleasant stare, her arms were pinned behind her, and a sticky reddish brown substance dripped across her chest onto her lap and into a thick pool on the tiles under her seat. On the floor in front of her lay a silver machete with an inlaid ivory handle.

23

The headline in Monday's paper ran, ASIAN PROFESSOR KILLED, POLICE FOCUS ON KHMER ROUGE.

"Popular professor of Asian studies and crusader for Asian women's rights, Cecily Chen was found brutally murdered tonight, less than twenty-four hours after leading a march protesting violence against women."

I dictated the lead to Whit over the phone as I waited for the police to tell me I could go. Brannigan made me promise not to describe the long knife found at Cecily's feet.

"It may not be the murder weapon," he confided. "Only tests will tell that for sure."

"Will you give me an exclusive on the arrest," I asked, "if I hold back that information?"

Brannigan shot me a searingly hostile glare, but eventually relented. "I can't make any promises, but I'll consider it."

What I didn't tell him, though I realized he was

thinking the same thing, was that the weapon lying there on the gray tile reminded me of another one I'd seen. My mind slipped back to Stephen hissing *"Get out."* And the ornate weapons on his wall. One had been a machete like this one, with a silver and ivory inlaid handle. Belonged to a minor Cambodian prince, he'd told me.

Mark, who'd heard the call on his police scanner and had appeared on the scene a step behind Brannigan, hovered in the background while the police questioned me and waited while I made a statement at the station house. When I left, he was on me like glue.

"Let me drop you at home," he offered as I left the warren of police offices in the basement of the Town Hall. I responded with a twinge of remorse.

"Thanks. I'm a little shaky."

He swung open the door of the Miata and I got in, still thinking of the papers I'd taken from Rok. What would happen when he found they were missing?

"I should have asked you along when I went to meet Cecily."

He backed the car out of the parking space and steered the Miata down Main past the gloomy near-mansions that lined the streets in this section of Greymont. The police radio, which he always kept on, crackled sporadically.

"Yeah," he said after a few moments. "I should have asked for your okay on that rewrite."

"It would have been the polite thing to do," I responded, a bit of frost creeping into my tone.

Mark laughed. "Speaking of manners—the next

time someone's about to make chop suey out of you, and I step in, you could maybe say thanks."

"I thought I did."

"Really? All I remember is some remark about a thick head."

We drove in silence for a couple of seconds. He hung a left, three blocks from my house. "You're right," I finally said. "That was uncalled for."

"Partners?"

"Yeah," I murmured. "Partners."

When we arrived at my house, Billy met me at the door, took me in his arms, and we just held each other. In shaky whispers I described the scene in Chen's house, the gruesome corpse with her throat cut, and the police search of the duplex. I told him about Brannigan leading me outside where I nearly threw up before the cold air saved me. "You're good, Szabo," Brannigan had said. "Not many reporters can take what you just saw."

I hadn't answered, not letting my panic and weakness show. Now, though, once Mark left, I wept, for Chram, for Ly and Song, for Phroeng, for Billy, and for myself. So many questions filled the air in the dark bedroom. Outside, the icy ground shone like a sugar glaze in the moonlight. Perhaps our love was like that glow, reflected from one cold surface to another, an echo from a star so distant that nothing was left of its heat but a fading glimmer.

"We've got to talk over this Vivi Cairo deal," Billy said quietly after we had lain there for a long time in silence. "She called again."

Memories of the crisis days twisted inside like the pain from an old soldier's wound.

His hand tightened on my shoulder.

"Please, Billy. Not now. Not tonight."

I turned away and pretended to go to sleep. I listened to his breathing for a long time. I might have slept fitfully. I might have lain awake. I didn't know. Finally, I got out of bed. The rhythmic sound of Billy's light snore calmed me as I dressed in old jeans, a turtleneck, and Nikes, and drove once more to the *Eagle* offices. Although it was four A.M., Whit was there already. I went upstairs to watch the final edit of the front page with the headline screaming of Chen's death and allegations of Chram's possible collaboration with Khmer Rouge laid out in full.

I had just returned to my monitor when I ran into Mark.

"Great news," he said excitedly. "You know those kids who saw 'Loony Toons'?"

"Yeah?"

"I found them at the video parlor last night after I dropped you off! I've been going back every chance I could and they finally showed. They agreed to give me their names. One of their mothers confirmed the story. She saw the same guy several times at the place."

"Has anybody been able to identify him?" I asked.

"Not yet, but I'm working on it." He made a thumbs-up sign, his clean-cut athlete's face broadening into a self-confident grin. I didn't tell him I knew the loony guy's name. He would find that out himself. I wondered how long it would take.

After he left I picked up the phone and dialed Cletha's number.

"I promised I'd let you know when Prith's name came up," I told her. My breath caught and the blood rushed to my ears.

Cletha's voice was dry. "It's come up?"

"Yes."

"All right."

I hung up, numb, helpless, and alone.

I was getting ready to go home when Hal Gaffney called to congratulate me for my fine reporting. He'd just read the Khmer Rouge story.

"It's about time you took an unbiased look at the refugees."

"Thanks, Hal," I muttered, demoralized. He was the last person I wanted praise from. He kept talking about the vagrants, the thugs, the welfare.

"Hal," I said after a moment, "you're in the Chamber of Commerce. Do you know of a company called Delstar?"

"It's a development firm based in Boston. They own property in town. Why?"

"Do they control the Sandwich Shoppe building?"

"I'm not sure. Why?"

"Someone tried to stop Chram from leasing the space. I wondered if you knew about that? Or participated—"

"Zoë, sweetheart," he said angrily, "will you stop

trying to hang this thing on me!" He slammed down the phone.

I packed my stuff and walked up to Town Center Realty, where I interviewed the agent who had talked to Chram Touch about the restaurant site. Chram had gone so far as to take a lease but had never returned to do the final paperwork. The realtor confirmed that Delstar owned the property and that another potential lessee had come forward just days before the murder.

"I assumed she couldn't raise the money," the realtor said. "She seemed very eager and had put together what I felt was a sound business plan. Several co-sponsors were willing to vouch for her. Really, all we needed to close the deal was a check. I called her . . . it may have been the morning of the day she was murdered. I'd just gotten the other offer and wanted to let her know. She insisted she'd have the money by the end of the week. I agreed to wait. To be honest, I liked her. I wanted her to succeed."

"Who made the second offer on the space?" I asked. The answer she gave was as unexpected as it was perplexing.

That evening, I was just finishing washing up after dinner when I received the call from Brannigan.

"Okay, Szabo," he said. "You want to be in on the action. I've got my suspect."

"There's been an arrest?"

"We're going to make one."

"Who?"

He sighed. "Be at the Fair residence in half an hour."

I put down the phone, nearly sick.

Wind scattered the clouds across the full moon as I drove the old Civic to the far northern part of town, past open farms and fields illuminated by the pale nocturnal glow. Beyond was a fringe of hills, farther still the mountains.

The wind tossed the silhouettes of evergreens and bare maples. It whistled faintly, a plaintive, high-pitched sigh. A sudden gust shook the car and the sigh grew into an angry bellow, rushing through the trembling boughs.

When I pulled into Cletha's circular drive, two police cars sat there, lights flashing furiously, blue, white, and red. My agitation increased as the prospect of facing Cletha began to loom. She would certainly never speak to me again. Maybe Billy was right. Greymont was so small, so traditional, so close-knit. We were too brash for this type of life. Most of the refugee supporters actually had begun to avoid me, some going so far as to cross the street when they saw me coming. If Whit knew I had stolen papers, he'd probably fire me. Topping it all off, Song had phoned today after reading the Khmer Rouge piece and told me she never wanted to talk to me again. I didn't think the call had been inspired by Rok, although I couldn't be sure. Now I was about to confront the only person besides Billy who provided a link between my present and my past. After tonight, she would probably no longer be willing to call herself my friend.

I was checking my camera for the third time when I heard a light rap on my window. I looked up and saw Brannigan. I rolled down the glass.

"She's getting him now," he said.

"Are you sure he did it?"

"We have adequate evidence to make an arrest." He turned abruptly and joined the uniformed officers in front of the house. On the porch I saw Bob Sodermeier, the chief of police, speaking with Larry Weiss, Greymont's most prominent progressive lawyer. I left my car and approached the group.

The door to Cletha's farmhouse opened. With the point-and-shoot camera and its built-in flash, I took several shots as three policemen accompanied Prith out the door and down the path, his hands in cuffs behind his back. I snapped a close-up of Cletha walking behind them. Another of Brannigan bending to speak to her. And another of her staring up at him, horsey teeth clenched in a grimace of anguish.

Prith said something to her in Khmer and she responded. At the door of the police car, she hugged him tightly. He put his head on her shoulder and sobbed, shuddering with fear. God, I thought, he was so thin, so fragile, as emaciated as a skeleton. Then Sodermeier, an old friend of Cletha's, gently patted her back and motioned Prith into the car. Prith began to struggle, but Cletha murmured something to him and he stopped. The entire process took no more than two minutes. Brannigan turned and spoke to

Cletha. I took photographs, waiting a few seconds between each for the automatic flash to recharge. Then Brannigan ducked into the sedan with a plainclothes detective behind the wheel and drove off behind the police car carrying Prith. Sodermeier and Weiss followed in a third car.

Cletha shivered in her woodsman's parka as they departed. I slipped the camera into my pocket. Her mouth still in a grimace, she stared down the road at the blue flashing lights receding into the distance. No sirens. Just the wind wailed.

A few feet apart, we watched the taillights slowly vanish.

"Zoë?"

"Yes."

The wind blew snow in our faces. The gusts raged so fiercely that we had to shout to be heard.

"I thought it was you." She spoke through still-clenched teeth, her voice tough and dry as it had been on the phone the previous night. "Have enough pictures?"

I cringed at the sarcasm in her tone.

"For now."

Frozen to the spot, I felt unable to leave, yet unable to speak. I wanted to explain, but whenever words began to form in my mind, their inadequacy made me falter. The gusts of wind tossed the treetops and their shadows danced a crazy, jerking tarantella.

Cletha finally broke the silence.

"I suppose I owe you thanks for the warning. It was a help."

"I don't know what to say," I attempted weakly. "I'm so sorry."

"You go home to your kids."

"Do you want a ride to the station? I can wait with you."

"No. Larry will take me down later."

I was reluctant to leave her alone, despite my guilt. If only there were something I could do to help, I kept thinking.

"Did he do it?" I asked.

The wind made the trees cry out, and then there was silence.

"Absolutely not," she whispered hoarsely.

"How can you be sure?"

I waited to hear about an alibi, evidence, Prith's denials. She said nothing.

"Do you have any proof?" I asked.

"Yes."

"What?" I asked when several moments passed without any elaboration.

She shouted her response. "Faith!"

"Is that all?"

She nodded, a sob caught in her throat. I was stunned. I'd assumed she had more to go on than that.

I put an arm about her, which she stiffly allowed.

Downtown, I elbowed my way into the police station in the midst of a crush of reporters, including Mark. Together we listened as Brannigan made a statement. Refusing to speculate on a motive, he said he had information placing the suspect at the mall near the time of Chram's death. The weapon found yesterday bore traces of the same blood type as Chram's, as well as Cecily Chen's. Some had seeped into the delicate inlay. The knife belonged to Stephen Giles, but he'd reported it stolen several weeks before Chram's killing. It had been tested for prints; Prith's and Chram's were the only ones on it. Before it had been stolen, Stephen had exhibited it on the wall in his living room, where many people had access, including Prith, who'd visited Stephen several times in the fall. The police were doing more refined blood typing now.

"Stephen Giles's prints weren't on the knife?" I asked.

"No."

"Isn't that odd, since it belonged to him?"

Brannigan's pained look evolved into a glare. Mark was asking about Giles, too. "Didn't the fiancé have a motive, access to the weapon, and no alibi for the time of death?"

Brannigan cut the interview short. "As the investigation develops we'll have further comment, but for tonight, ladies and gentlemen, that's all."

In the story I played up the drama of the arrest, giving up any hope of shielding Cletha. Chram's murder had been front page news for over a week, another victim had been felled, and at last a suspect had been caught and charged. Mark fumed that I had stolen what should have been his story. I offered to let him share the byline. He accepted, but only after I agreed to let him rewrite the lead and add more details on the police side. In the meantime, Kate developed the film. She and Whit showed me the picture they were going to run: the one of Cletha holding Prith weeping on her shoulder in front of the police cars, his hands in cuffs behind his back.

24

When I arrived home, I found Billy in the living room, sitting in a straight chair, headphones on, picking at his bass, playing riffs in the dark. Exhausted from the ordeal of the past twenty-four hours, I threw myself down on the old corduroy couch. A tape loop in my head kept replaying my encounter with Cletha after Prith's arrest. Her words echoed with the monotone banality of punk rock at its most alienated. Cletha's Quaker reserve, her strength, the intensity of her feelings hidden by her quiet stoicism—all amplified the meaning of her meager words: "I suppose I owe you thanks for the warning. It was a help." Her stiffness when I embraced her said so much more than her words. She had tried to provide a refuge for Billy and me, just as she'd done for Song and Chram and Prith and so many others. Yet all her effort, all her stoical persistence, had resulted in what? Two grisly deaths, the arrest of her foster son, and . . . Billy and me, what would become of us?

The wind blew outside, whistling as lonely as a train. Reflections cascaded as the dark clouds rushed across the moon. Billy bent down and switched off the amp. He plucked at the electric bass strings. All I could hear was the thin wiry sound of the unamplified strings.

Finally, his voice broke through the thick blanket of emotion and unspoken thoughts.

"I talked to Vivi about an hour ago."

I said nothing, my consciousness unwilling to face the confrontation that seemed as unbearable as it was inevitable.

"Her manager wants me in the band. They're sending a contract on the two songs she wants to record. If they get good air play . . . The tour is in the planning stages. Might be as short as a month.

"So," he added after a pause, "what do you think?"

My throat felt thick, my heart constricted. I tried to think of noncommittal things to say. Inside me, a voice whispered to beg him not to take the offer.

"You and the kids could come along. Might be a gas. They're talking Europe. . . ."

"It's tempting," I admitted, hearing the words as if someone else were speaking.

Half his face was illuminated by moonlight, the other half dark. My eyes traced the silver line of his cheek and jaw. I sat up, leaned forward, and allowed myself to continue:

"But I'm ready to stop running. There are people here I admire. People like Cletha and Whit. People who stand for something even if it's not going to win them money, fame, or awards. They're the kind of people I want my kids to be surrounded by as they grow. People with . . . I don't know, all those small town virtues that aren't very glamorous but which endure."

The dark breezes whipped noisily through the bare branches of the oaks and maples outside our doors. A cloud covered the moon and Billy's face was engulfed by darkness. I could hear him breathing, thinking.

"If you knew how much I want this."

"Can't you sell the songs and beg off the tour?"

I let my voice drift wistfully. I waited for him to answer, but he said nothing.

My clock said 4:30 A.M. when I realized it was no use trying to sleep. My mind kept racing, repeating the discussion with Billy, the moments of Prith's arrest and Cletha's resignation, the vivid memory of Cecily Chen tied to the chair with her throat cut, the huge, wide-bladed machete with the ivory-inlaid handle, even Brannigan saying pointedly that they would be scraping my brains off the asphalt in some alley. Then the memory loomed of Rok in the blue Ford. Song's call saying she never wanted to see me again. Beside me, Billy turned, snoring. I got out of bed.

What bothered me the most was Cletha. I felt so bad that this terrible thing had happened to her. If Prith was proved the murderer, she would never forgive herself for having brought him over here, knowing, as she must have, how compromised he was by the Khmer Rouge connection. But what if he hadn't done it? What if someone had cleverly taken advantage of his mental weakness, of his possible psychosis, and of his inability to express himself in English and possibly Khmer? A more perfect patsy to hang a murder on couldn't be found. One thing made me doubt his guilt, and that was the way Cecily Chen had been killed. I was perfectly willing to believe he could give way to irrational fury and kill someone, but not that he could sneak into a house like Cecily's, surprise her, tie her up, and slaughter her so neatly, the murder weapon laid at her feet like an offering. It was more like an act of necessity than of rage.

I found a pair of jeans and a sweater and went into the bathroom to dress. I slipped on the running shoes I'd worn yesterday. For what I was about to do, I had to wear clothes I could move in. I looked in on Smokie and Keith. Careful not to rouse them, I closed their doors and tiptoed downstairs.

About a quarter mile from Cletha's, I turned onto a dirt road that led to a network of backwoods trails which linked up with the Appalachian trail at the very north end of town, heading up toward the Vermont border. The wind had died down and the air had turned warmer.

I pulled the Civic behind the evergreens, so it wouldn't be visible from the main road, and reached over to the glove compartment to get a flashlight. The latch had jammed. After banging a few times, the door fell open, but then I couldn't get it closed. Finally, I gave up and left it hanging. I slipped the flashlight into the roomy pocket of my parka, locked the car, and started to hike into the woods toward the back end of Cletha's property. The sky was dark, but the moon shed enough light so I could make my way, with the help of memories of hikes Billy and I had taken in the area and a small compass, which I checked at intervals in the beam of my flashlight.

Mist rose from the banks of snow in the low areas. The dripping trees were black against the fog. Following the beam of my flashlight, I moved quietly along the narrow, poorly-marked path. Cletha had nearly a hundred acres, most of it woodlands, and this trail, which Billy and I had hiked several times the previous summer, went close to the house.

After a ten-minute walk on the snow, which had been packed down by cross-country skiers, my light shone on a turning point. The trail went off to the left, but I went right, through the high snow of back country, under branches and through snowy underbrush. With each step my feet sank deeper. My beam lit odd things along the way: a tangle of branches etched white with snow, dead blossoms from the previous spring hanging off a wild laurel encrusted with ice, the prints of sparrows near a frozen stream bed. At last the beam caught a broken line of rusty barbed wire tangled around a thick maple trunk. At the base of the tree an old stone wall marked Cletha's property line. I flashed the light along the wall and found a break in the barbed wire. Beyond, thick woods led downhill. Inching my way under the top strand of rusted wire, I crawled headfirst, sat on the rocks, and pulled my legs through one at a time.

After stumbling along next to the stone wall for what seemed like a very long time, I saw an opening in the trees. I followed. My light glanced along an open clearing of snow. A pale gray streak glowed along the eastern horizon, helping me find my way through the woods. At last, through a thicket of evergreen boughs, I spotted a light in the distance. The dial of my watch said 5:44. Soon it would be daylight. I wanted to avoid detection and get out of there before sunrise. I sneaked down to the rim of trees, able to see the outline of the house in the murky predawn. I stole along the edge of the woods, shielded by trees, my flashlight off. There was still a trail of footprints, which I followed even though the light was very dim.

Yes, this seemed to be the wall of pines where I'd come upon Prith. I began to trace a circle. Yes, here was where he had seemed to conjure himself out of thin air. Looking up and taking the risk of momentarily shining my flashlight beam, I saw a branch about eight feet over my head. Moving the light along the branch I found the huge trunk of the tree, about four feet from where I stood. The trunk was split. The two halves shot together straight up for about sixty feet. I couldn't see the top, but there were many branches coming off the old hemlock. Its higher reaches were well-shielded from view.

I tucked the flashlight into my pocket, wiped the slush off my Nikes, and unwrapped the rope that I'd taken from the car and coiled over my shoulder. It took a couple of tries, but I was able to loop the rope over the lowest branch and tie a knot. With some difficulty, I hoisted myself up to the split in the trunk. I hadn't climbed a tree in a long time, but the logic of it was still in my bones. One summer when I was a kid, my parents had rented a house in the country, and I'd spent much of my vacation in the boughs of the tallest tree, reading books and enjoying being able to look down at the lowly world. Compared to that tree, the hemlock with its many branches going off in all directions was a cinch, once I made it past the notch. My sense of time and place vanished. I twisted my body between the branches, pulling higher. Every few branches, I took out my light and shone it around, searching for anything that might serve as a hiding place. There were no knot holes. I checked thoroughly. No baskets or scarves hanging from the branches. But I kept hoping.

I climbed higher. Soon I was above the line of treetops and I could see down over the road and fields and Cletha's farmhouse, small in the distance.

I climbed higher. The dawn was slowly turning the blackness into deep gray, and I didn't have to shine my beam quite as often. In Cletha's house a light went on in the kitchen.

The branches had become less firm under my feet. The trunk had grown thinner and swayed as I moved. The sky seemed ever closer and the earth seemed to be very far down, a soft shadowy blanket bejeweled with lights twinkling in clusters here and there. I could make out the streetlights of the town center in the distance, the white beams of a car going down the road, and then red dots after it passed. To the west a bracelet of lights along Route 88 led toward Sheffington. Clusters of pink floodlights surrounded the black towers of the State University. To the south were the softer gas lamps of Greymont College. Beyond, the sky was growing paler. The moon had set. The stars twinkled occasionally through gaps in the cover of benevolent clouds.

Toward the top of the tree I found an abandoned squirrels' nest. It was a large basket-shaped dome made of twigs and leaves. My beam moved along the outline of the nest. I couldn't find any opening. I swung around to the other side of the tree, swaying, and shone the light again. Finding a good foothold, I was able to lean against a strong branch. There. The hole was about the size of my fist. I slipped my light into my pocket and, with some trepidation, slowly put in my hand. I reached deeper inside and felt something soft and smooth.

I pulled myself up until my face was level with the nest. I reached out. Again my hand touched what felt like cotton. My problem was that it took both hands and feet to hold myself in position. Moving around again, I managed to get a little more secure, hooking one arm around the bough and reaching with the other.

I managed to grab hold of the cloth this time. I felt what seemed like a ball of material, a kerchief of some kind. Testing, I discovered something hard inside this ball.

Finally, I stuffed the kerchief in my pocket and slid

down the tree until I found a thick double branch I could comfortably drape my legs over. I propped my back against the trunk. Both hands were finally free. I opened the kerchief on my lap. Inside there was a memo pad not unlike the one I used to keep my reporter's notes. I opened it, dug into my pocket for the light, and shone the beam on it. Drawings with exotic curling characters that looked like Khmer script were illuminated in the dim yellow circle. These were not the idyllic village scenes Cletha had described. These were different. These were of mutilated bodies. Of people doing unspeakable things to each other. One depicted a woman, her tongue cut off, a necklace like a web of golden vines in her hand. At the center of each web was a lotus with a round, pearl-like center. Beside her was a perfect likeness of Chram, only younger. She was taking the necklace, in the other hand holding a knife.

I was wrapping the book back in the kerchief when I felt something drop onto my jeans. At first I thought it was a twig or a pine cone, but it glittered in my light. I adjusted the beam. A golden lotus, a pearl at its heart, glowed flawlessly against the black fabric.

25

I managed to descend the tree without incident. After shimmying down the rope, I untied it, coiled it over my arm, and set off. In the gray light stretching up from the eastern horizon, I made my way easily through the brush. Sooner than I expected, I found the stone wall.

When I reached the blazed trail on the other side of the wall I fell into a slow jog, watching my footing over the rocks and packed snow. The sunrise painted the cottony clouds orange and fiery gold. I unlocked my Civic and the engine charged right up for a change. Feeling a surge of fondness for the old car, I patted the dash and then headed slowly along the icy road till I hit the pavement of the back highway that merged into Stanhope Street.

When I arrived a little after seven, the office was in a whirlwind of activity. Everyone seemed to be there, even Sharon, who was carrying two boxes of muffins, danishes, and doughnuts into the kitchen. Fresh coffee was brewing in the automatic drip maker on the counter.

I was just beginning to focus on sources to call for comments on the arrest when my line lit up. It was Gaffney. He just started right in, not even bothering to mention his name. His familiar voice had the high-pitched insistence of the dentist's drill setting on the keyboard that Smokie loved.

"We've been ahead of you all the way on this murder. How much more violence is it going to take before we take a close look at immigration policy?"

"I've got that down as a direct quote, Hal. Now I need background on you. What went on between you and Chram when she worked for you? Did you lend her money for her restaurant?"

"On the record. And I want this printed, every single word of it. I met Chram Touch two years ago when she worked in my bar. She was one of the lousiest employees I've ever had. I would have been better off with a trained monkey. There was no way she could run a restaurant. She could barely take an order. I'd sooner throw money down a sewer than lend it to her."

"Did you ask someone to intervene, to try to stop her?"

"Why bother? She was bound to fail."

"Hal, I'd like to discuss this in more detail. Can we meet?"

"Absolutely. I'm sick of your innuendoes. Let's get it all out on the record."

"You want to meet here?"

"Come down to my bar. We can talk in my office."

"Let me make a few calls and I'll get back to you."

I dialed Stephen and reached the housemate. "He's not talking to the press."

"Tell him it's Zoë Szabo and I urgently need to confirm something with him."

After a few seconds, she said, "He won't talk to you."

"I've found information that he must see," I persisted.

I heard Stephen's voice. "You've got one minute."

"I've come across something new. Can we meet?"

"What did you find?"

"Do you think Prith is the murderer?"

He paused. "Probably."

"But you're not sure."

He said nothing.

"The knife was yours. When did he steal it?"

"I'm hanging up now."

"Stephen, I've found some pictures—"

There was a long silence. I listened to the faint whisper of static. Finally, I heard him breathe. "Okay. Let's talk."

"Where are you going?" Whit asked as I was on my way out the door. His temper seemed short, his skin red with pressure.

"Research."

"Round up Kate. I want the two of you to go to the Touch household, ask for their reaction to the arrest. Be back by ten, so we can put it in the paper today. Do your research after deadline. I'm sending Mark to Town Hall. Gaffney and the town manager are giving a press conference. You can meet him there after you file the Touch story. I want you sticking together."

"But I have to talk to Stephen and . . . I might have new information."

"Do it later. I'm waiting for your story to transmit the front page. I want the Touches above the fold."

"They've had publicity up to the gills," I protested. "Can't we leave them in peace?"

"No." He raised his eyebrows, color heightening. "You'll get the long answer after deadline."

I backed off, suppressing my outrage. After calling Gaffney and Stephen to postpone our meetings, I headed downstairs to find Kate. So much for showing my newfound treasures to Whit. My only consolation was that Song was probably still so furious at me she wouldn't let me within miles of her parents.

"What's eating you?" Kate asked when I stopped by her desk.

"No comment. Grab your camera. We're going to the Touches' for pictures."

As we dashed out the door, Mark was galloping in. The three of us nearly collided.

"Hey, *qué pasó*, Szabo?"

I told him where we were headed. "You're going to the press conference with Gaffney?"

He nodded.

"Ask him why he tried to block Chram from renting her restaurant space." I hesitated. "Listen, maybe you can meet me later," I added. "I've set up meetings with him and Stephen."

Mark lightly jabbed my arm. "Welcome to the team, Szabo."

"Take advantage. It might not last long."

He jotted down the times I'd set for the meetings, assured me he'd be there, and Kate and I ran off.

Bou Vuthy and an apprentice monk were guarding the door of the Touch apartment. They were speaking to reporters and keeping them away from the family. Rok was being kept hostage in his townhouse by the hordes of media folk collected not only around the front door, but also behind the building to catch anyone trying to escape out the rear.

His shriveled body impassive in his saffron cloak, Bou Vuthy surveyed the cameras, reporters, and mikes with bemusement. When I approached, his eyes narrowed.

"Leave them in peace," he murmured to me.

"I must talk to Song."

"Not today."

"Please, *Loak Sang*, could you ask if she'll see me?"

Other reporters crowded around, pushing Kate and me forward. The monk stepped back, trying to avoid the crush of bodies.

"Zoë!" a voice cried from the second floor window.

I looked up. It was Song. Photographers started snapping pictures and she pulled back behind heavy curtains. Reluctantly, Bou Vuthy let me through.

"I've been trying to call you," she said hurriedly as

she greeted us inside the door. We'd just squeezed past the press of reporters and slammed the door shut. "The police say they're sending someone to help with the reporters. But I think it's too late."

I put my arm around her shoulders. We embraced. "I'm so sorry," I whispered, "about the Khmer Rouge story. I'm sorry I let you down."

"But now, you see," she said, visibly relieved, "they've found out the killer and he will be punished." She stopped for a second, noticing Kate. "What's she doing here?"

"We need a photo."

"Will this be the end?"

I nodded. "I hope so."

She went to find Ly and Phroeng, and we followed.

Ly, her round body noticeably weak, smiled tepidly when Song brought me in to talk with her at the table. Phroeng was in a daze. Auntie Saw grumbled to herself in Khmer as she worked at cleaning the kitchen.

I greeted them with a *sompeah* that was by now becoming second nature and explained that we were here to get their response to the arrest of Prith Prahn.

"Do you believe he killed your daughter?" I asked both Ly and Phroeng, with an apologetic glance toward Song.

"Yes," said Ly in translation. "This maybe can be over now. Finished."

When I asked Phroeng to speculate on what might have been in Prith's mind, he seemed utterly bewildered.

"Why do you think he killed your daughter?" I asked.

"He says," Song translated, "he thinks maybe there was a bad spirit that got into Prith and made him do it."

"The Cambodian people," said Ly in English, "many bad thing happen. The bad thing—here." She pointed to her shaven head.

Kate caught a picture of Ly's gesture.

"What will you do now?" I asked.

The mother and father turned to each other after they heard the translation and exchanged a tired gaze. The father finally shook his head and murmured a few words.

Song said, "He says he'll drink some and forget."

"Come here," I murmured to Song. "I have to show you something I found. You're not going to like it."

"Was it in Rok's desk?" she asked me. We moved to the living room, while Kate kept her parents busy in the kitchen taking pictures. "Zoë, he's furious. He knows you stole his papers. I'm afraid what he might do to you. Even though you said those things about Chram . . . I don't want anything to happen to you. Why didn't I guess it was Prith?"

"I'm going to turn these over to Brannigan, but first you have to know what it is. Because . . . others will see. I thought you had a right to know and to prepare"—I nodded toward the kitchen—"them."

I withdrew the black kerchief from my pocket, unwrapped the sketchbook, and opened it to the drawing of the woman holding the necklace.

"Do you recognize this? Or either of the people in the picture?"

Song opened her mouth. She recognized Chram instantly. Her large black eyes went from the picture to me.

"Zoë," she said, "what does this mean?"

"I have no idea. I thought you could tell me."

She slowly shook her head back and forth.

"Do you recognize the other woman—not Chram?"

"No."

"You recognize the necklace."

"It's the same one that Chram gave me."

"Who do you think that woman is?"

"I don't know." Something glinting in her dark pupils told me this wasn't the entire truth.

"Who was she?"

"I never met her."

"But you've seen her. You've seen a picture."

She shook her head violently. Finally, she whispered, "Take it away. Burn it."

"I'm going to give it to Brannigan."

"When?"

"I don't know. Soon."

Song put her head in her hands. I wanted to comfort her, to explain why, but there were no words adequate to the task. I remembered the words of the monk. *Metta*. Forgiveness.

26

Shortly after four, I got a call from Eleanor Kerr, telling me something that made me uneasy. "I received notification by mail today," she said, "that Chram's final citizenship hearing has been delayed. Not that it matters now."

"Did they say why?"

"Something about needing further information. You know these government documents. It was a form letter with a box checked for the reason for the delay."

She had phoned Brannigan to tell him, and again my thoughts went to the sketchpad in my pocket with the gruesome drawings and the likeness of Chram. It was time to put my theories to the test. After checking my schedule, I called Billy.

"How about we get a baby-sitter and go out for an early dinner," I suggested. "We can talk about Vivi's offer without interruption."

Billy agreed to meet me at Gaffney's bar around

six. That would give me time to see Stephen and confront Gaffney. It was possible, I conjectured, that Gaffney had a personal reason for his attack on the refugees. The real estate agent had confirmed that Gaffney had inquired after the restaurant space Chram wanted. Mark had promised to come to both interviews. His size alone would lend protection if the pictures provoked unpleasant reactions. I paused momentarily, remembering the warnings I'd received from both Whit and Brannigan. In any event, I thought, patting my pocket, I had the cell phone. If anything went terribly wrong, I could call the police.

Last, I remembered something I wanted to ask Song and dialed her number. "She wen' out," Ly said. "So-ee, you take care her?"

"Yes, don't worry. Where did she go?"

"She say library, but she take no book."

"Okay," I promised, "I'll check."

After a hurried search of the library, with no sign of Song, I decided to go ahead with my plans, figuring I'd call Ly later to see if she'd turned up. First, I had to get Rok's papers translated and there was only one person I trusted to do the job.

It was nearly five when I parked at the north end of the fortress-like Botwick Arts and Sciences Building. At this time of year the campus was mostly shut except for professors' offices and labs, and I saw only a few other cars in the lot, Peter's new Volvo, a couple of Camrys that probably belonged to professors, and an old American model, which I didn't recognize.

Inside, the labyrinthine hallways were only dimly lit. I passed to the southern wing through a glassed-in tunnel with panoramic views of the boxy concrete structures of the ugly state campus, blanketed in a layer of icy snow in the fast descending twilight.

Peter's office was the only one in the building that appeared to be open. I looked in, calling, "Hello? Peter?"

Since there was no response, I went in. Peter's tweed overcoat hung on an old wooden coat tree near the file cabinets. On the wall behind the desk, covered with papers, were framed photos and prints. To kill time, I moved to the wall and examined the pictures. There was one of Peter's wife, a matronly, tall woman with a resolute smile and red hair piled on top of her head. There was Peter in a tuxedo receiving some award, looking proud and hearty as he so often did. There were some of him at the refugee camps in Thailand, touring with Bou Vuthy, teaching, shaking hands. There was one of Cletha with the squalid huts of the Thai camp spread out in a red and brown vista behind her. I took down the photo of Cletha, who was smiling and sunburnt despite the wide-brimmed straw hat.

Studying it with a twinge of regret at our estrangement, I sighed sadly, then reached up to replace the picture on its hook. As I did, I noticed that the cardboard backing seemed loose. Two thin metal pieces had worked out from the frame. I pulled one of them, trying to refit the point in the wood frame. As I attempted to fix it, something seemed to get in the way. Pulling off the cardboard, I suddenly saw what was causing the problem. An envelope had been stuffed between the photo and the board holding it in place. Unable to suppress my curiosity, I removed it, refit the frame, and rehung the picture.

A brief examination revealed that the envelope hadn't been fully sealed. I picked at the flap with my fingernail and it lifted without even the slightest tear. Inside were four old photographs. One was of a Cambodian man I didn't recognize. One was of a Buddhist temple. The third was of a young man with dark brown hair, bushy eyebrows, and a square-set face who greatly resembled the man in the snapshot I'd seen at Stephen's. I studied the man, tall, big-boned, with those thick eyebrows.

Suddenly it dawned on me that this was a young Peter Albright. He was standing in front of a grand building bearing a sign: HOTEL METROPOLE. The streets and buildings looked like old pictures of downtown Phnom Penh. With him was a group of Americans and Asians, much like those in the snapshot I'd come across at Stephen's. They were smiling into the camera. A few waved. One was the Chinese woman who seemed to be a ringer for a young Cecily Chen. In back of her was another woman, fragile and quite beautiful. She stood three steps behind Peter. It was the same woman I'd seen in the snapshot at Stephen's and her jewelry again made her stand out. My breath caught in my throat when I examined the last photo. It was a close-up of the fragile Cambodian woman. She was quite young and rail-thin. Her cheekbones were pronounced, eyes fringed with thick lashes, her glance at once demure and beguiling. She wore an elaborate necklace which appeared to be a web of vines and lotuses. At the center of each was a pearl. I extracted the sketchbook and the fragment of jewelry from my pocket. The likeness between the woman in the photo and the one depicted in the drawing, the one with her tongue cut out, was uncanny. Though the photo was fairly small, and I couldn't be certain, the jewelry appeared to be a perfect match.

Part of me didn't believe what my eyes insisted was so. I put that together with what I'd learned from the real estate agent, what I'd deduced from the cold-blooded way Cecily Chen had been murdered, and the little I'd gleaned about Peter's past from my cursory search of the *Eagle*'s back files. Even Springsteen's music had been screaming this answer to me, though I'd done all I could to ignore the message: about being "Born in the USA" and being sent off to war—in Peter's case a covert war in Cambodia; about the "Fire" that made us all succumb to enticements we tried to resist; about secrets that we desperately needed to hide, but which drew us inexorably to the "Darkness at the Edge of Town." Although I wasn't completely surprised, I was disillusioned and shocked that this lurking suspicion had suddenly been confirmed. Perhaps it was the sense of *knowing*, the belief pervading the very air of this university town that *knowledge is power*, which gave me a kind of foolhardy courage.

I closed the drawer. As I did, my glance wandered to the coatrack by the file cabinet. I hadn't noticed before, but partly concealed by Peter's tweed overcoat was a long brown woman's coat. Dangling near the sleeve were the soft wool tassels of a lavender scarf that I knew well. It was Song's. Had she come here to confront Peter after recognizing the woman in Prith's sketch? Had she seen one of these photos?

Suddenly, I heard a sound in the hall. A coldness began to creep toward my core.

The door opened and I saw the bushy white brows and gray-green eyes that I'd once considered so friendly and cheerful. Peter Albright stared at me with an expression of dismay.

"Oh, Dr. Albright," I said warmly. "I need your help."

His tall frame relaxed tentatively. "Zoë, I'm afraid it's not a good time."

"This won't take a minute. I just need a comment on Prith's arrest."

Peter shook his head mournfully. "Poor boy. So sad," he murmured. I noticed that his slacks were smeared with dirt and that the tail of his shirt hung out in the back. His cheeks were flushed from exertion.

"Do you think he murdered Chram?"

"Isn't that what the police are saying?"

In the moments before he entered the room, I'd moved away from his desk, thrusting his photos into my pocket. "I found some papers of Chram's. They might hold a clue as to the reason for her killing. Perhaps they have something to do with Prith . . . or . . . Rok. You mentioned his gambling."

"Yes. Do you want me to take a look at them?"

I slipped my hand into my pocket, pressed the record button on my tape machine, and touched my cell phone for reassurance. Help was within reach. Not exactly Lois and Superman, but a reasonable facsimile. I extracted the notes I'd found in Rok's drawer.

"If you could translate these," I said, "it might explain the reason for the murder."

He took the papers and skimmed them. Agitated, I planned my exit, but then something inside me, some new will or strength, decreed that I *had* to find Song first.

"Has anyone else seen this?"

"Oh, yes. Whit has a copy," I assured him in my most confident tone.

"Well, I don't see how these can help. They have nothing to do with Prith. It seems to be an agreement between Chram, Rok, and Saw." He breathed heavily, his faded gray eyes taking me in guardedly.

"What about?"

"That restaurant of hers. It seems Rok offered to fund it if she married the son of his friend. It's unsigned. I suppose she wouldn't go through with it."

"Just one more thing. Have you seen this?"

"What?"

I opened the sketchbook to the page I'd shown Song, the one with the beautiful woman, her tongue cut out, holding a necklace toward Chram. His muscular hand trembled as he took it. He studied the drawing, his eyes glazing. Spittle formed on his reddening lips and his face grew deathly pale.

"Where did you get this?" he whispered hoarsely.

"Do you recognize anyone?"

My back was against the door, my hand behind me, reaching toward the knob. If he made a move, I would run.

"My, God. Where did you get this?"

"Then you have seen the woman before?"

He took a staggering step toward me.

I held the doorknob tightly in my fist. "Who is the woman?"

Blotches of red stood out on his beefy cheeks and his forehead went white.

"Peter," I urged, somewhere between compassion and fear, "what was her name?"

His large body shuddered. He staggered dazedly toward the desk and steadied himself against it, bowing his head.

"Peter," I said, moved by his distress.

His bulky body grew rigid as he remembered that I was there with him. He took a deep, rasping breath. "She was a woman I loved . . . deeply."

"How did you meet her?" I asked hesitantly.

"She worked as a translator for some of the embassy people. Very few of us stationed there spoke Khmer. We conferred often, and . . . it started out, I suppose, as a dalliance on my part. But she was a brave and intelligent woman. By the time I left I'd become much more serious than I was willing to admit—to myself or to her."

He gasped slightly, and his face reddened, stained with emotion.

"So," I whispered, "it was you." I didn't want it to be true, even as I spoke. As strange as it seemed, I still liked him. He had worked so tirelessly for the Cambodian refugees, had been such a useful source, so good-natured and hearty, always ready with a quotable phrase.

He was lost in memory. "She wanted me to take her along, begged. But my wife . . . how could I explain? We had to leave in such a rush."

"Leave Phnom Penh?"

He nodded. "It was chaos, pure chaos. Who was to know what would happen? I thought, we all thought . . . it wouldn't be so bad, not for Cambodians. Just Americans. Some embassy staff even wanted to stay on. You understand?"

"You didn't have the advantage of hindsight."

"No," he agreed eagerly. "That's it, precisely. After the war, I scoured the camps. I searched everywhere. I carried her picture. I questioned thousands, thousands of people. No one had seen her. And then, long after I'd given up, I found Prith."

He suddenly began to heave in huge, racking sobs, like an enormous beast crying out in pain. A long time passed while he wept.

"What I don't understand, Peter," I said softly, "is how Prith was connected with—what was her name?"

"Yom," he told me, breathing it out as if it were a word that he hadn't spoken in many years. Like a great secret. The name settled into the room as if it belonged there, as if it had been waiting through the decades to be spoken in just this manner, with just this reverence. I was stirred by the power the name had over Peter. It was almost ennobling. He breathed it again. "Yom . . . "

"You showed Prith her photo?"

"No, I'd stopped looking for her. I'd given up hope. After Prith came, he began to have nightmares. Episodes. He wouldn't confide in Cletha, so I offered to listen. I spent an afternoon alone with him, listening to his ravings, and as he told me this story, I began to realize he was talking about Yom. He knew her name. He showed me that sketch and the necklace. . . . I'd given it to her as a parting gift. If I hadn't, she might still be alive." His hollow forced laugh reverberated against the concrete walls of his small office.

"Prith showed me the piece of necklace," he whispered huskily. "He had a fragment. He'd smuggled it in. He described how Chram had killed Yom, twisting a knife, while they watched. Prith was . . . horrified. . . . Yom had kept the necklace hidden, used bits of it to trade for food and safety. Chram spied on her. She threatened to tell. Yom gave her the necklace in return for her silence, but Chram told anyway. Chram killed her in cold blood. She admitted the whole story to me. Prith had witnessed the killing. She'd given him pieces of the necklace as a bribe. He kept them hidden. He was terrified of her.

"I wanted her deported. I notified colleagues in the State Department that there were questions about her past. At the very least I could keep her from being naturalized."

Peter stopped speaking, staring off into the past. The silence was pierced by a strange high-pitched sound. It took a few thickheaded moments for me to realize that the source of the sound was my cell phone. Peter's eyes moved down toward my jacket.

I grabbed the phone and tried to answer, fumbling with the unfamiliar equipment. Peter's hand grasped mine, tightening on my arm. His strength took me completely by surprise. A sharp pain went through my wrist and elbow as he snapped back my hand and the cell phone dropped on the floor and skidded under the desk. The ringing had stopped.

An aeon or two passed in that instant. Images of Billy, Smokie, and Keith flowed into my mind, and suddenly all the dread I'd felt about Billy going out on tour seemed absurd. Time slowed down. I felt a great fatalism, a sense that I could possibly save myself with my wits or some miracle could intervene. At the same time the realization gnawed that the odds I would ever see my family again were just about nil.

I turned to Peter, attempting to make eye contact, to make him see me as a fellow human being.

"How?" I asked softly, in an effort to make the quiver in my voice reflect gentle understanding rather than the terror coursing through my veins. "How did this awful accident happen?"

His eyes seemed to plead for sympathy. For a few moments I thought I wouldn't be able to reach him, but then he spoke. "All I wanted," he explained as if I were able to absolve him, "was to have her leave the country. I didn't want her to die. You have to believe that."

"I do, Peter," I said gently.

"She called *me*. I agreed to meet her out there in the parking lot. We'd met there before. We'd hashed this out a number of times, ever since Prith confided in me. When I got in the car, she pulled the knife."

"She had the knife?"

"She was no innocent. Stole the thing from Stephen. He suspected she'd taken it. I gave him a photo of Yom, told him to show her, see what she'd say."

"Stephen . . . knew?"

"Why do you think he ditched her? It was a shock, of course. At first he didn't believe it. He'd put up with a lot, but that—even he couldn't stomach it.

"I wanted her to leave the country on her own. She laughed in my face and shouted obscenities. She tried to blackmail me. I told her to get out of the country before I let the world know what she'd done. She said I was guilty. Me. Me! She threatened to write letters to my colleagues. She wanted money. From me! Money. Nasty person. She had a very ugly side not visible to Americans. I gripped the knife. She shouted at me . . . dared me to kill her. 'You've taken Stephen away,' she said, 'You've stolen my citizenship, my restaurant, my dream. You've taken my life. Kill my body, too.'"

He exhaled in one long shuddering breath.

"I wrestled the knife from her, raised it, and let it

sink into her chest. It was remarkably easy. I let it sink in again. And again. And again."

The air rattled in his lungs.

"She was dead so quickly. I couldn't believe how fast death came, compared with all the suffering she'd caused."

He nodded, his neck slack.

"And Professor Chen?"

He looked toward me. "That couldn't be helped. She'd known Yom. We'd been friends, the three of us, a long time ago. She found some old photos. She figured it out. She insisted I give myself up. I told her I'd be damned if I was going to rot in jail for the murder of that piece of filth."

"It doesn't bother you that Prith might go to prison for crimes you committed?"

"I'll tell you something about Prith. I've seen cases like his before. Nothing could bring him back. Might as well have left him sitting in a gutter back in Thailand. Hopeless case. Cletha's gone soft."

"And Song?" I asked holding my breath. Albright's bulk stirred. His head turned toward the rack and he gazed at her brown coat and lavender scarf. Fear turned my legs and arms to ice.

His breath had slowed.

"What have you done with her?"

"You were the problem," he said. "You wouldn't stop asking questions. I thought Grandfather would stop you, focus you on the Khmer Rouge, but you kept poking your nose where you had no business. Asking again and again."

I spun and tried to turn the knob, when I felt his body press behind me. I turned and kicked him hard in the crotch, but I just missed the spot that would cause the most pain. He slapped my face so hard that it stung.

"Where's Song?" I screamed at the top of my voice. I hoped against hope someone would hear, though reason told me the building was deserted.

"Where is she?" I repeated, hearing and not believing the strength of my own voice. I felt as if I were somewhere close to the ceiling watching a woman braver and more powerful than I act out a part in a film. But there were no cameras. There were no lights. I was alone. The ice in my veins began to pump again. I screamed for help.

His viselike grasp twisted me backwards. Cold steel pricked my throat, a sharp pain and a wetness that could only be blood. I gasped and in an instant my courage fled.

He slammed me against the door and, as I fell, the light went out. He roughly shoved me out into the black hallway, jabbing and knocking me, his grip twisting my arm behind me, the other hand pressing the knife at my throat. We clambered down series after series of stairs until we finally reached the basement. The blade bit my skin at my larynx, threatening to sink deeper.

I was propelled through the door of a large storeroom marked, HAZARDOUS WASTE AREA. AUTHORIZED PERSONNEL ONLY. Panting heavily, Peter thrust me down. I stood up and dove at him. A sudden sharp pain stabbed at the back of my neck. I fell to the floor and began crawling away, trying to hide among the dark objects. A faint nausea crept over me, and then everything swam in a gray haze.

I don't know how much later it was when I came to. I was sprawled out on a cold concrete floor wedged between what seemed like tall shelving units. A red light glimmered in the blackness. It was an exit sign at the far end of the cavernous space.

I lay there, thinking I was alone, wondering how badly I was injured, and if this would turn out to be my last conscious moment. Again, I longed to embrace my children. And Billy. My head felt dizzy and a clammy sweat broke out despite the cold. I heard the noises—the rasping, heavy breathing of a large man. And then a soft, muffled moan.

I forced myself out of my stupor. My head ached horribly. As my eyes adjusted to the dim light, I made out the shadowy shapes: old lab furniture, shelving units, file cabinets, desks and chairs piled high, filling nearly a quarter of the huge space. Around me, taking up most of the remaining area, were waste drums, piled two and three high. I rose to my knees, hidden by the black barrels, given courage by the bleakness of my situation. The adrenaline set to work, dulling my pain, as I heard the unmistakable sound of Peter Albright's voice. He was muttering unintelligibly to someone. His breathing was labored.

Able to see almost nothing in the darkness, I began to creep around the barrels, following the sounds. I snaked through the maze of discarded objects, until I could make out the dark form of Peter Albright about twenty feet away. He bent over a body, which seemed to struggle as he tried to force it into a huge drum. *Song!* I thought. The pounding of my heart clashed with the angry throbbing in my head. I felt suddenly faint.

A few yards away, I could just discern the shadowy piles of materials destined for the dump: plywood, giant spools of wire, old two-by-fours, and a cache of copper pipes. I edged toward the pipes, staying in the shadows. The professor continued scuffling with the figure I thought might be Song. She fell forward like a rag doll, seeming to lose consciousness. Peter lifted her body and pushed her into the large drum headfirst.

I inadvertently sucked in my breath. Peter stopped suddenly. I forced myself to freeze while he glanced around, looking for me. Finally he turned back to his awful task. I crouched behind the debris, inching my way toward the pipes. I had nearly reached my goal when the silence was shattered by thunderous banging from somewhere in the distance.

Peter turned in the direction of the sound. Again, the banging. Then, shouting. I took advantage of the momentary diversion and made a run for the pipes. It seemed that someone shouted my name from outside, but I wasn't sure. I didn't know whether to scream for help or keep silent. If I made any noise, Peter would surely get to me before any help could break through the door.

"Zoë?" the distant voice called.

I ached to shout back, but I was terrified of what might happen.

Only a few feet away, Peter Albright suddenly turned toward me.

I screamed for help.

The banging thundered and the shouting grew louder. At the same time Peter moved in my direction. I lunged toward the pipes, which clattered noisily as I fell into them. My fingers curled around a cold length of metal. Gripping hard, I gritted my teeth and turned just in time to see Peter's huge body rise above me.

All at once he dove at me. I jumped away, pipe held high, uttering a karate cry.

The dagger glinted as he raised it. With all the force I could muster, I brought the pipe down onto his head.

He let out a guttural *"ugh"* and fell with a thud.

I slowly became aware of banging and shouting outside, of some heavy object being rammed against the metal door. An overwhelming feeling of anger and relief surged through me like water gushing through a dam that has just given way. My body trembled and I was bathed in sweat.

The basement door crashed open and a shaft of yellow light pierced the darkness. I was vaguely aware of heavy footsteps racing down the stairs. Shadows of figures loomed across the high concrete ceilings. Lying on the floor in a heap, Peter appeared to be unconscious. But when the hall light hit his face, I saw his eyes gleam. With the dagger still clutched in his hand, he struggled to rise to his feet. Baring my teeth, I raised the pipe once again and aimed directly for his skull.

Before I could let the weapon swing, a muscular hand caught both my wrists. I fought against the arms that restrained me from bringing the pipe down on Peter's head with full force.

Then I saw Detective Brannigan, pistol in hand, silhouetted above the professor. Relaxing my grip, I allowed Mark, who still held my wrists, to remove the pipe from my hands.

A muffled voice called from the drum. A police officer opened the lid and Song wriggled free. She gazed at me, eyes wide with terror, a gag stuffed in her mouth. I ran to Song, and the officer helped cut the ropes behind her hands.

Mark began snapping pictures, while Brannigan knelt over Peter Albright.

"He told me you were dead, Zoë," Song cried, when I removed the gag. "He said no one would ever look here. He was going to leave me here to die."

The police swarmed into the basement, while Brannigan issued orders and called for an ambulance. Mark continued to take photographs of Brannigan, Peter, and Song. Finally, he turned the lens on me.

"So, Polanski," I said. *"Qué pasó?"*

"You didn't stick to the plan," he retorted angrily. "We waited an hour for you at Stephen's. Then at Gaffney's. Nobody knew where you were. If Billy hadn't called you on the cell phone, we'd still be there. Luckily, Stephen recognized Peter's voice, and we called Brannigan. We've been all over this building, searching for the past hour. Do you know how big this place is?"

I was about to object, when I spotted Billy descending the basement stairs. We ran toward each other, and he wrapped me in his arms. Later, as the medics lifted Peter Albright onto the stretcher, Song, Billy, Mark, and I watched in awe. His large body quivered like a mortally wounded beast, and I worried for the first time that he might die.

Not long afterward, we opened the double doors and walked down the steps of the main entrance to the building. Parked on the road along the wide sidewalk were a row of police cars, blue lights flashing, sirens wailing. TV units bathed the area in artificial daylight. For a moment I wondered, as if in a terrible dream, what crime had been committed.

Hal Gaffney waited with Stephen, who held Ly close, supporting her heavy body. Song ran straight to her mother. Weeping freely, Ly stroked her child's hair and cheeks and Song, too, burst into tears. Stephen did his best to comfort them. For a brief moment, I observed Gaffney, moved by the spectacle of the two weeping women, lift his arm, as if to reach out with a compassionate touch. Then, noticing my gaze, he grew self-conscious and shrank back, realizing perhaps that solace was not his to bestow.

At the station, Brannigan replayed the tape. I handed him the sketchbook wrapped with the jewel in the kerchief and Peter's photo of Yom. After a debriefing, I was told that Peter had suffered a severe concussion and a broken shoulder, but the blow I'd wielded wouldn't kill him. Brannigan said, almost solicitously, "You're damned lucky."

"I know."

"Do me a favor. Next time you dig up something incriminating, let me interview the suspects."

I gave him my word.

Brannigan allowed me the honor of breaking the news to Cletha. I used his phone to inform her she could come and collect her foster son. All charges were being dropped.

Reserved as usual, Cletha thanked me, expressed concern about my ordeal and Song's, but there was still a note of distance that I sensed would take time to bridge.

Billy and I spent hours sorting things out that night. After he heard the story of my adventure, we held hands quietly, beginning to realize how close we'd come to losing each other.

"Billy, if you were frightened tonight, maybe you can understand how I felt when I got that horrible call last year from Kyoto. I thought you were going to die. You'd been slipping away, growing more and more distant. And then I thought you might be completely gone. I'll never forget that flight to Japan. Never. As long as I live. And the first sight of you in that hospital bed."

We sat at a quiet table in the dining room of the Lord William Inn. A fire blazed in the huge brick hearth.

"I'm sorry," he finally said. "I'm sorry for the pain I caused you."

I didn't know whether the tear on my cheek sprang from the ordeal I'd been through that day or from the relief I felt at hearing those simple words. They couldn't erase the pain. Nothing could do that. But acknowledgment might be the first step toward forgiveness. What was the word, Bou Vuthy's word? *Metta*.

"This gig with Vivi is tempting," Billy added, "but I can do without the tour. I made you a promise. I'm going to keep it."

"Whit might give me a couple of weeks leave of absence," I responded with a surge of good will. "We could all go."

Billy shook his head, his fine-hewn features glimmering in the light of the candles. "Maybe next time."

At home I ran upstairs and held my sleeping children in my arms. Smokie's fine hair was so sweet, Keith's expression so soft, so innocent. What was it, I wondered, that tied us so tightly to our children, that gave us such exquisite joy just to watch them sleep, to see them play and laugh, fill the air with their shouts and music, to see them thrive? There was nothing like the threat of loss to make you appreciate those small but utterly irreplaceable gifts.

Much later, I retired to the study with a steaming mug of chamomile tea, swept the piles of paper, kids' paintings, and music charts off the card table, plugged in the laptop computer, slapped a tape in the Walkman, and started to write.

I wrote compassionately. I wrote with contempt. I wrote courageously. I wrote with fear. I wrote enthusiastically. I wrote with reluctance. I wrote about darkness and lies. I wrote about dreams and betrayal. I wrote with fire. I wrote through the night into the morning. I wrote while the tears rolled down my cheeks. I wrote from the beginning through to the bitter end.

27

Together Brannigan, Cletha, Song, and I pieced together the fragments of what had happened. Yom's murder had been hidden deep in Prith's subconscious until the day he saw Chram at the wedding, when the memories came flooding back, triggering hallucinations and a reliving of the event. Peter had offered to help. Listening to what seemed like ravings to everyone else, Peter realized that Prith was talking about something that had really happened. When Peter heard about the necklace, he knew instantly that the woman he'd been seeking for over a decade was dead at Chram's hand. In an effort to get Chram deported, he contacted friends in the State Department and US-AID, the agency he worked for while in Phnom Penh during the years before the Communist takeover, but found to his dismay that he would have had to reveal the embarrassing facts of his obsession. Instead, he attempted to force Chram to leave on her own. She responded by blackmailing him.

No one would ever know for sure what exactly transpired in their last meeting, whether he went to meet her with the intention of killing her or whether she threatened his life as he claimed. And no one would know for certain whether Chram had stolen the knife from Stephen, as Peter insisted, or whether he had taken it himself.

In the search of the Botwick basement storage area, the police found stuffed in a hazardous waste drum the bloodstained coat Peter had been wearing on the night of the murder and his blood-covered gloves. University officials admitted reluctantly that anything sealed in the containers would have been shipped off to a disposal site in Georgia without inspection. So Albright nearly got away with the murder.

The photograph that Cecily had stumbled upon pictured Peter, Yom, and Cecily herself. She had known Peter during the war, when she'd worked with USAID. As Peter had told me during his rambling confession, she had begun to suspect him. Not wanting to embarrass her colleague if her suspicions proved groundless, she made the mistake of going to him before mentioning her concerns to the authorities.

The big question concerned the weapon. How did Prith's fingerprints get on it? And why were there no others? Prith told us that he'd touched the weapon along with the others in Stephen's living room long before Chram had stolen it, and Peter had worn gloves during his crimes.

Prith's attack on me with a stick was explained by Cletha. A Cambodian superstition held that ghosts could be warded off by repeating certain words while breaking a stick. When I had appeared, saying Chram's name, he'd taken me for a ghost come to take possession of his soul.

Peter's confession and arrest had a depressing effect on the refugee supporters. Tensions within the Cambodian community and among the various factions in town increased. Cletha began a prolonged and exhausting battle to keep Song and her family in the country. The depth of their Khmer Rouge involvement remained unresolved. Stephen stayed on to finish his doctoral thesis and continued to stand by the family. Despite lingering tensions between us, he finally allowed an interview in late February, during which he discussed his relationship with Chram.

His attachment had been deeper and more passionate than he'd let any of us see. Trying to stop the marriage, Peter Albright had made veiled insinuations about Chram after he'd heard Prith's revelations, confiding that "friends in the State Department" had information that she had collaborated with the Khmer Rouge. On their last day together, Stephen had confronted her with this accusation. She'd admitted it was true. They'd fought. He told her he wouldn't marry her. She'd begged and pleaded. He offered her the check for the restaurant lease. She threw it down, telling him she didn't want his money, she wanted him. He'd been cold, telling her it was no longer possible. Later, returning on the night she died, he'd decided he couldn't abandon her. But it was too late.

When the police questioned him about her murder, he resolved not to shame her family and he'd kept the allegations about the Khmer Rouge secret. Though Stephen had begun to suspect Peter, not knowing the extent of Albright's involvement with the woman in the photograph, he hadn't believed his mentor capable of such a brutal deed.

That spring Hal Gaffney, still railing about Khmer Rouge sympathizers, ran for Select Board and was elected, much to the chagrin of Cletha and, I suspected, Whit, though he was too much of a newsman to admit it.

Brannigan received kudos from Boston for breaking the case, which everyone had considered unsolvable because the body had been found so many hours after the time of death. He granted me several hours of his time discussing police procedure, which was of invaluable help in my preparing a long article on the murder for *Rolling Stone*.

The cheeriest news was a call I received from Song not long after the first anniversary of Chram's death, letting me know that she'd been accepted, on full scholarship, to Yale. To celebrate, Aunt Saw and Ly cooked for days, preparing a huge Cambodian feast, and invited the entire newspaper staff.

Happy endings are for fairy tales, not stories about genocide. Phroeng drank heavily at the feast, made awkward comments, and wept over a photo of Chram on the family altar. The candles burned as angrily as ever among the offerings of betel chew, cigarettes, rice, fruit, and flowers.

Rok was surly. I'd heard rumors that the police investigation had led to the temporary shutdown of his gambling business. But Saw's energy and liveliness brightened the party, and once even Rok cracked a smile. Musicians played. Saw danced and told stories. And there was laughter. Billy sat in with the Khmer musicians, trying to add a bass line to traditional Cambodian tunes. Keith and Smokie played with Song's young cousins. The sun shone and the air smelled of the coming of spring.

Yet in the midst of the celebrating I felt the presence of the ghost when a gust of March wind blustered and the branches scratched at the windows. The breeze sighed through the new buds, blossoms about to burst through winter's dead wood. Would she ever find peace? Or would she wander forever through the timeless mist, searching for those who had cast her adrift?